Broken Beats

An Illusion Series Novel

D. Kelly

D. Kelly

Broken Beats
Copyright © 2019 D. Kelly
Editing by – Tiffany Fox – Beyond DEF
Cover design by – Regina Wamba – Mae I Design and Photography
Formatting by – Brenda Wright, Formatting Done Wright
Photographer – The Glass Camera
Model – Graham Nation
Shawn Lucas and Ryder Stone appear courtesy of Siobhan Davis
Copyright © 2019

Dee Kelly www.dkellyauthor.com

This book contains mature subject matter and is not appropriate for minors. Please note this novel contains profanity, sexual situations, and alcohol consumption and potential triggers.

Dee Kelly
P.O. Box 940123
Simi Valley, CA. 93094

ISBN: 13: 978-1-7326394-7-8

D. Kelly

Table of Contents

D. Kelly

The **Acceptance Series** –

Breaking Kate – Book One
Catching Kate – Book 1.5
Releasing Kate- Book Two
Loving Kate – Book Three
Christmas with the Houstons – Book Four

Standalone Novels

Chasing Cassidy
Sharing Rylee
The Evolution of Us
The Last Resort Motel – Room 13
Dating Roulette – Pre-order available now – Coming July 9th 2019

The Illusion Series

Just an Illusion – Side A
Just an Illusion – The B Side
Just an Illusion – EP
Just an Illusion – Unplugged
Just an Illusion – Encore

Illusion Series Spinoff Novels

Interlude – Jordan's story
Broken Beats – Darren's story
TBA – Eli's story coming fall 2019

http://www.dkellyauthor.com/all-books

dear readers,

Thank you for purchasing *Broken Beats*. Darren's story has been one I've wanted to tell for a few years now, and I hope you will all enjoy it. I'd like to take a moment to address new-to-me readers. While this book can be read as a standalone, the story is part of a larger world. There will be many spoilers from previous books, and I strongly advise reading the complete Illusion Series in order. This may not be an issue for some of you, but the choice is yours. If you would like to back up and read the rest of the books, I've listed the reading order below:

Just an Illusion – Side A

Just an Illusion – The B Side

Just an Illusion – EP

Just an Illusion – Unplugged

Just an Illusion – Encore

Illusion Series Spin-off Novels

Interlude – Jordan's story

Broken Beats – Darren's story

TBA – Eli's story (Coming Fall 2019)

D. Kelly

For Danielle –

Thank you for allowing me to ask the questions few people would understand and for giving me the absolute truth. You helped bring an authenticity to this story that I hope everyone will appreciate.

D. Kelly

The wound is the place where the light enters you

– Rumi

D. Kelly

prologue

Darren

Widower.

I hate that word. I've spent my entire life striving not to hate. Not to give anything such immense control over my feelings. Then I think of this one thing, and it fills me with rage. Every. Fucking. Time.

When someone's spouse dies, they become a widow or a widower. They've now been labeled. It sounds unkind, cruel even, but maybe that's because some people perceive it that way. I've seen people flinch when they hear it. Kind people whisper when they say the word out loud knowing it's a sensitive subject. This one single word carries so much power, and why not? It means one of the worst things in life has happened to you.

Then there are people like me who were never afforded the chance to sign a marriage license and file it with a courthouse. We don't get a word. Somehow, that makes it worse for me. Do I *want* to be a widower? Of course not. I want the love of my life back, not heavy with the weight of death and covered in blood like she was the last time I held her. But … if I'm not a widower, what am I? I feel like one. My heart aches like one. I wish my soul mate were still here to share my life, to share our daughter's life.

Are the vows Belle and I shared under the moonlight any less important than those shared by others who have a legal document for proof of marriage? In the eyes of the law, yes, they are. But in the language of love, hell fucking no.

My best friend Mel is a widow, and she hates the word too. She was with her husband about the same amount of time I was with Belle. With the luck of time on their side—as brief as it was—they had a wedding. Although she's found her way out of the darkness with the help of her new husband, she'll always be Noah Weston's widow.

Do you know what's fucked up? I consider myself a widower, but I'm not. As much as I hate the word, I wish I had that label. I wish I had the right to say I was Belle's husband. But I don't, because ceremonies of the heart don't carry weight in the real world. When people found out Mel was a widow, they would say things like, "I'm so sorry. What a horrible tragedy to lose your husband so young." When I say I've lost my fiancée, people reply, "That's a shame, but you're young, and you'll love again." What the fuck? Is it a married-versus-unmarried thing? Or is it a man-versus-woman thing? Are people so old-fashioned they assume a woman should grieve forever? Or do they think men can't love as deeply and have an easier time moving on?

Loving Belle was what I was born to do. I knew it the night we met. I'd always thought being one of the best drummers in the world was my destiny. I'd have tossed my sticks and never looked back in exchange for Belle's life. Hell, I'd have swapped buses with her so Cadence would have her mom and I'd never feel this kind of heartache. Belle was so much stronger than me; she'd have found someone else to share her life with, like Mel has.

Unfortunately, I can't change the past. I spend every day honoring Belle by making the best life possible for Cadence and always putting her before anything else. Some days it's hard to believe she's already six. She was only four months old when Belle passed away. Cady is the spitting image of Belle, and when she smiles, my heart fills with love. I've done my fair share of fucked-up things in this life, but my little girl is my reward for every good choice I've made.

Cadence and Mel's son Nate are attached at the hip. His dad, Noah, was also killed in the accident that took Belle. Belle had big dreams of the two of them growing up and getting married. It's not hard to imagine things could play out that way; their bond is already strong.

Our band spent ten years traveling the world on buses and planes, sometimes even trains. We were only two months away from completing our last U.S. tour when the accident happened. I've gone over that night a million times in my head. Because Cadence was teething and no one had been getting much sleep, we'd rearranged our sleeping arrangements that night. The guys and I had napped on our bus in the afternoon, and Belle stayed with Mel and Noah on their bus that night so she could catch up on her sleep. It's the only reason Belle was on a different bus than Cadence and me.

Since then, I've put Cadence first and foremost. I don't date, but I do fuck. I'm not interested in a relationship, not now, and likely not ever. Sometimes, I wonder how Mel was able to move on, but it makes sense when I see her with my best friend Sawyer. The kind of love they have usually comes once in a lifetime, but Mel found it twice. God must have been making amends to her for taking Noah.

Noah was the heart and soul of our band Bastards and Dangerous, and brother to Sawyer, Wyatt, and me. If all of that wasn't awful enough, the accident stripped away my future. Instead of planning our wedding, I was searching through debris. By the time I found Belle, she was gone. Later, I found out she'd likely died immediately after she was ejected from the bus. There was a lot of blood from where the back of her head hit the ground, but when I scooped her into my arms, she looked like a sleeping princess waiting for her prince to kiss her. I tried … Lord knows I tried. The first responders and our security guard Mac spent nearly an hour coaxing me to put her down. I begged, pleaded, and offered my soul to any higher being who could hear me, but it was no use.

It was the night the air disappeared from my lungs. All of our hopes and dreams were shattered in the blink of an eye. I've done my best to move forward. Belle's motto was "live today, like there's no tomorrow," and I try like hell to honor that for her.

Six months ago, I was living a little too much and drinking a bit too hard. I spent almost every weekend at the beach house drowning in Belle's memories, fucking random girls at the bar, and coming home to drown myself in more alcohol. There was one night I didn't go out, but I did drink and make a terrible mistake. It was an especially hard day. I'd registered Cadence for kindergarten and pretty much lost my shit.

I made a choice I can't take back—one I've regretted every day since. It's an irredeemable sin, and it's going to cost me my best friends. The old Darren would have never done it, and if he would've, he'd have confessed immediately. This Darren is scared. I'm a fucking coward but with good reason. I've lost more than my share already, and so have my friends. When my secret comes out, we're all going to lose again because Sawyer will never forgive me.

Things have changed. I'm home more on the weekends. I haven't had more than three drinks in one day—I was drinking up to three drinks an hour some nights. Overall, my head is on straight. Maybe that's why random fucks aren't appealing lately. The loneliness is always right under the surface. I'm constantly surrounded by people, but I've never felt more alone. This is life without Belle ... and it fucking sucks.

Darren

Six months ago

"Daddy! Me and Nate are big kids now!" Cadence and Nate walk side by side with a bounce in their step next to Mel and me. We've just finished registering the kids for school and are heading back to our car. Sawyer stayed home with the rest of their kids so it wouldn't be such a production.

Mel flashes me the look. It's one we've mastered together and share each time our kids hit a new milestone without Noah and Belle.

Mel smiles down at her. "You sure are, Cady. You guys are going to love school."

She tugs on my hand and I crouch down, giving her my full attention. "Can me and Nate be in the same class?"

"Yeah, I don't want to go to school if I have to be alone." Nate crosses his arms and looks at his mom with a thoughtful gaze. He may be five, but he's an old soul like Noah was.

Mel bends down and looks them both in the eye. "We can't promise you'll be in the same class, but we can promise we'll ask and do our best to make it happen. You guys saw the classrooms. They're right next door to each other, and they share the same playground. Even if something happens and you're not in the same room, you'll still be sharing recess and lunchtime." She pulls them both into a quick hug and blinks back her tears.

"Don't cry, Auntie Mel. We'll be okay."

I swallow over the lump in my throat. Moments like these always throw me for a loop. Cadence is so much like Belle, but they only shared four brief months together.

"I'm sorry, Mommy. I'll go to school." Nate is near tears. He's a bit on the emotional side sometimes. Noah was too, and I can easily imagine he was like this when he was Nate's age.

"How about we all go get some ice cream to celebrate? After that, we'll drop you off with Grandma V for the weekend." Grandma V is Belle's mom, Veronica. Since Mel's mom passed away when she was young, Veronica is the closest thing to a mom she has. The kids cheer in excitement as we head to the car.

"Have I mentioned lately how lucky we are to have you in our lives?" Maybe I'm a little emotional today too.

Mel squeezes my hand. "I'm the lucky one, Darren. What if you'd been an asshole and had taken Cadence far away when Belle died? I would've been devastated."

"I'm an asshole, but not that kind of asshole. We need you as much as you need us."

She flashes me a smile as she unlocks the car. "I love you too, Darren."

At the ice cream shop, we let the kids have their own table next to ours. They talk excitedly about their toppings and flavors, and I miss the days when that could be my biggest concern.

"Are you okay, Darren? You seem a bit lost today. Is it the public school thing? I thought you were on board with it."

"Nah, it's not about the school. I'm perfectly happy sending Cadence to public school. We all went to public school. I want that for them, that sense of normalcy, you know?"

Mel snorts. "I'm not sure it's normal to have a guard parked in front of the school all day."

We all wanted the kids to go to the neighborhood school. It's been five years since the band stopped performing and a lot of the paparazzi have died down. Celebrities are always in the spotlight. Fans notice us, and people still want updates about our lives. It's why we're always one bad photo, one compromising situation, or one scandal away from a full-fledged press frenzy.

Sawyer, Mel, and I decided early on not to keep the kids hidden. Wyatt and his wife Anna don't like their kids' photos out there for the world if they can help it, but that's their family and their call. They may be changing their tune, though, because they were followed a few weeks ago and had to increase their security again.

As for the three of us, we put out our own photos and have noticed the press tends to leave our kids alone. When they're already visible, they're not a story. It probably helps that Mel maintained Belle's entertainment blog with updates after she died. She only stopped posting to it in the last year, opting to turn it over to an up and comer who would run it the way Belle always intended.

"They'll never know the guard is there," I reply. "That's for *our* peace of mind. We both know the possibility of stalkers is a real danger. But it would be a real danger at a private school as well."

Mel licks her spoon and nods. "Well then, what's the matter? You don't seem yourself today."

I push away my empty bowl. "I've just been missing her more than usual lately."

"Daddy, look! Is my tongue blue?" Cadence sticks out her tongue, and Nate immediately follows suit.

"What about mine, Uncle Darren?"

"You've both successfully given yourselves Smurf tongues. Finish eating your ice cream, and maybe it will stay blue long enough for Grandma V to see it."

They both giggle and squeal as they dig back in, and I give my attention back to Mel.

"Darren," she begins hesitantly, "are you sure you're not ready to date again? No one understands your heartache more than I do, but I'm worried about you. Belle wouldn't want this."

"I'm as much in love with Belle today as I was five years ago. If that changes someday, I'll reassess how I feel. For today, I'm going to be sad she missed another milestone, but happy Cadence and I are together for it."

Mel's expression softens and her eyes glaze over. "Noah would've been researching schools for at least the last year, if not longer. He'd have a list of pros and cons and would probably advocate for private school. Sometimes I feel like I'm failing Nate because I don't put that kind of thought into things. I've always followed my gut."

I don't mean to laugh, but it just comes out. "Noah was overkill at times. You're a great mom, Mel. Don't discredit yourself. We have to do what we feel is best for our kids. If it works, great, and if it doesn't, we do better next time."

Her eyes sparkle as she pulls wet wipes from her purse and motions the kids over to wipe them down. "Okay, Mr. Philosophical, point taken. What are you going to do with your free weekend? Let me guess, back to the beach house?"

"Give the lady a gold star."

"I want a gold star too, Daddy."

"Me too," Nate mumbles as Mel drags the wipe across his mouth.

"Sorry, guys, all out of stars. But do you know who *does* have gold stars?"

"Who?" They ask excitedly, in unison as usual.

"Teachers," Mel answers with a smile. "You'll get gold stars at school but only if you're good students, do your work, and follow all the rules."

"We can do that, Mommy. Right, Cady?" The solemn expression on Nate's face kicks me right in the gut. Maybe I'm missing Noah a bit extra today. We may not have been brothers by blood, but that never mattered to us.

"Yup, we'll get lots of stars, Nate." Cady laces their fingers together, and they walk hand in hand back to the car.

We are so fortunate to still have them with us. These kids survived the accident because they have a greater purpose in life. I'm not sure what it is, but I can't wait to find out.

Later that evening, I grab a blanket and head down to our spot on the beach. It's where Belle and I had sex for the first time. The place we took Cadence to the last Fourth of July we were home from tour. That was the weekend we set our wedding date, and the memory is sharp and clear in my mind.

"She's out." Belle smiles sweetly as she bundles our little girl up in her carrier.

"Come here." Belle cuddles into my arms as we look up at the stars. "Mary May and Bobby" by Joe Purdy plays softly from my phone.

"Marry me."

She tips her head toward mine and grins. *"I thought that was already a given."*

"It is, but I want us to pick a date. We've done it your way, Belle. We've given our love a chance to grow, we waited to meet our daughter, and we're planning our future. What are we waiting for?"

Belle sighs. *"Nothing, but I continue getting stuck on the legalities of it all, you know? Why do I have to pay for court documents and file paperwork to prove I love you and want to be with you? Why can't we have that with each other? Right here, right now, under the stars with our daughter, the universe, and God as our witnesses?"*

I flip to my side, and she turns to face me.

"Can't we have both? We can get married now and seal our hearts. I'm yours, Belle, for as long as you'll have me. And then how about Thanksgiving weekend we get married at our house? I

want a day to share with our friends and family. What better day than Thanksgiving?"

"Your grandma will have a heart attack if you actually marry the black girl."

"It won't be any worse than when my dad married the Mexican girl down the block."

"If you say so." She trails her fingers down my arms.

"Belle, I want the three of us to be a family. I want you to share our last name. Call me old-fashioned, but I want to know I have legal rights as your husband if something were to happen. And I wouldn't mind shoving my head up your dress and sneaking a lick of your sweet pussy while everyone assumes I'm tugging the garter from your upper thigh. Peeling the dress off you at the end of the night will be pretty hot too, but so would pushing you up against the wall and fucking you while you're still wearing it. Getting the bride dirty is such a hot fantasy."

She presses her head against my chest and laughs. "You're so fucking dirty, but dammit if that isn't one of my favorite things about you. God made you for me, Darren. We can bind our hearts tonight and combine our legal entities in November."

I caress her cheek with my thumb and lower my lips to hers for a quick kiss. Cady is a light sleeper and I want to do this before she wakes up.

"Belle Dixson, I didn't know what love was until you. When I first saw you, I was drawn to you immediately. I wanted to know everything about the gorgeous, petite woman in front of me who was larger than life. The night we fucked for the first time, I finally understood how my dad was so sure my mom was the one for him. This incredible awareness washed over my entire being, and I knew you were the only woman I ever wanted to bang my bongo again."

Belle giggles at my much-used euphemism for sex.

Taking a deep breath, I continue. "You're the bravest woman I know. We did things a little backward, but I wouldn't have it any other way. I want to explore the world with you and fall in love with all the hidden wonders of the world together. I'm going to love you for the rest of my life and probably well into the next one too. I don't think it was a coincidence you and Mel were the ones to interview the band that night. I'm pretty sure we've been fated for each other all along. Marry me, for now and eternity."

Belle tries so hard to keep her emotions in check, but tears stream down her face, and she doesn't try to stop me from wiping them away. "Yes, I'll marry you, for now and always."

She inhales deeply and entwines her fingers with mine.

"Darren Miller, the old Belle would laugh at the idea of being fated to anyone. Mel and I are lucky to have you and Noah. Both of you love so completely at times it's hard to believe this is my life now. The first time Bastards and Dangerous landed on my radar, I was drawn to you. I thought it was a harmless celebrity crush until the night we met. I realized harmless was far from the truth. It felt like a piece of myself that had been missing my entire life had finally been given back to me. I couldn't explain it. Maybe that's why I was so careless about not using a condom. But even that choice proves the universe had a bigger plan for us because we two became three, and I've never been happier."

Belles words coat my soul in an incredible amount of pride. I can't believe this strong, beautiful woman is marrying me. I'll never forget this night as long as I live.

"I never want you to think I was opposed to marrying you. It's just ... what we share between us is all-encompassing. I'm not making much sense, I know, but marriage feels like the end in a way. It's the thing you do when you've taken all the other roads. I didn't want us to lose what makes us special by agreeing to some ritualistic ceremony where my family wants us to jump the broom and your family wants to lasso us together. I don't care about traditions; I only care about you. I don't want to lose what's special about us while we're arguing out the details between our families. This night is what I'm going to carry with me. My heart is yours, Darren, for every moment of this life and until I find you in my next one. I love you more than I ever thought possible. Your love has opened a whole new part of me I can't wait to fill with adventures and memories that will stay with me long after we're gone from this

earth. Marry me, Darren. Be my husband, my partner in life, my co-parent, and my ride or die."

We both laugh, but then she focuses her bright eyes on me. "See, that right there is why this works. We're supposed to be serious, but when I can't do it and crack a joke to ease the moment, you laugh with me. You've never made me feel anything other than loved and accepted for who I am. I've never been with a man long enough to truly let down my guard and be myself around him, but with you, that's all I've ever been. I love you."

I wrap my arms around her and pull her flush to my body. "I love you, and I'm going to love being your husband. Kiss me, wife."

Belle wraps her arms around my neck as our lips meet. Her mouth parts and our tongues meet passionately. Her needy whimpers go straight to my dick as we devour each other. With each stroke of her tongue against mine, our connection strengthens. I can't imagine a time when kissing her won't be my absolute favorite thing to do. Although, slipping into her sweet pussy would be right up there with kissing.

Cadence whimpers, and we slowly break our newly created bond. "She's fine," I say, peeking over Belle's shoulder. "Must be a dream."

"Or maybe she saw us starting to get it on and was letting us know she doesn't need the visual."

"Considering how opinionated her mother can be, that is a likely possibility."

"Hey, that's not a nice thing to say to your bride on our wedding night. Just when I was thinking I might have a garter in the house, I could dig up too."

"I take it back." I pull her closer to me and kiss the top of her head. "I could get used to this. I never used to look forward to the end of our band, but spending days like this with you is definitely softening the blow."

Belle snuggles into the crook of my arm. "You guys won't let the band end. You're far too talented. The fans will be happy to have new music even without the tours. Trust me on that. Music is always evolving. Now, I do have a request."

"A request from my wife on our wedding night? Whatever it is, the answer is yes."

She bites her bottom lip and hesitates before speaking. "Would you mind not telling anyone about this?"

Is she serious?

"Why?"

"So much of our lives are public. I want something for us. Only us. Not Mel or any of our friends. Not Sawyer either. Can we just have this for me and you? We'll tell them the night of our wedding because today is the only one I ever want to celebrate. July second will now and forever more be the day we combined our hearts and our lives. Thanksgiving will be the day we decide to share it with the world."

"If it makes my wife happy, it'll be our secret."

Belle kisses me, and my worries melt away. "Thank you. I just want to relish this feeling a bit longer. But come Thanksgiving, I'm going to blast it to my blog as soon as the wedding is over. All those Darren fans out there hoping you're going to break up with your baby mama need to know you're finally off the market for good."

"Sexy, protective, jealous, and devious. You've got all the signs of a stage-five clinger yet I'm not afraid of you. Why is that?"

"Hm, I'm not sure. Maybe you've always had a secret fantasy of having clinger of your own. One who will adore you, bang your bongo, give birth to your beautiful children, and tell anyone who gets in the way to fuck right off."

"Now that sounds like exactly what I was looking for in a wife. No wonder I picked you."

Cadence cries, and Belle jumps up to care for her. I'm in awe as she pulls her from her seat, clutches her against her chest, and murmurs soothing words to her.

"We should go back; it's starting to get chilly. For the record, Mr. Miller, don't get it twisted. I picked you almost ten years ago; you just didn't know it yet."

"Well, Mrs. Miller, when you put it that way, you are definitely my own personal clinger. I wouldn't have it any other way."

Tears stream down my cheeks as I pull myself from one of my favorite yet most painful memories of Belle. I've never told a soul what happened that night, and I'm not sure I ever will.

Darren

It's close to ten by the time I return to the house. Pulling a bottle of gin from the cabinet, I toss back a few shots. Gin isn't my usual go-to, but it works the fastest, and I'd like to be numb tonight.

I'm anxious this evening. I miss Belle something fierce. Instead of drinking alone, I probably should have gone to the bar and gotten laid. It wouldn't have been hard; even though the band isn't putting out new music anymore, groupies are still a dime a dozen. It's not the first time lately groupie sex hasn't seemed appealing to me, and it likely won't be the last.

The gin shots kick in quickly, and I'm drunk and feeling no pain within the hour. I left the sliding glass door open, allowing the echoes of the waves crashing against the shore to flood the house. The air flowing into the room is chilly, so I've also got a fire burning. Music plays through the surround sound, and I'm finally back in the present after spending so much of my day lost in the past.

Grabbing a beer, I put away the gin. If I drink any more of it, I'm going to hate myself in the morning. It's warming up in here more than I'd like, but I don't want to shut off the fire. Instead, I remove my shirt and toss it to the floor. The flames dance seductively, and I lose myself in their beauty. It reminds me of being snowed in up at Sawyer's cabin in Big Bear. His cabin is the perfect place to be stranded with a date. Snow, sex, solitude, and a roaring fire—it doesn't get much better than that.

The sound of a door closing echoes through the house, and Rory saunters into the living room like she owns it. Rory is Sawyer's baby sister, and sometimes I think she forgets her brother doesn't live here anymore. Then again, neither do I, but everyone knows this place is my weekend sanctuary.

"Hey, Darren!"

"Rory, what are you doing here?"

She flashes me her signature grin but doesn't say a word until she plops down next to me on the sofa. Her vanilla scent is laced with more than a hint of whiskey. "Truth? I forgot my new address, and this was the only one I could remember to give the Uber driver."

Typical Rory. She's seven years younger than me, and it really shows sometimes. Or maybe I'm just feeling old as I creep closer to thirty-five.

"Are you drunk?"

She holds her fingers about a half-inch apart. "Just this much." Then she spreads her arms wide. "Or maybe this much. I haven't quite decided yet."

She kicks off her heels and slowly crosses her perfectly sculpted legs. My cock twitches, and I take a long draw of my beer. Rory is like my little sister, but she's also an undeniably sexy twenty-eight-year-old woman.

"Well, you can crash in your old room."

Her sparkling green eyes meet mine. "I'd rather sleep in yours."

Oh, hell no ...

"Very funny, Ror."

"I'm not laughing, Darren." She flips herself onto my lap, spreading those sexy legs wide open, her pussy pressing against my cock. This can only end one way—badly. My dick doesn't seem to realize that because I'm hard as a rock, a fact she's well-aware of now.

"Time to stop messing around. This can never happen, and we both know it. We're practically brother and sis—"

Her mouth covers mine before I can finish the sentence. Fuck me, she tastes like the sweetest sin. Instinctively, I lower my hands to her ass as our tongues duel for control. I squeeze her ample cheeks, pulling her tighter to me, and she slows her attack, allowing me to lead. Rory's whimpers are like a drug to my senses.

Sex has always been my favorite high and my biggest weakness. Sawyer will kill me if I fuck his sister, but when she moves against my cock, the devil on my shoulder wants this moment with her. Fortunately, there is a part of my mind that still realizes out of all the bad choices I've made in life, this would probably top them all.

"Rory, stop. We can't do this."

She drops her forehead against mine and catches her breath. The scent of her desire lingers between us, setting off an entirely different kind of need. All I can think about is how she'd taste on my tongue. Suddenly, she leans back, her gaze filled with fire. The song changes to "I Feel A Sin Comin' On" by Pistol Annies. What are the fucking odds?

Rory grins. "I've wanted you since I was fifteen. You're the man I thought of when I masturbated the first time and so many more times after that. Darren, I'm a grown fucking woman. My brothers don't get to tell me who to kiss, and they sure the hell don't get a say in who I get to fuck."

She grinds against me and only our clothes separate her sweet fucking pussy from my cock. I'm losing ground fast. She's a woman with needs—needs I can easily take care of for her.

"This could never be more than one night, Rory. I don't want to be that guy, but it's all I can give you. And Sawyer—"

"Can never fucking know. My lips are sealed." Smiling, she leans forward and traces my lips with her tongue. "I can handle one night, but the question is, can you?"

"Little girl, this rock star aced his one-night stand final a decade ago. You sure you're ready to swim in the deep end?"

There has never been a worse idea in the history of bad ideas, but as I'm about to push aside how drunk and horny I am in favor of being an adult, Rory smirks and slides down my legs onto the floor. She unbuttons and unzips my pants in record time. In one smooth motion, she pulls my cock from my boxers and strokes me.

Her eyes meet mine and lead me straight into temptation. "Fuck the deep end, Darren. I'm about to drown you in my ocean."

Rory lowers her head and slides her mouth down my length. She cups my balls with one hand and squeezes my thigh with the other. Her ministrations are a wet dream come true. I weave my fingers through her hair and guide her deeper. Her eyes water, but instead of backing off she pushes herself farther and moans with pleasure.

"Jesus, Rory …"

She pulls back and meets my gaze. "Can you get it up more than once a night, old man?"

"I'm not that old. I've got stamina for days."

Nodding, she licks her lips and circles the tip of my cock with her tongue, lapping up my pre-cum. "Good, because I want you to come in my mouth. I've waited too damn long to know what you taste like, and I don't want to miss a single fucking drop."

Holy shit. Her words light my fuck-fuse and all cognitive reasoning is gone. I push her head back down until I'm fully seated at back of her throat and her lips meet the base of my dick. This woman is a sex fiend, and once she's finished sucking me dry, I'm going to return the favor. Going down on her is going to be my absolute fucking pleasure.

"Rory, shit … if you don't stop, I'm going to come."

Her eyes meet mine as she sucks harder and faster, making my body crave everything she's giving. Tingles shoot up the base of my spine, and I chant her name as I come. Every aftershock through my body is reciprocated with an eager moan as she swallows my release.

Rory leans back, once again licking those perfectly plump lips of hers, and I lift her into my lap. Shifting my hand to the back of her head, I pull her lips to mine and kiss her deeply. I slip my free hand under her skirt and slide my fingers against her wet heat. She's fucking drenched, and my cock twitches back to life.

I turn us around and lay her down on the couch. After hiking up her skirt, I pull off her panties and toss them to the floor. She spreads her legs wide, and I lick my lips at the sight of her glistening cunt.

"Rory," I meet her lustful gaze with mine, "if you want me to fuck you after this, you'd better scream my name when you come."

She bites her lip and nods. "Won't be hard."

Dammit, I already feel myself drowning in her ocean. It doesn't matter though; it's only for tonight. My heart is no longer mine to give. It belongs to Belle and always will.

Hours later, I wake up needing to take a piss, and for a moment, I'm completely disoriented. My head pounds, and my heart races as my eyes begin to focus. This isn't my bed. I sit up and say a silent prayer, already knowing it's in vain. I turn my head slowly and look over my shoulder. *Fuck.* A very naked Rory is asleep next to me.

I don't even see my clothes as I make my way to her bathroom. Once I finish, I splash some water on my face and wrap a towel around my waist. When I step back into the bedroom, she looks up at me.

"It's a little too late for modesty don't you think?"

I'm never drinking gin again as long as I live. "Rory, we need to talk."

She sits up and has the decency to cover herself up. "Darren, calm down. It was only sex."

"You're practically my sister! It never should've happened. I'm sorry, that's shitty to say, but fuck ..."

I take a seat on the edge of the bed, and she scoots next to me.

"Look, last night was fucking hot, but we agreed it would be a one-time thing. You've been in my head since I was a teenager, Darren. I had to know once and for all."

My heart lurches in my chest. A teenage fantasy come to life. Could this get any fucking worse?

"Know what, Ror?"

"If I'm wrong about who I'm supposed to be with," she says softly. "Don't worry, I wasn't wrong, and it's not you."

This situation is so messed up, all I can do is laugh. "You fucked me to rule me out as an option? I'm not sure if I should be offended or give you a high-five. I hope it was worth it because I'm sure your family will disown me after this."

This is all my fault. I drank excessively to numb my pain and ended up depleting my own damn common sense. I'm not sure I've ever regretted sex with anyone, but this might be the biggest mistake of my life.

"That's not going to happen. My family doesn't need to know everything about me. I'm sorry I was deceptive, but to be fair, you seemed as into it as I was. That was some of the best sex of my life. That thing you did with your tongue … ugh … just … damn."

"Okay, then tell me what the goal was because I feel like I'm missing a huge piece of the puzzle."

With a sigh, she leans back on the bed. "I've been seeing someone, and I think he could be the one. But he knew I had feelings for someone else and backed away from me."

"You've had feelings for me that have interfered with your relationship?"

"Partially, it's just—" Rory takes a deep breath. "Have you ever wanted something for so long that you felt like you were stuck? It's not like I was *in* love with you, but I do love you. We obviously have chemistry. Fucking you was by no means a hardship."

She's awful at this. "Gee, thanks."

"Gah, I'm sorry. That sounded bad. I've always wondered if all those pent-up feelings I had for you could be more than just sex. I couldn't let him walk away without finally having an answer. If he's the one and I lose him for something that isn't meant to be, that would be pretty dumb, right?"

I'm not sure I'm sober enough to keep up with this conversation.

"If you had talked to me prior to last night, we probably could've figured this out without crossing so many boundaries. Are you telling me the truth? You're sure this was a one-off and I'm not your one?"

She sits back up and looks at me with the adoring expression I always thought was sisterly love. I want to be disgusted with myself for what happened between us, but we're not actual family, and it would make what we did tawdry, and it wasn't. But it never should have happened.

"Cross my heart, Darren. I'll always love you, but this was definitely me closing a door." I release a deep exhale, and she snickers. "I'll try not to be offended."

"Whoever he is, you should fight for him. If he pushed you away to be sure you were happy, even if it wasn't with him, that's love. We both know how fleeting it can be. Don't throw it away."

She covers my hand with hers. "I'm sorry for dragging you into this. Do you think we'll be okay?"

"We'll be fine, but I need to be the one to tell Sawyer at some point."

"No, you can't. We've all lost too much, and Sawyer is," she sighs exhaustedly, "Sawyer. There has to be *something* you've kept from him over the years. Whatever that is, vault this secret with it."

"Okay, but only if you promise to get your man back."

"Deal. You're an amazing man and one of the best fathers I've ever seen. I know how much you adored Belle and how hard it was to lose her. You deserve so much more from life, and so does Cadence. It's time for you to come back to the land of the living. All the way back. Some lucky woman out there is waiting for her heart to sync to yours."

"Rory—"

"Don't talk to me like a kid you can caution. If Mel and Sawyer could find love, so can you. But you won't know till you open your heart and mind again." She stands with the sheet wrapped around her lithe body and kisses the top of my head. "All I'm asking is for you to consider it. You're a catch, D," she looks over her shoulder before stepping into the bathroom, "and you fuck like a porn star."

I laugh as she closes the door, a sign of her dismissal. I'm happy to take the out. Heading toward the kitchen, I pick up my clothes along the way. After grabbing the gin from the cupboard, I pour it down the sink. Never again will I drink myself into a gin stupor.

Darren

Six months later

"Once upon a time, there was a beautiful princess named Belle. Belle was funny and feisty, and one of the prettiest princesses in all the kingdom."

"Just like Princess Amelia, right, Daddy?" Cadence asks.

"Yes, both princesses are equally pretty and funny. More importantly, they're kind, generous, and filled with laughter and love. Plus, they're the very best of friends."

"And they live in a rock and roll kingdom, right, Uncle Darren?" Nate queries from his bed.

Story time with six-year-olds can be a bit trying, but I will never run out of patience with these two or with the story our families tell them night after night.

"That's right, Nate. Their kingdom is a musical wonderland."

"And it's filled with humans and angels, right, Daddy?" Cadence has been trying to clarify this recently.

"Correct, it's a magical land where angels and humans live together in harmony."

Cadence sits up in her bed, her face taking on a serious expression. "Can we go there, Daddy? I want to visit Mommy and Uncle Noah."

"No, Cady, we can't go see them because we're not angels yet."

"Nate's right. You can't go there in person, but you can visit the kingdom in your dreams." Oh man, they're overly tired. I need to nip this in the bud before they brawl.

Cadence yawns. "Okay, Daddy, we'll finish the story tomorrow. If I see Mommy in my dreams, I'll tell her you love her too."

"With all my heart and soul. Goodnight, sleepyhead." After tucking her in and kissing her goodnight, I do the same to Nate.

"Night, Uncle Darren." He mumbles as his eyes close completely.

"Night, Nate."

Nate and Cadence have shared a room since they were just over a year old. When Mel and Sawyer moved from the beach house into their house by the creek, the kids didn't handle the separation well. Luckily, Sawyer bought the house next door as soon as it went on the market.

My house needed renovations before we could move in. During that time, we shuffled the kids back and forth a lot. Recently, we've been preparing them for the upcoming changes that will happen when they start school. The biggest upset will be sleeping in their own homes during the week and only having sleepovers on the weekends. We know it's going to be rough, but it's a necessary change.

When I make it back out to the living room, I collapse on the couch. Sawyer and Mel are each feeding one of their twins. Sawyer eyes me suspiciously. "You're that tired from putting two kids to bed? Try doing it with five."

"No thanks, that's your idea of a good time."

"Actually, my idea of a good time is making them, but putting them to bed isn't as exhausting as you're making it look." Sawyer laughs. "Or maybe I've just got more stamina than you, old man."

I sit up and scrub my face with my hands. "Cadence asked me about humans and angels again. Maybe they're too young for this."

"Darren," Mel says softly, "Cadence is a curious little girl. It's natural to ask if she can go where her mom is. Our kids have a good grasp on the fact they each have a parent who is no longer with us."

"Maybe, but I hate this feeling."

She nods and reaches for Sawyer's hand. "We all do. If we could give them Noah and Belle, I don't think any of us would hesitate. That's why building their lives with stories and our memories is the next-best thing. If you want us to back off with Cadence, we can."

"Nah, it's okay. I'm just having a moment. I hate that she'll never have Belle, but she has us, and we're pretty awesome."

Sawyer scoops a sleeping Greyson from Mel and takes both boys to the nursery. Now that they're nine months old, they're much easier to tell apart. Grey looks like Sawyer, and Joey looks like Nate.

"You've seemed happier the past few months, and you've been drinking less, at least it seems like it. You guys had a long week getting things together in the studio; maybe you need a night out. Why don't we keep Cady tomorrow and you go have some fun? It's been a while hasn't it?"

I haven't gone out since before I fucked Rory. I've been focusing on me. Instead of drinking and fucking, I've been working out and spending more time in the studio playing music. Plus, with school starting soon, spending more quality time with Cadence has been my top priority.

"It has, but I'm good."

"No, you're not," Sawyer says, coming back into the room. "The only songs you played in the studio today were by Metallica. You were working out some serious aggression. What's up?"

This Rory thing is eating away at me, and I want to tell Sawyer because I'm not sure how long I can deal with the stress of it. "I haven't been laid in about six months or so. Maybe I need a release."

Mel arches her brow. "That's unusual for you. What's going on, Darren? You can talk to us."

More and more, I feel like the odd man out. Everyone is dating. Hell, even our bodyguards are settling down. I'm not looking to date, but lately, I'm lonely.

"I'm probably having a mid-life crisis. I think I'll take you up on your offer and go to Just an Illusion tomorrow night. Want to come and play some pool, Sawyer?"

"I would, but we're watching Sebastian for Allie and Jordan. Hit up Wyatt; I'm sure he'd love to go."

"That's a good idea. It's probably been a while since he's had a night away from Anna and the boys."

Mel yawns, and although it's only a little after eight, I follow.

"On that note, I'm going home. I'm exhausted. Call me if you need me. Otherwise, I'll see you in the morning."

"Later, Darren." Sawyer pulls Mel to her feet and into his embrace.

"See you tomorrow, D, sleep well," Mel adds before kissing her husband.

I pause when I get to the main entrance of the house and take in the photos on the walls. Maybe Cadence and I should do something similar. The representation of love and family makes this house more of a home. Plus, each time I see Noah and Belle's faces, it doesn't seem to hurt as much.

Haddie

"Are you really going to do it, Haddie?" My friend and co-worker Marina looks at me skeptically.

"Richie died three years ago this weekend, and I have to go say goodbye. It's time to move on." If I tell myself often enough, maybe it will make it true.

"I know I bust your balls, but it's only because I love you. Are you ready to let him go?"

His smile invades my memory; it was my favorite thing about him. "I'm not sure I'll ever be ready, but the choice was taken from me the night of the accident. I'll always love him, but I'm lonely. If I can say goodbye, maybe I can step out of my comfort zone and consider going out on a date."

Marina pulls me into a hug. "I'm proud of you. Do you want me to come with you?"

"No, but thanks. I've got to do this alone." I sigh. "Enough sadness for today. Where would you like me to hang this?"

"Right by the pencil sharpener would be great."

We're spending our Saturday afternoon decorating Marina's kindergarten classroom. School starts soon, and she's trying to get her room finished early.

I'm one of the district psychologists. Normally, I work at the district office, but our district was chosen for a pilot program this year. I've been assigned to Marina's school.

Each school in our district will have a dedicated psychologist on site. Due to the influx in bullying, disabilities, homelessness, and hunger throughout the state not to mention fear stemming from active shooter drills, the powers that be think this will help students and teachers. I'm excited because I think this program will be a great success.

Typically, our caseload is insane and we run from school to school. I'm looking forward to more of a relaxed environment and working with kids who know I'll be here for them.

Marina spins in a circle, checking out our progress. "I'm exhausted and starving. Can I buy you lunch for helping me?"

"Have I ever turned down food? Even though I probably should, I'm not going to."

"Stop, Haddie. You're perfect as you are—curvaceous and insanely gorgeous. Richie loved you for you, and anyone else worthy of you will too."

We gather our belongings, and she locks up the room before we head for the parking lot.

"Richie loved me when I was thinner. Even *he* might be repulsed by me now."

Marina narrows her eyes at me. "Stop it. You had severe injuries. It took you almost a year to recover physically. You're still recovering emotionally. You're so much more than a number on a scale."

"Have I mentioned lately that I love you?"

"It could bear repeating."

"I love you. Thank you for being my oldest and dearest friend."

She unlocks the car, and we get inside. "You're welcome. Now stop with the old. You're giving me a complex."

After lunch, Marina drops me off at home. Grandpa left me his bungalow when he passed away five years ago. It's nestled away on a little cul-de-sac, and my favorite thing about it is the backyard. There are so many plants and trees; it feels like a small tropical village. I've got comfortable patio furniture that circles a fire pit, enough room for a table under a covered porch, and a barbecue off to the side.

Richie and I were excited to make this our home once we were married. He was old-fashioned and didn't believe in living together before marriage. He slept over often, but he never wanted a drawer to call his own until we sealed the deal.

Before Richie died, he was saving up to open a restaurant. He'd just gotten a job as a chef at an upscale place in Santa Monica, and we were out celebrating the night of the accident. After that, life wasn't the same. My parents flew in and helped with my recovery, and one of the first things I did was buy a massive jetted tub and remodel my bathroom to accommodate it.

Due to my injuries, I was in the hospital for a few weeks, and I missed his funeral. Richie's sisters came and sat with me at the hospital off and on. His parents never really liked me much, but even if they had, I wouldn't have expected them to delay his services on my account. I wasn't the only one who needed closure.

I kick off my shoes and quickly sort through the mail. A soak in that big tub is exactly what I need right now. Then I'll nap, shower, and get ready for my night.

As I put the finishing touches on my makeup, I look at my reflection. At least my skin looks flawless—on the inside, I'm a nervous wreck.

I've got on a red, long-sleeved V-neck shirt that accentuates my cleavage, dark denim jeans, and a pair of black boots. I open my rideshare app and request a car before I chicken out.

Most people would go to the cemetery to say goodbye to a loved one, or even to the crash site. Not me. I want to go to the bar where we had our last date. Thoughts of our night at Just an Illusion have comforted me since the accident. We had one last incredible night. Right before the accident, Richie and I were laughing. Those are the memories I want to keep close.

I haven't been to the bar since he died. I'm going to have a good time for both of us. Grabbing my leather jacket and purse, I lock up the house just as my ride arrives. With one last deep breath, I get inside the car and prepare myself for the evening.

The driver lets me off right outside the door, but I walk around the building and check out the artwork before going inside. Just an Illusion is in an industrial park, and the outside of the bar is spray painted with some of the best artwork in the area. From what I've heard, there's a waitlist to be one of the featured artists. Jordan, the owner, switches out the art every six months and showcases the artists on the bar's website. It's such an eclectic way to let other people shine.

The bar is packed. Before I left the house, I checked the website to make sure they didn't have live music tonight. It's usually loud enough without the band; I didn't want to say my goodbyes at a concert.

I need to eventually get to the pool room, but for now, I work my way to the bar. Jordan's eyes meet mine, and he raises a finger to give him a minute. I scan the bottles behind the bar trying to decide what I want to drink when someone taps my shoulder. I turn around slowly and am quickly engulfed in one of Jordan Weston's famous hugs.

"Haddie, I didn't think you'd ever grace my bar with your presence again. How are you?"

He pulls back from our hug with his hands on my shoulder and looks me up and down.

"That's new." I point to his wedding ring. "Well, maybe not new, but new to me. Last time I was here, you guys were engaged and expecting."

Jordan smiles, whips out his phone, and opens the photo gallery. "Sebastian is almost four now. Allie and I were married ... not too long after your last visit."

Jordan and Richie talked often, and he and Allie came to see me in the hospital.

"He's adorable! You and Allie must be proud."

"Haddie!" Allie nudges Jordan with her hip and squeezes in for a hug.

"Is that—?"

Allie backs up with a huge grin on her face. "Yup, it's a baby bump. We thought it was time Sebastian has a brother or sister."

Jordan puts his arm around Allie's shoulder. "What can I say? We Westons like to multiply. Do you think you'll be coming in more often? We've missed you around here."

"I'm not sure. I'd love to say yes, but tonight is about saying goodbye. This was the last place we were ... you know, before ..." I take a deep breath and exhale. "Anyway, I'm hoping to put my life back on track. Maybe date a bit? I'm not sure."

Allie squeezes my arm. "It's okay. Take it one day at a time. We'll take you when we get you. If you'll excuse me, I need to use the restroom. It was lovely seeing you, Haddie. Don't be a stranger."

Jordan watches Allie wade through the crowd and turns his attention back to me. "Unfortunately, we're working tonight, so we have to get back. I'll make your drink first. What can I get you?"

"Vodka on the rocks, please."

"You got it." Jordan says before he maneuvers his way through the crowd to get back behind the bar.

"Do you want a double?" he asks, popping the ice into the glass.

"Yes, that's a good idea."

When I pull out a twenty, he shakes his head. "This one is on me."

"Don't be silly." I slide the money across the bar.

"I'm not being silly," he replies, ignoring my offer. "I'm being a friend. Use it to do something nice for someone else."

"Thank you." I put the money back in my wallet, and he waves as he works the bar. Taking a deep breath, I grab my drink and walk around the club. I look up at the pool room, but I'm not quite ready yet.

When I finish my drink, I'm on the opposite side of the venue. The bar over here isn't quite as crowded.

"As I live and breathe ... If I blink, will you disappear?"

"Hey, Sasha, long time no see."

Sasha is one of the bar managers and always good for a laugh. She leans over the counter, boobs front and center, and pulls me into a one-armed hug.

"Vodka rocks, huh? Some things never change. Want another?"

"Sure. How's life? Are you seeing anyone special?"

She winks at me as she grabs the bottle of vodka. "Ha! You know my motto: too many dicks and not enough time. One day I may find the elusive magical cock, but until then, I'm having a blast test driving different makes and models."

I laugh as she passes me my drink. "Good for you."

"So ... first time back, huh?"

"Yeah, I'm about to go up and relive some memories and bring myself back into the present if I'm lucky."

Sasha squeezes my hand. "Luck has nothing to do with it. Life gave you the shit end of a stick, but now you're going to close the door on that chapter, remember it with love, and reclaim your life like the badass bitch you are. You've got this, Haddie."

"Thanks."

I reach into my purse, and she shakes her head. "Jordan would kill me if I took your money."

"How does he expect to stay in business if he won't let patrons pay?"

Sasha laughs. "He won't take *your* money. The rest of these people are *all* going to pay. Plus, we've got an awesome tipper in the house tonight, and that makes J happy."

"It's now or never. Thanks for the drink, Sasha."

She waves. "You're welcome."

I walk around to the end of the bar and head up the stairs. With each step, my heart slams against my chest. I swear I hear his laughter in the air. It's impossible, I know, but it's a nice thought.

I lean against one of the tables and look at the pool table in the corner. Instantly, I'm lost in the memory of our last night together.

chapter 5

Darren

Wyatt left a few minutes ago because his kids are sick and he felt bad for leaving Anna alone. I get it; I wouldn't have wanted to leave Cadence if she were sick either.

Now, I'm hitting balls and debating about moving on to something harder to drink. My Spidey sense goes off as I chalk the cue. After so many years of surveillance by fans and press, my self-awareness sensors are on point.

After sinking the eight ball, I raise my eyes to meet the gaze of a woman nearby. Since Belle, my type has been anyone who doesn't remind me of her, and this girl fits the bill. Her eyes hold a deep intensity, and I can't help but be intrigued. I don't think I've fucked her in the past. She's nothing if not memorable.

"Wanna play?"

She startles as if just noticing me, and her bright-green eyes sweep over my body. I'll forgive her for staring because she's hot as fuck.

"Nah, it's cool. Thanks though," she answers with a bit of uncertainty in her voice.

Setting the pool cue on the table, I step closer to her and lean against the table. "You sure? You've been keeping an eye on me for a while now. If you don't want to play, there's only one other thing I can think of. You wanna bang?"

Her pouty lips separate as she gasps. All right, maybe banging isn't what was on her mind, but it's not the worst thing I've ever said to a woman.

"Is that how you come on to women? I mean, I'm not judging, but that kind of shit doesn't work with me."

"So why are you watching me? I'm guessing you know who I am. Do I intimidate you or something?"

Her eyes grow wide. "I'm sorry." She picks up her drink and downs it quickly. I don't know what it is about this girl, but she intrigues the fuck out of me.

"May I?" I motion to her table. She bites her bottom lip but nods. "Can I get you another?" I flag down the waitress before she can reply.

"The usual, D?" she asks with a smile.

"You know it, and my friend will have ..."

"Double shot of vodka on the rocks, thanks," she adds softly.

Once we're alone again, I reach my hand across the table. "Let's start over. I'm Darren, and you are?"

Her cheeks flush a light pink, and she reaches her perfectly manicured hand across the table and shakes mine. "Haddie. Nice to meet you." The server promptly delivers our drinks, and once again we're alone. "Wow, that was fast."

"The owner is my friend, more like a brother, so I don't ever have to wait long."

She squeezes the lime into her drink before taking a sip. "Jordan is a good guy. I'm pretty sure he must know the whole city."

I flash her a grin. "I'm sure he probably does. Do you come here a lot?"

She shakes her head. "Not anymore. I used to come here a lot to play pool."

"Did you? Now I feel slighted you didn't want to play with me." I wink.

"It's not you, I swear. My fiancé ... ex, I suppose ... he taught me here. At that very table, actually. I wasn't looking at you ... not that you're not nice to look at or anything," she mumbles. "Anyway, I was lost in memories and didn't really notice you, just what you reminded me of."

The best thing about meeting people in bars is being able to be myself and never seeing them again. People tend to open up, and for a few hours, I can push past the lingering ache in my chest.

"How long have you been separated?"

Sadness crosses her face. "We aren't. It's been three years now."

"Well, Haddie, you're a gorgeous woman. You must have men beating down your door. What gives?"

"Ha!" She blushes and begins to shred her napkin. "I'm far from gorgeous, but thanks for trying to make me feel better."

"I'm not." Haddie *is* beautiful. Her blond hair cascades past her shoulders in bouncing curls. The green of her eyes pops against her eyeliner. Her full red lips would be better served wrapped around my cock. She's rocking the curves, and I can't help but picture myself buried between her thighs.

"He died," she spits out rapidly.

"Oh." And the ache is back. Nothing has ever hurt as much as losing Belle and Noah. Even though six years have passed, it's still fresh.

"We were here that night. Playing pool and having a good time. He was the designated driver, and I was wasted. It was raining, our car hydroplaned, and that's pretty much it. I survived, and he didn't."

"I'm sorry," I whisper. She's a kindred spirit.

"Me too. Tonight is the first time I've been back to this bar. I wasn't going to come, but I felt like I had to. I missed his funeral, and I need closure. I felt like this is the place I would get it."

"I hope you do." I toss back the rest of my drink and meet her sorrowful gaze. "I lost my fiancée six years ago, and that ache never seems to go away. I got to keep a piece of her though. My daughter was only four months old when the accident happened."

She gasps and covers her mouth with her hands. "I'm so sorry." Her sympathy is genuine, but I find it hard to believe she doesn't know this already, especially since she knows J.

"Haddie, do you know who I am? It's okay if you do. I'm just curious."

She finishes her drink and looks back at me. "Should I? Are you an actor or something?"

I laugh. "Or something. I'm the drummer for Bastards and Dangerous, or I used to be."

"Oh my God." She gasps again. "I ... um ... I know your story. Who doesn't? It was national news, but I've never been the kind of person to pay attention to ... How do I say this without sounding like an asshole?"

I chuckle. "I like assholes. Just say whatever you want to."

"I don't follow pop culture or celebrities and stuff. It's never been my thing. Don't get me wrong, I love movies and music and stuff, but ..."

"But what?"

She shrugs, "Well, it's just your job, right? I'd hate to have people following me around at work, down the street, or wherever, so I've never seen the appeal of knowing someone's business like that. I don't need a window into the life of a stranger, you know? I've got enough stuff of my own to deal with."

This girl just went up about ten notches.

"That's a good answer, Haddie. You sure you don't want to bang?" I give her an exaggerated wink, and she finally laughs. It's a beautiful sound, and it momentarily stuns the pain in my heart.

"You're funny. I'm going to ask you something, and you don't have to answer, but ... I don't know any other younger people who have lost someone. How soon did you start having relationships again?"

"I don't. Not real ones, anyway. I had sex just shy of a year after, and I wish I'd waited. Sex fills a need, but it doesn't fill the void. A relationship might. I'm not sure though. So ... you haven't moved on?"

"No," she replies, shaking her head. "No sex, no relationship. At first, I couldn't, but lately ..."

"You miss being intimate with someone."

She nods. "Not just that. I miss sharing interests and making memories. I was standing there watching you play and remembering, but I was also missing that connection. I wonder if the pain will go away or be less intense if I make new memories with someone else. It's hard to wrap my head around the idea though."

It's like she's plucking every word from my deepest thoughts.

"Haddie, I've never been one to let an opportunity pass. You're a cool chick, and for some reason, we were meant to meet. I think you should give me your number and we should go out. On a date ... or ... you know, as friends. Whatever you're comfortable with."

She points back and forth between us. "You want to go on a date? With me?"

"You're the only Haddie I see."

She starts to smile but bites her lip. I reach up and gently pull her lip from her teeth with my thumb. "You've got a beautiful smile. Don't hide it."

"Give me your phone," she says, and I pass it to her. After adding her number, she hands it back to me, and I hit the call button. Seconds later, her phone rings. "You didn't believe me?"

"I did, but now you have my number. Call or text me anytime. I've got a sitter tonight, so I need to get home. Do you need a ride?"

"I'll catch an Uber, but thanks."

"You sure? I don't mind."

"Yeah, I want to stay a bit longer to try to let go of some of these memories."

"Good luck. It was nice meeting you tonight, and I will be calling you soon."

"It was nice to meet you too, Darren. I'm looking forward to our ... night out."

I let my hand graze over hers as I walk away. I want to kiss her, but there's something about her that keeps me in check. I haven't felt this kind of connection since the night I met Belle.

Thinking about that will only make this harder. I have to move forward and make new memories for Cadence and me. It's what Belle would want, and Cady deserves it.

Over coffee the next morning, Mel and Sawyer keep giving me funny looks. At first, I try to ignore it, but with my guilt about Rory weighing heavily on my mind, I can't ignore them for long.

"What?"

Sawyer snorts. "You don't realize it, do you?"

I wipe at my mouth. "Do I have something on my face?"

Sawyer laughs and nearly chokes on his coffee.

"A smile," Mel answers with a grin. "You look truly happy, Darren. Want to share?"

"Do I always look like a miserable son of a bitch or something?"

"Pretty much," Sawyer says and then grumbles when Mel smacks his shoulder.

"Did you meet someone?" Mel presses.

"Or did you get some really hot sex?" Sawyer wags his eyebrows, earning a glare from his wife. Sawyer leans forward and kisses her. "Don't give me that look, Princess. We have hot sex all the damn time."

"No sex, but I did meet someone last night. Well, I got her number. We're supposed to go out. Maybe as friends or maybe more, I'm not exactly sure."

Sawyer's jaw drops. "Holy shit, you're nervous. You must really like her. Is she hot? Does she look like Belle?"

This time, Mel shoves his shoulder hard. "Darren, you don't have to answer any of that." She nails Sawyer with a death glare. "None of her physical attributes matter, do they?"

Sawyer blushes. "No, sorry. Damn, I sounded like a dick, didn't I? I think I reverted back to the days where we were tag teaming girls." Sawyer cringes. "Sorry, Princess. You know what? I'm going to make some more coffee; I think I need it."

When Sawyer comes back to the table, I address his questions. "Maybe I'm nervous. Dating as a single dad isn't something I've given much thought. Moving on from Belle has never been a consideration. Lately, I've been sad about nothing, and I think it's because I'm lonely. Random fucks just aren't cutting it these days. Hell, they're not even appealing."

Mel nods. "This girl appeals to you?"

"She does. She lost her fiancé a few years ago."

Mel gasps. "Oh, how sad."

"I guess I felt a connection to her when she said that, but I felt something before too. She didn't even know who I was at first. She's gorgeous. She has long curly hair and these big green eyes. She reminds me of a blond Ashley Graham. She's fucking sexy. I'm not calling it a match made in heaven or anything, but she's the only person I've wanted to take on a date since Belle. That has to mean something, right?"

"I think that means a lot," Sawyer answers.

Mel's eyes meet mine. "It means everything. I'm happy for you, and Belle would be too."

Sawyer promised the kids he'd take them to the studio today. As much as I love music time with the kids, I head home instead. I sit on the couch for thirty minutes and write texts, only to delete them. Other than Belle, I haven't dated since high school.

With Haddie, I'm completely out of my element. I don't want to play games and wait to text her. If I want something, I'm going for it before someone else snatches it away from me.

Finally, I decide on simple and blunt.

Hi, it's Darren from last night.

I'm not sure why I thought I'd get an immediate reply, but it takes about a half-hour before I get one.

Haddie: Hi, it's Haddie from last night.

Cool, she's got jokes. I can work with this.

Haha sorry, that was probably lame. How was the rest of your night?

Haddie: It was ... sad ... but cathartic ... healing.

The hardest things usually are.

Haddie: That's true. How was the rest of your night?

Yes! She's engaging. This is a good sign. At least, I think it is.

It was fine. Came home, listened to some tunes, thought of you, and went to sleep.

Haddie: Me? Why?

Because you make my dick jump and my head spin. I can't say that though. I need to go with something smoother until she knows me better.

You're captivating. It's been years since anyone has sparked my interest like you do.

Haddie: Oh

Is that a good Oh or a bad one?

Haddie: Sorry, that wasn't very captivating at all, was it? I'm really bad at this. It's been a long time since I've done this.

How about we be bad at it together? In person.

My pulse quickens while I wait for her answer. Why is talking to someone new so stressful?

Haddie: As friends ... or like a date?

Whatever you prefer. I want to get to know you, but if I had my choice, I'd call it a date.

Haddie: We can call it a date and if it's a bust maybe part as friends?

Like that's going to happen.

It won't be a bust, but if it is, sure. I've got the kids tonight. Would Friday work for you? I can do it sooner, but I don't know your work schedule. Do you work?

Ugh, did that sound rude? Do I care if she doesn't work?

Haddie: Yes, I work. I'm a contributing member of society in case it was bothering you. Friday is fine.

Wasn't bothering me at all. Can I make you dinner at my beach house? Sometimes going out can be difficult. I'd like to get to know you before putting you through that in case you don't like me. It wouldn't be kind to torture you.

That was probably TMI, but she should know what she's getting into.

Haddie: That bad?

Not so much these days, but it's hit or miss.

Haddie: Sure, dinner at your house is fine. Send me the address and the time.

Would it be okay if I pick you up?

Haddie: I'm fully capable of driving, or do you not want me to have your address?

Damn … I didn't think she'd go there.

Call me old-fashioned. I might not be able to take you out yet, but I'd like to have some semblance of a real date.

Haddie: You're a gentleman deep down. Good to know. I'll send you my address later. Just let me know what time. See you Friday.

Seven sharp. See you then.

And just like that, I have a date. A huge part of my heart feels like I'm betraying Belle. There's another part that knows she'd want this for me. I'm not sure why, but Haddie makes me happy.

Haddie

"Holy Christ on a cracker, Haddie! You have a date with a rock star!" It's Monday afternoon, and Marina and I are setting up my new office.

"Shh. I'm sure he doesn't need everyone knowing his business, and I sure as hell don't want people in mine. You get to know because you're my best friend. This is only between the two of us."

Marina plops down in the chair across from mine with a dazed smile. "I can't believe my best friend snagged the last eligible bachelor from Bastards and Dangerous, and you didn't even know who he was. That's like ... an epic origin story for fairy tale love." She sighs in a swoon-worthy way, and I swear I can see hearts dancing in her eyes.

"I hate to break it to you, but the only origin of this story is I met a hot guy at a bar and he—"

"Yes?" she prompts. "He what? Spill, Haddie ... I'm dying here. Let me live vicariously through you."

I chuckle at her theatrics. "He's got a great smile, and his eyes are as blue as the Caribbean Sea. There's no doubt in my mind he's a player. Dude has great game, but I gave him my number because there is something right under the surface that's familiar."

She quirks a brow. "That's it? Familiar? What does that even mean?"

With a sigh, I lean back in my chair. "I'm not sure, but it feels like I can trust him. I wish I didn't. He's rich, famous, and gorgeous as sin, and I'm—"

"Don't say it. You rag on yourself way too much. You are gorgeous, my friend, and if he asked you out, he thinks you're as amazing as I do."

"It doesn't negate that I'm a plus-sized woman. I'm sure the press will have a field day with it. I can picture the headlines now."

The two of us sit in silence for a moment as the gravity of the situation sets in. She can't tell me I'm wrong. Hollywood likes pretty people, and while I'm not a dog or anything, extra weight is still a gossip topic.

"Haddie, ever since Richie died, you've been focused on your size. When you were with him, you never worried about that. I don't know if you're projecting your insecurities about love and life onto your size or what, but you need to stop. It's not healthy, babe."

"First, that's not true. I did worry in the beginning, but we were young and in college when we met, and I was about twenty-five pounds lighter. Second, it's not like I haven't tried losing weight. With all the adhesions and scars from the accident, any kind of stomach toning or firming exercise is kind of out the door. And third," I lean back in my seat and sigh, "he's next-level, Marina. Hollywood royalty. Anything above a size eight in his world gets people talking. I like him, but do I want to open myself up to that kind of scrutiny?"

She frowns. "Dating any celebrity would come with a whole new world and rules. You're going to have to always dress nice, have your makeup done, and make sure your hair perfect, which it usually is."

"Ugh, you're not making me feel better. This is a disaster."

"Not necessarily. He's aware of the world he lives in, and you never know how he feels about the press. I doubt he would've asked you out if he was concerned about it though. Besides, you don't even know if you will click. One date at his house doesn't seem like a big deal. Plus, he's not a big star right now. They're focusing on releasing bands, not putting out new music."

I lean forward and meet her gaze. "And you know that how?"

Marina grins, and her eyes twinkle with delight. "Just because you don't follow celebrities doesn't mean I don't. Darren and his brothers built some studio in honor of their brother who passed away. They're helping young indies work their way up in the industry by putting an honest team behind them."

"See? This is exactly why it's a bad idea to date him. Everyone knows everything about most aspects of his life. If we were to get serious, they'd know about *my* life. I don't know if I want that kind of future."

"Well, that's a choice only you can make. If you could have something special with him, like what you had with Richie, would you want it? This time, you'd actually get the happily ever after." Knowing this is still a sensitive subject, her voice drops an octave at the end.

"Yes, I think so, but his fame—"

"Is off-putting." She waves her hand dismissively. "We've established that already. What if he weren't famous? Would you then?"

"If we click as well as I think we will, yes."

"Essentially, you're punishing him for his job. That's not very fair."

And just like that, I've been put in my place.

"Touché."

Later in the evening, my phone buzzes as I'm enjoying a glass of wine in my back yard.

Darren: We should get to know each other before our date. Maybe it won't be as awkward.

I'm game ... what do you want to know?

Darren: What do you do for a living?

I'm a child psychologist, and I work for a local elementary school.

Darren: *Wow*

Darren: *I mean that in the best kind of way*

Darren: *This is stupid, can we talk?*

Smiling, I press talk on my phone.

"Thanks for calling. I tend to say what pops into my head at all times. At least on the phone, you can hear my voice and know I'm not being an ass."

I laugh at his nervousness and am thankful I'm not the only one who's bad at this. "I didn't think you were being an ass. If anything, I'm sure I'm pretty boring to you."

"Seriously? That's what you think? Not at all. You went to school and got a degree. As long as you enjoy what you do, that's all that matters. Do you like your job?"

"I love my job. Helping kids is what I was born to do."

A tapping sound comes across the line, and I can fully imagine him rapping his fingers to a beat in his head like he did the night at the bar. Music must flow through his soul.

"I must seem like a big loser to you, huh?"

"Whoa … why would you think that? You're one of the most successful musicians in the world."

"I don't have a degree or a job anymore. Some days I feel like I'm just existing."

"My friend mentioned you own a studio and produce bands. That doesn't sound like 'just existing.' Like you said, what does it matter as long as you're happy? You take care of your kid and have a stable home. Are you happy?"

He pauses, and silence greets my ears.

"I'm content … but I want to be happy again."

My heart flutters at the tenderness in his words.

"Then you will be."

He chuckles. "That simple? You say it and it shall be?"

I take a sip of my wine and push back on my porch swing. "Nothing is ever simple, but it seems like we're both trying to find the same thing. I can't make you happy, but our journeys are similar. I'm all for walking beside you while we try to find it."

Darren hisses. "Don't be so sure about that. For the first time in a long time, I want happiness again, and that has something to do with you."

"Why? You could have your pick of women."

"Yeah, but I picked you. Haven't you ever clicked with someone and wanted to know more? That's what I felt when we met."

"I'm pretty sure you tried to get into my pants."

He laughs heartily. "You're right, I did. If I'm lucky, maybe I'll still have a shot at that. What can I say? You're hot, and I'm sexually deprived. Damn, don't take that wrong. Let's just not rule out sex yet."

"Clicking with someone is important though. If there's no initial ..."

"Spark?"

I take another sip of wine. "I was trying to avoid the cliché, but yeah. If there's no spark, why try?"

"I don't think it's cliché. I think it's chemistry. You either connect with someone or you don't. We did. At least, I think we did."

Everything about Darren and me is a contradiction. He's thin and fit, I'm curvy and chunky. He's rich, and I work for the public school system. This couldn't be any stranger.

"Haddie, are you there?"

"Yeah, sorry." I finish my wine and put the glass on the patio table next to me. "There was a spark. I wouldn't have given you my number if there wasn't."

"Really?"

"Why is that surprising? The *last* thing I want to do is give some creeper my number." He laughs until it sounds like he's wheezing. "Care to share what's so funny?"

"This, us, it's so ... normal. I love it. For almost fifteen years my life has been about who I am. Women have only wanted to know me because of my status. Except for Belle. Well, she wanted to know me, but it was her job. We just happened to click too. I'm sorry if I doubted you; it's an unfortunate side effect of fame."

He's so down to earth it's impossible not to like him.

"It's okay. I have my own insecurities; it's part of life."

"Oh yeah? Like what?"

It takes a second to breathe. There's no way I can delve into my issues this fast. I'm not about to make him run yet.

"Nothing I want to talk about right now. When I know you better, I'll share."

"Deal. I have an important question to ask. Does it bother you that I have a child?"

Oh man, that one hits me right in the feels. "No, not at all. I mean, I don't want to meet her anytime soon or anything, but that's completely for her benefit. I don't think kids should meet the people their parents are dating unless that person is significantly important and the relationship is progressing into a long-term situation."

Darren exhales loudly. "I'm happy to hear that. Cadence is the most important thing in my world right now. I have to be careful with her heart because it's mine to protect."

My eyes fill with tears. I wish every parent loved their kids and wanted to protect them as much as he does. "She's lucky to have you. I've worked with kids who haven't been as fortunate."

"*I'm* lucky to have *her*. She was on the bus that crashed about an hour or less before it happened. I could've lost both of them, but for some reason, she was spared. I'll never take her life for granted." Darren pauses. "This call is becoming depressing, and that wasn't my intention. If I can confess a secret, I just wanted to hear your voice."

"Are you sure? I thought you were still trying to get into my pants."

He laughs, and I relish the sound over his sadness a few seconds ago. "That will always be a goal. You should make getting into mine one of yours. I've got skills between the sheets, you know."

"Oh my God, I'm sure you do. I mean, maybe some current STI testing should take place if this date goes well. I'm sure ... well,

I assume … please don't take this wrong, but I'm guessing you've been with more people than me."

I need more wine.

"What? You think I was a whore because I was a rock star? Haddie, talk about presumptuous."

"I'm so sorry. I shouldn't assume."

I'm completely mortified and glad he's not here. His laugh greets my ears, and I realize he's fucking with me.

"I have current tests. Our label used to test us twice a year. I've kept up the habit. I'm also a lot more discretionary lately on who I hop into bed with. I've had a healthy sex life for a long time. I hope that won't be an issue for you. If you've had an equally healthy sex life, it won't bother me one bit."

"This is such a bizarre conversation. I have recent tests too. *If* we get to that point, I'll show you. I haven't had sex with anyone but my vibrator since the accident. I wasn't ready."

Damn, that was a lot of word vomit. I know he understands, but it's embarrassing to admit.

"Thank you for trusting me with that information. If I push you too fast, tell me you're not ready. I like sex, probably more than I should, but it's not a deal breaker for me. You're worth the wait."

I wish I knew him better to know if his swoon level is always this high or if he's only like this when he's trying to fuck someone new. My instincts tell me he's the real deal though.

"Thank you."

"I have to pick up Cadence and my nephew Nate from their grandparents' house, but can I call you tomorrow?"

"I'd like that. Goodnight, Darren."

"Night, Haddie. Sweet dreams."

chapter 7

Darren

"Run, Nate, before they get you! I'll save you!" Cadence squeals excitedly.

"Beat on the Brat" by The Ramones is playing all through the house and Sawyer, Wyatt, Jordan, all the kids, and me are hitting each other with inflatable baseball bats. This is one of their favorite games and likely proves we're probably not the most mature dads around, but it's fun, and that's the important part.

Wyatt's son Jake and Jordan's son Sebastian are teaming up trying to take down Wyatt. In the blink of an eye, I'm greeted with laughter and attacked from behind.

"I got you, Uncle Darren!" Nate runs toward Sawyer to help Cadence, and I give up and collapse on the couch. We've been at this for about an hour, and I don't think we'll ever win. These kids have endless energy.

"Whoa! What's going on in here?" Mel cries from the entry of my living room as she places Noelle on the floor. Sawyer scoops her up, and she giggles uncontrollably. That girl loves her daddy to pieces.

"Mommy, come beat Daddy with the baseball bat too," Nate urges.

Mel shakes her head but grins at the sight before her. She sits next to me, and we watch as the dads fall one by one to the floor in surrender. The kids cheer, clap, and high-five each other.

"Okay, guys, how about you all watch a movie in the playroom." I'm already on my feet knowing they'll all knock out in about fifteen minutes.

A chorus of cheers goes up, and with the exception of Nate and Cadence, they all run ahead of me. Cadence simply holds out her hand and Nate reaches for it. They walk hand in hand to the playroom.

I look behind us to find Mel taking photos of the moment. These kids will have photos of memories they can't possibly remember when they're older. If they ever do get married, it's going to make a great story for their kids.

Once the kids are settled, Mel snuggles up next to Sawyer.

These two are so fucking romantic. Never in an overly ridiculous way but their love shines. I suppose, if I were to fall in love again, maybe I'd be the same way. Time waits for no one.

While the kids watch their movie, we start going over some studio business. It's great to work with the people who are in my life every day. Impromptu meetings with the kids are the norm, and besides being convenient, it keeps us close. After about thirty minutes of discussion, I look down at my phone. I click on the video feed from the playroom and all the kids are already sleeping.

"They're out already," I say, showing them my screen.

Somehow, while I was checking on the kids, their topic of discussion turned to having more kids. For some reason Mel is staring at me.

"Nope, Cadence is all I need. Besides, Jordan and Allie are popping out the next Weston in a few months. You guys get that baby fix with them. My swimmers are off limits."

"Besides, he'd need a woman for that first." Wyatt chimes in and Mel bites her bottom lip. "Wait – is there a girl? What the hell am I missing?"

Jordan turns his attention to me too, "I'm with him, what am I missing?"

Sawyer reaches for Mel's hand. "On that note, we're going to run home and have a quickie while the kids are asleep and my mom has the twins. Hate to run ... but later. Call us when the kids are up, unless it's in the next thirty minutes, then be a good uncle and give me time to come first."

Mel's mortified voice carries through the hall, "Jesus, Sawyer ..."

"Oh, come on, Princess, it's not like they don't know we fuck. Look at all our damn kids."

The three of us laugh as the door closes, and then I finally give them the information they're waiting for.

"I met a woman at the bar over the weekend. We have a date on Friday."

Wyatt and Jordan exchange cautious glances. "Way to keep it low key. Why the secrecy?" Wyatt is mad, and I guess I can't blame him.

"Not secrecy, just being cautious. She's nice, and she's also lost her fiancé. The date is sort of a trial for both of us. If it's a total bust, there's nothing to talk about. If it's not, then I was going to share."

Jordan's brow furrows. "What's her name?"

"Haddie."

He straightens his stance. "Blonde, curvy, sweet as can be, and sexy as all get out? Did you meet her at my bar?"

This doesn't sound good. "Yes, all of that, and yes, at your bar."

Jordan massages his temple, and Wyatt's eyes bounce between us. "Darren, please don't fuck with Haddie if you don't really like her. She's a good woman, and she's been through a lot."

I forgot Haddie mentioned knowing J. "How long have you known her?"

Jordan sighs. "Remember my friend Richie that died a few weeks before my wedding? Haddie was his girl, so I guess about five years or more? She nearly died in that accident, and her recovery was brutal. Just be sure before you get deep with her. I'd hate for her to fall for someone who ... fuck ... you know what I mean."

Anger burns low in my gut. "Someone who what? Doesn't know exactly how she feels?"

Wyatt interjects, "I'm going to let you two hash this out while I go outside and call Anna to check in. Don't kill each other, there are kids sleeping in the other room."

Once Wyatt leaves Jordan sits across from me, but he doesn't talk until we hear the front door close. "Look, Darren, I'm going to give it to you straight. I know you fucked my sister a few months back."

My eyes widen, and my palms begin to sweat. "Jordan, fuck ..."

He laughs. "Man, you and Rory are the least of my concerns. She came to the bar drunk and told me all about how she seduced you in order to figure out her feelings. I'm not going to tell Sawyer, but at some point, you should because if Rory spilled to me, she's going to spill again. If it's any consolation, I'm not mad. I know my sister is a force to be reckoned with, especially when she gets an idea in her head."

"It's eating away at me, but wrecking my friendship with Sawyer would kill me. I don't remember a time he hasn't been my best fucking friend."

He nods. "I get that, and like I said, I'm not telling anyone. I wouldn't betray Rory like that, and you know, the bartender is really like a poorly paid therapist. I tend to keep all sorts of secrets. Back to Haddie though—"

"I like her, J. I don't know her well, but I'm trying to get to know her, and she's different. We have ... something. Chemistry, or whatever. I've been miserable since that shit went down with Rory, but Haddie is the first person who has made me happy, legitimately happy, since Belle."

Jordan looks me over as if assessing my character. "Okay, you know where I stand. If two people I care about can find happiness with each other after what you've both been through fuck, I'm all for it."

"Thanks, man."

He leans forward. "Has Haddie mentioned anything to you about your fame or anything?"

My body stills. "She didn't know who I was."

Jordan laughs. "That doesn't surprise me in the least. Look, I don't know if this still applies and hell, it's most definitely not my place to say, but at the beginning with Richie, she was insecure about her size. Just keep that in your head because with your fame, if this is something that still bugs her … you know what, just ignore me."

"Man, I'll never understand women. I'm not sure there is a woman on the planet I wouldn't be attracted to in some form. I'll keep it in the back of my mind, but it's not an issue to me, and I hope it's not an issue for her anymore. There is so much more important shit to worry about in life than who has a few extra pounds or a few gray hairs, or other superficial shit. But I absolutely respect if she has that concern. Thanks for the heads-up, J."

"Daddy, Jake farted on my head." Sebastian shuffles into the room, rubbing sleep from his eyes and Jordan stifles back a laugh.

"Like father like son," I mutter.

Jordan snorts and scoops Bastian into his arms. "Isn't that the truth? We need to get back to the bar and pick up Allie. Tell Sawyer I'll check in later. I don't want to interrupt them. Keep me posted on Haddie and if you do end up talking to Sawyer about that other thing… let me know, and I'll do damage control. He might be pissed, but he'll always love you."

"Thanks, J, later Bastian, come back and play with your cousins again soon."

He high-fives me over Jordan's shoulder. "Bye, Uncle Darren. See you next time."

Six years ago, I was on a world tour without a care in the world, now most days I feel like I'm running a preschool. I never would've imagined how much I love the now and how little I miss those touring days in comparison. I only wish Belle were here to be a part of it.

A lot has changed in the last few months, and maybe I should be thanking Rory for it. The night I spent with her made me realize how sad and desperate I'd become. Belle would have detested that version of me. Now I have a shot at bettering myself and maybe even dating someone special again. The unease I've always felt when thinking about dating isn't as strong right now, but I wonder if that will change if it actually happens.

"Hey, I was just thinking about you."

The sound of her voice eases my anxiety over calling her.

"Good thoughts, I hope."

"Okay, more like wondering if I should text you since you hadn't texted me yet. That's stupid, right? If you didn't want to talk, you'd tell me."

"You can call or text any time you'd like. I've got the kids tonight and was trying to get them down for the count before I bothered trying to have an uninterrupted conversation."

"You mention kids in the plural form often. Do you run the neighborhood daycare or something?"

"Sometimes it feels like it, but no. All of us in the band settled down around the same time. Babies started coming, and now I've got lots of nieces and nephews. We're a huge family, so I'm rarely alone, and I like to keep Cadence around them as much as possible."

She hums on the other end of the line. "That makes sense. After losing her mom, I can see family being extra important."

"Exactly. The night Belle and Noah died was also Nate's birthday. Before Mel and Sawyer got married, we all lived together at the beach house. Nate and Cadence have shared a room since they were a little over a year old. They're best friends. When Mel and Sawyer moved, the kids didn't handle it well. Neither did I. The house next door went on the market and Sawyer swooped in and bought it for us. We're working on weaning them apart because they start school soon. They have to get used to sleeping in their own houses."

"How sweet. They're like built-in siblings."

I practically choke on my water. "Um ... no, we're not going that route, which is why getting them to sleep separately now is a good thing."

"Come again?"

"Belle fantasized they would grow up and get married one day. We're trying to let whatever is going to happen unfold naturally. But the way they gravitate toward each other is ... well, hard to explain. Cadence is fiercely protective of Nate and always has been. They hold hands and say the sweetest things about each other. Mel has albums full of cute moments she's captured on film. She says they're memories, but we know she's secretly plotting the slide show of their wedding already. None of us will say it, but I'm pretty sure we'll all be crushed if they don't end up married."

"And if they don't end up together?" Her cautious tone amuses me. I bet the psychologist in her is analyzing the hell out of this.

"Then they don't. They'll likely be the best of friends, and we'll have an album documenting their friendship from the start."

Her loud exhale makes me smile. If nothing else, she cares. "How many kids are there?"

"Hm, let's see. Sawyer and Mel have four, Wyatt and Anna have two, Sawyer's older sister Diane has four, Jordan and Allie have one and one on the way, and I have Cadence."

Haddie gasps. "Oh my God. I don't know why I didn't put two and two together. You're Jordan's brother."

"Yup, not by blood, but the Westons are family. Even though our lives have taken a different path than we all originally thought, we're extremely close. How about you? What's your family like?"

"I'm an only child. My parents are great, but it's just us. I don't a lot of friends. Richie was the social one, and after he died, it didn't feel right to try to hang around them and be a reminder. Plus, it's not like I was in the headspace for friendship. I do work with my best friend. Marina teaches at the school I'm assigned to this year."

I don't like how she's so isolated, but it would make dating her much easier without having to worry about her friends leaking things to the press for a payday.

"I'm an only child too."

Our conversation pauses, but not uncomfortably.

"Darren, are you okay?"

"Yeah, just thinking. When I pick you up on Friday, would you be upset if my security team drove me?"

She inhales sharply, and I can picture her breasts heaving as she does it. Fuck, I have to adjust myself. Even thinking of Haddie's tits turns me on.

"It starts that fast, huh? First date out the gate and there's already a chaperone?"

I hate hearing the defeat in her voice. As much as I love everything about being famous, having a normal life sounds extremely appealing these days.

"It doesn't have to, but on the off chance someone got a whiff of our date, it's going to be a thing. I have to face reality. I'm just trying to protect you."

It would kill me if something happened to her because of me.

"Oh," her voice softens, "thank you for looking out for me. I'm fine with you picking me up however you need to. This is just so … surreal, I guess."

"Fuck, Haddie, I'm sorry. If you want to back out, I get it. With Belle, it was part of the protocol. She was an industry reporter, so she knew what to expect. Other than Belle and girls from high school, I've never dated. I have no idea what this is like, so—"

"We'll figure it out together."

And just like that, she eases my fears again.

"How did you know you were ready to date again?"

It sounds like she's pouring a glass of wine.

"It's been a slow process. One day I woke up less sad. Progressively I found myself smiling more and being generally happy overall. I think the kicker was the morning I woke up and looked at his picture and I smiled instead of immediately bursting into tears. I started remembering him in good times, instead of images of that night. Even still, it took about nine more months to finally build up the courage to go to the bar and say goodbye. How did you know?"

Ugh, this is where it gets tricky.

"Less than a year after Belle died, I had sex with someone. I spiraled downward after. I thought if I got it over with, it would be like closing a chapter of my life and I could move forward."

"I take it that didn't happen?"

I hold back a groan. "Not even close. Eventually, I was ready for sex, not for anything more. I never thought I'd want to date again, but about a year ago I started spiraling downward. Making bad choices, drinking a lot, fucking more often."

She hisses.

"Sorry, but I don't want to lie to you."

"It's okay. Keep talking."

"Six months ago, I was drunk and did something I can't take back. I'm grateful for it, though, because it made me realize I needed to change. But if certain people find out, not to mention the press, it could destroy me. The next day, I poured out the gin and decided to get my head right."

I lie back on my pillows and look at the ceiling.

"Did it work?"

"I think so. I realized I was spiraling because I was lonely. Everyone around me has someone to love and some have families. I finally admitted to myself that Belle isn't coming back. I have the best of her in Cadence. Her smile, her personality, she's all Belle. Maybe it's selfish to want more."

"No, don't say that," Haddie says firmly. "People like you and me ... we have the right to be cautious. If I find love again, I'll appreciate it more this time around. I regret some of the stupid arguments Richie and I had. I can't pretend they didn't happen, but it was time wasted."

"I understand completely. I only had a year with Belle, and we spent most of that time via Skype. We cherished every second, but we didn't have very long. Sometimes I wonder how it's possible to miss someone so much that I only had for such a short amount of time."

"Ah but that's the thing about connecting with someone. Once your person has imprinted on your soul, it doesn't matter if have them for a fleeting moment, or a lifetime, your heart has already recognized your mate."

I grin from ear to ear. "Sounds like you might be a bit romantic, Haddie."

"Maybe, I am."

"Did you write the songs for your band too? You're pretty good with your words."

"You obviously don't listen to our music, or you wouldn't ask that. We weren't a swoony kind of band. Except for the last album – it was acoustical, and Sawyer was falling in love and wrote a pretty swoony ballad as the title track. What's funny is he didn't even realize he was falling before it was too late."

"What happened?"

"Get comfortable if you want to know; this could take a while."

I spend the next few hours talking to Haddie all about the band and our past and Sawyer's love life. By the time we hang up, I'm exhausted and exhilarated. Only one more day until our date.

chapter 8

Haddie

"What are you wearing? Send me a picture," Marina huffs through the phone.

"Dark jeans, flowy royal-blue blouse, black canvas sneakers in case he wants to walk on the beach, and random jewelry." I pause doing my makeup long enough to take a selfie and send it to her.

"You look super cute. Casual but not sloppy, cute but not trying too hard. Totally hot enough to see all his tattoos up close and personal if you choose to."

I've seen the tats on his neck and arms, but Marina made sure to send me a shirtless photo from one of his shows. I've never been a fan of so much ink, but it looks good on Darren.

"I should cancel. This is stupid, Marina. I'm out of my depth. He wants to travel, which is cool, but he's seen so much already. Why would he want to be a tourist with me when he's got to be a seasoned pro by now?"

"Girl, you're overthinking everything. I read an article once where he talked about his desire to travel the world. He said as cool as it was to travel to so many places with the band, it was all work and no play. They never got more than a few hours to sightsee. How messed up is that?"

Shit, I'd never even considered that. Celebrities give up so much for their art.

"That sucks, and I'm over here stressing about one date."

"Stop overthinking this. What if he's the one? Do you think it was a coincidence you decided to say goodbye at the exact time and place where he happened to be? You've both lost someone, and maybe you're meant to find love again together."

"Stop it. You sound like a Hallmark movie."

"No, I sound like I believe in destiny."

"I need to take this one date at a time. Anything more is overwhelming and terrifying. Everything about his life scares me. He's rich, famous, has freaking bodyguards and a paparazzi patrol, *and* he's a single dad."

"Do you hear that?"

"Hear what?"

"Let me turn it up," Marina offers. "Cry me a River" by Justin Timberlake blasts through the line, and I grin.

"Haddie, this man has his shit straight. He doesn't live on his mama's couch. He has priorities and responsibilities, and he likes you. Yeah, you'll have to deal with the press, but he's pre-emptively protecting you by coming to get you with his guards."

I groan as I shut off the lights in my room. "You're right, it's one night, and it could be fun."

My doorbell rings, and Marina screams, "He's there! Don't keep him waiting. It's going to be amazing. Grab your purse, toss in some condoms, and call me tomorrow when you get home."

"No condoms, no sex. I'll text you when I get home *tonight*." I end the call and answer the door.

Darren leans against a post on my porch and eyes me appreciatively. "You look gorgeous. Are you ready to go?"

My eye catches the black Cadillac Escalade with blackout windows waiting at the curb. This can't be real.

"Sure, let me grab my purse and keys. Do you want to come in for a second? It's not much, but it's mine."

Darren steps inside and looks around. "Don't be nervous." He grabs my hand, giving it a light squeeze. "I like your house. It reminds me of the one I lived in when I was in elementary school. What's your favorite place or thing about it?"

My heart has been thumping against my chest since he grabbed my hand. "The back yard. Want to see?"

He entwines his fingers with mine. "Lead the way."

I flip the switch to turn on the twinkly lights, and he carefully follows me into the yard without releasing my hand.

"This is incredible; it's like a private oasis."

"Thanks, this is usually where I am when we talk. I'm thinking I might put in a Koi pond in the spring."

He nods. "I can totally picture it."

Darren runs the thumb of his free hand across my cheek before leaning forward and kissing it. "Thank you for showing me your favorite place. Now I know where to imagine you when we're on the phone."

I'm completely dazed and fighting hard not to bring my fingers to my cheek. It's like I can still feel his lips lingering there. That's insane. It's been a long time since a man has touched me and my body is short-circuiting or something.

"Do you want to go, or ..."

"I'd rather stay here, but I made you dinner, and Ryan and Aria have plans after they drop us off."

Darren still has my hand in his but lets me go up the porch steps first. Just as we step inside, he groans.

"You okay?"

He shrugs. "I'm fine. My cock is a bit uncomfortable. Fuck, Haddie, your ass ... We should go because I'm trying really hard to be a gentleman tonight."

Laughing, I grab my purse and toss my phone and keys inside. He finally releases my hand and pops his head outside before giving me the all clear. He grabs my hand again and leads me to the car after I lock the door.

A pretty girl in the front seat turns toward me as Darren and I climb into the back. "Hi! I'm Aria, Ryan's girlfriend. You must be Haddie." She smiles, but the hulk of a man next to her practically growls.

"Aria, babe, we talked about this."

Darren snorts. "Relax, Ryan, you guys are family. Haddie, Ryan is one of our top two security guards and one of our best friends. He has an issue with being friendly while on the clock."

"Nice to meet you, Haddie. Darren pays me to protect him. If I'm sitting here shooting the breeze, I could miss a threat."

"Nice to meet you too," I answer.

Aria smiles adoringly at her man. "Ryan, you wouldn't let anything happen to anyone. You're always alert, even off the clock." She kisses him on the cheek and puts her seatbelt back on, and I do the same.

"No, he wouldn't," Darren interjects." I've seen this guy in action many times. He's badass. Anyway, we're intruding on your date night. I should be thanking you for helping me out."

Aria turns her head toward us. "Are you kidding? This is awesome. I feel like a super spy up here. I'm totally going to make a song out of this too. Besides, we go out all the time and you haven't been out ..."

Ryan nails her with a look, but Darren just laughs. "It's okay, Aria, she knows I haven't dated anyone in five years."

A relieved sigh fills the car. "Sorry I almost let the cat out of the bag. I just get excited for love."

Darren squeezes my hand and smiles while mouthing *She means well.*

Aria babbles to Ryan along the way, and I'm content to look out the window and watch the scenery fly by. The reflection of the setting sun on the ocean is sensational.

"This is my favorite time of day," Darren murmurs.

I turn and give him my full attention. "How come?"

"I'm not sure. Sawyer loves the sunrise, but I've always felt the best things in life happen after dark."

"That's interesting. I've always liked this time of day because it means I can unwind. The stress of the day melts away, and I feel like I can finally exhale and be me."

"I can see that," Darren answers. Ryan turns down a driveway and pushes a button to open a massive set of gates. When the SUV comes to a stop, Darren helps me out, and we say our goodbyes.

"They're cute. Have they been together long?"

Darren leads me inside the house, and it's all I can do not to gasp. Not only is it immense but it's incredibly gorgeous. Floor-to-ceiling windows line the entire backside for a breathtaking view of the ocean. It's a stark reminder we live in completely different worlds.

"Maybe a year? Now that we don't tour anymore, our security team can finally have lives too. It's hard to settle down with someone when you're constantly on the go. We knew how hard it was for us to date, but they didn't pick fame."

"Maybe not, but they picked their career. We can't always harbor guilt for other people's choices, no matter how much we may want to."

Darren turns and pulls me close. "I'm glad you're here. Can I get you a glass of wine?"

He smells like the ocean and fresh air. "I'm glad I'm here too. I'd love a glass of wine. Anything you have is fine; there isn't much I don't like."

"A girl after my own heart."

I wander around the living room and end up in front of a shelf with some photos. There is one of him, a baby, and his arm is around a beautiful woman.

"Does that bother you?"

I turn around and accept a glass of red wine from Darren. "Is that Belle?"

"Yeah, that picture is from Noah's wedding."

"She's stunning."

He nods. "She was. I'm sorry, I should have put it away."

"Why? It doesn't bother me. She was a huge part of your life."

"She was, but I'm hoping we can avoid living in the past tonight. Are you hungry?" Darren leads me into the kitchen where a bottle of cabernet sits on the counter and the scent of tomatoes and garlic wafts through the air. It smells amazing. "I can have dinner ready in about fifteen minutes."

"Can I help?"

"Nope, but you can talk to me while I cook the pasta. It's nothing fancy, just spaghetti."

It's surreal to watch him work so easily in the kitchen. "Did your mom teach you to cook?"

He laughs. "She tried. I can make some family recipes pretty well. I've picked up a few things since Cadence was born, but Mel taught me how to make this. She made meals on the bus when we toured. Even with limited kitchen space, she managed to make things that were far better than any of the food we were eating on the road."

"Even at the end? I mean, you had to be eating better food by then."

He pulls a salad from the refrigerator. "You'd think, but no. We had some upscale restaurant meals, which were great, but it was still restaurant food. After a bunch of fancy meals, it comes to a point where you crave something homemade."

"Don't let a food critic or a chef from a five-star restaurant hear you say that."

"Know a lot about restaurants, do you?"

I take a sip of my wine and hum my appreciation. He smiles at my response, easing my nerves. "I know enough. Richie was a chef and dreamed of having his own restaurant."

"Shit, I'm sorry." Darren tops off my wine after popping some bread into the oven.

I wave dismissively. "It's fine. We're going to stumble a bit until we know each other better. I guess this isn't the typical 'best way to get over someone is to get under someone new' scenario." My laughter bubbles to the surface as my face heats.

"Well, I'm not opposed to getting under you, or getting you under me." He waggles his eyebrows, and I laugh even harder. I think we've officially broken the ice.

"You're a shameless flirt."

His blue eyes lock on mine. "Only with people I like. I don't beat around the bush either. I want to fuck you, but at the right time and when you're comfortable."

Hot damn. I have to be blushing, and the wine is not helping.

"Can I get some water?"

He grins sinfully but slips behind me, his chest against my back, and places his hands on the bar on either side of me. Leaning close to my ear, I feel his breath against my skin. "I like you, Haddie. Get used to it."

Goose bumps break out on my skin, and my nipples tighten. I'm not sure how I'm going to make it through this date with my clothes on, but I'm going to try.

"Your pasta ... I-I think it's done," I stammer as the water boils over the edge of the pot.

Darren backs away and tends to the stove. Within minutes he's plated salad, pasta, and bread for both of us. "Bar or table?"

"Let's stay at the bar. I like the casual feel of it."

He moves his stool catty-corner to me and digs in right away, but I push my food around on my plate.

"What's wrong? I thought you were hungry."

"I was. I mean ... I am." If I duck out now, can I save my dignity?

"Do you not like spaghetti? I can make something else." Darren pushes back both of our plates and moves to stand.

"No, it's not that. I love spaghetti. It's just ... I have issues." I look down at my hands and fidget with my napkin.

"Okay," he says hesitantly. "Talk to me, Haddie."

"I'm fat," I blurt out as tears fill my eyes.

Sucking in a breath, he steps in front of me and gently takes each of my hands. "I find you extremely attractive, Haddie. If you're hesitant to eat in front of me, I understand. Women of all sizes seem to have the same issue."

"That's supposed to make me feel better?"

Darren throws his hands up in defeat. "I don't know what should make you feel better. I like you *exactly* as you are. Food is part of life and, in my family, a way to bond.

"I'm the only child of a Mexican mother. She cooks for twenty people when there are only three. At Christmas, tamales are a week-long process. My mom and my tias cook up a storm, and if I'm home, I help. Cadence is already learning. Haddie," he tips my chin up and looks me in the eye, "can you let go of your fears and enjoy a meal with me?" The sincerity in his gaze is almost overwhelming.

"I'm sorry, Darren. It's hard being a big girl. It feels like people stare at me when I eat, and it's only added to my insecurities."

He rakes his gaze over my body and licks his lips before locking his eyes on mine. "You're what, maybe a size sixteen?"

My eyes widen, and he grins. "Maybe an eighteen in an off brand?"

My mouth drops, and he runs his finger across my lips. "Haddie, I'm attracted to all types of women. All shapes, sizes, colors, religions, you name it."

"It's all pink on the inside, right?"

He arches a brow and caresses my cheek. "Wow, and people say *I'm* crass. That wasn't even close to what I was thinking. I have a feeling once I know more of your past, I'm going to want to kill some of your exes. You said Richie was a chef. Was he a good guy?"

"I thought we weren't living in the past tonight."

"That was before I knew we needed to set some ground rules. Answer the question." As if sensing my hesitation, he adds, "Please."

"He was a great guy."

"Did your issues start before or after him?" He tilts his head and looks at me patiently.

"Before. Richie had to earn my trust and get me to a place where I believed he wanted me for me."

He smiles. "Then that's what I'll do too."

"Darren, I saw that photo of Belle. She was gorgeous, petite, and dainty, and I'm so—"

He presses his finger against my lip. "Don't talk about my date like that. Belle was beautiful in her way. You are beautiful in yours. Over time, I've become a good judge of character. I've fucked around for the last few years, and that was all that I did before I met Belle."

"Rock stars," I mutter.

The corner of his lip kicks up in a suppressed smile. "It's who I am, and I can't change it. You got to me the night we met. Sure, your shirt hugged your gorgeous tits perfectly. Your jeans showed off your voluptuous hips and incredible ass. Your plump lips with that red lipstick ... Damn, I wanted them wrapped around my cock like you wouldn't believe. But when we talked, your eyes held so many emotions I understood. Your words conveyed the pain of a kindred spirit. I wanted to know you and hold you. The last time that happened, I fell in love with Belle."

"I see."

He locks eyes with me. "Do you?"

I feel like such a shit. "Yes. I'm sorry about all of this."

He leans down and kisses my forehead. "No need to apologize. Eat dinner with me, and then we'll light a fire and talk. Unless you want to call this off?"

"No, let's enjoy the night."

Darren

Haddie and I have a nice conversation through dinner. I'm careful not to stare at her too much— just enough to keep her engaged. It sucks that she's so insecure, but I'm encouraged she likes me enough to tell me her fears. One thing is for sure: she has fight. If Jordan hadn't given me the heads-up, I think I would have been blindsided by her sudden meltdown.

"Probably not as good as Richie's, huh?"

She wipes her mouth with her napkin and smiles. "Actually, it's better. I loved him, but he put carrots and zucchini in his spaghetti sauce."

"That's just wrong."

"Right? I'd eat it to make him happy, but it wasn't my favorite thing."

She pushes her plate to the side and sips her wine. "Are you finished?"

"Yes, I'm sorry about before. I just …"

I top off her wine and mine. "You don't have to explain. We're good. One day, I may want to know that history, but let's enjoy the rest of our night. I'll rinse the dishes and meet you in the living room."

"Here, let me do it." I snag our plates before she can. "Go, you're the guest. It will only take me a minute."

"Bossy much?" she asks with a teasing glimmer in her eye.

"You have no idea."

Her chest heaves as she inhales deeply, and I turn toward the sink so she can't see my grin. Dating Haddie is going to be fun.

Once I've finished the dishes, I flick on the fire and join her on the couch.

"You realize the door is open, right?"

"Yup, I love listening to the ocean, and when the windows are open, the house doesn't feel so claustrophobic. But I also love a fire, so … best of both worlds."

She places her wine on the table and turns to face me. "Tell me about Cadence."

I smile immediately. "What do you want to know?"

"Whatever you feel like sharing. What is she like?"

I pull out my phone and show her a couple of photos. "This is Cadence and Nate playing drums and singing in the studio. They're so fucking talented. Nate has perfect pitch, and I swear Cadence is better than me with the sticks."

"They're adorable. They're going into kindergarten soon?"

"Next week," I reply with a sad sigh. "It just went so fast, you know? One day she was born and now she's six. In the beginning, I was filled with guilt because girls should have their mother and I had no desire to ever date again."

"Finding the courage to date again is hard." She places her hand on my knee. Haddie's presence is like a soothing balm.

"After Mel and Sawyer got married, I asked Mel to be the mother figure in Cadence's life. No matter who I end up with, if anyone, I don't think they could love Cadence like Mel can. She knew Belle better than anyone in the world, including me."

Haddie hums softly for a moment. "Did Mel agree?"

"She did, but she told me she'd step back if I found someone who wanted that role in Cadence's life."

"Are *you* okay with that?"

"Not really, but it's complicated. I know Cadence needs Mel. She calls her Auntie, not Mom. If I were to remar- um ... get married, I'd want my wife to be able to share the role with Mel. Each of them would be what Cady needs, when she needs it."

Haddie squeezes my knee. I love how she's so tactile. It's like she knows I need it or maybe she understands because she's been alone for a long time too.

"As long as you're honest from the get-go, it should work out fine."

"Do you think I'm wrong for expecting that?"

"You want the best for your daughter, and it sounds like Mel wants the same thing. She knew Belle well enough to remind Cadence of her mother's love. I know a lot of kids who aren't that lucky. You're a good dad."

I lean forward, never breaking eye contact. "Haddie, can I kiss you?"

Her eyes widen, but she nods. I'm not sure I've ever asked to kiss someone, but until she knows me, I don't want to scare her off. I slide my fingers through her hair and pull her mouth to mine. Our lips touch, and she stills, so I pull back.

"Are you okay? Do you want me to stop?"

"Don't stop, please ..."

That please goes straight to my cock. I want her to beg me to fuck her, but I trace her bottom lip with my tongue and part her lips instead. She whimpers as I nip the soft flesh with my teeth, and her breasts heave between us. She has the most amazing fucking tits.

Haddie laces her fingers through my hair as I dip my tongue into her mouth. She tastes like cabernet and smells like bubbles. Our tongues meet and touch hesitantly at first. I haven't taken a kiss this slow since I was a teenager, but there's something special about taking my time with her.

The pace picks up as we ease into each other, and I caress her cheek. "You're so damn sweet; I want to devour you."

She releases a whimper, but it's a plea to my soul. My mouth crashes back to hers, and with my free hand, I caress her breasts.

My cock hardens, but it doesn't matter as long as I can continue losing myself in this kiss.

By the time we separate, we're both winded. Her lips are nice and plump from me nipping and sucking them, and her cheeks are the perfect shade of flushed.

"Wow, that was ... wow." She giggles and buries her face in her hands.

I pull them away almost immediately. "Don't you dare hide that gorgeous face from me. Seeing that glow in your cheeks and knowing it's because of me is fucking hot, and it makes me even harder for you."

Her eyes dart down to my jeans.

I grin. "If looking doesn't satisfy you, feel free to cop a feel."

Her blush deepens, and she reaches out her hand only to pull it back.

"Don't be shy, not with me. I want you, Haddie, but I'm not an asshole. I only wanted you to feel what you do to me. Whatever happens between us will happen at your pace."

She brushes her fingers against me and pulls away slowly. "This is probably a stupid question, but have you ever waited for anyone before? I mean, you're kind of a big deal."

I lean closer and put my arm around her shoulder. "I haven't waited for sex. Belle and I had sex the first night we met, and that's when she got pregnant with Cadence."

"Oh wow."

"She was unexpected but not unwanted. That spark we talked about before, it hit the two of us like lightning. We were both fly-by-the-seat-of-our-pants,   grab-the-moment-before-it-disappears kind of people. I would've waited forever for her. We spent most of that year apart, but when we had time together, you bet your ass we made it count, but now ..."

She snuggles in closer, and I lean my head against hers as I watch the flames dance in the fireplace. "I'm a different person these days. I know how fast things can change, so I still seize the moment, but I'm more cautious. I knew you were special the night I met you. I'll wait as long as you need me to wait."

"I should confess something." Haddie sits up and cringes slightly. "This is awkward, but ... I get attached easily. I don't have a lot of friends or a big family like you do. It takes a lot for me to let someone into my world and when I decide to do it, I ..." She pauses and takes a deep breath.

I tuck her hair away from her face. "You what?"

"I fall hard and fast. It's how I'm built. When I was in college, there were guys who made bets about who could fuck the big girl first, stupid shit like that. I fell for the wrong asshole a few times. I stopped letting people in. It took Richie months to break down my walls. When I lost him, I lost the armor we'd built together and isolated myself again, but I'm tired of being alone, Darren." She blinks away the tears filling her eyes.

I pull her into my embrace. "You're not alone anymore. I'm pretty sure you're not the only one in this room who falls fast and hard."

"Yeah, but you don't all the time. Only when you feel something special."

She looks down, and I tip her head back up and look into her eyes. "Do you feel what I feel? Or am I just another potential asshole in your queue?"

"At first, I wasn't sure, but when you kissed me ..." Tears fall from her eyes, and she quickly swipes them away.

"It's okay. You don't have to answer me."

She shakes her head. "The thing is, I'm not sure if I've *ever* felt a connection like what I felt when we kissed. Does that mean—"

"Shh, it doesn't mean anything. Some sparks start off hotter than others, and some people have a slow burn their entire lives. It doesn't matter if you're with me or someone else, no one and nothing can negate what you had with Richie."

She leans forward and kisses me. I let her set the pace while happily enjoying this moment here with her.

"Oh my God, what time is it?" Haddie groans as she sits up.

"A little after seven in the morning." We spent the entire night talking and making out like a couple of high school kids and fell asleep around four. Her head was in my lap, and my arm was wrapped around her protectively. It was perfect.

She swipes at her eyes. "I must look like a disaster."

I pull her hand to my mouth and kiss it. "You look beautiful, just like last night. You can shower in my room if you want to, and then maybe I can take you to breakfast."

"As much as I'd like to take you up on that, doing the walk of shame straight into a restaurant might not be the best idea."

I laugh at the dire tone of her voice. "First of all, we didn't fuck so there's no shame. And secondly, the place I have in mind is low-key. I roll in there all the time rumpled from the night before and in desperate need of banana pancakes. It wouldn't be a big deal."

"I do love banana pancakes." She nibbles on her lip, and I pull us both to our feet.

"It's settled. We'll shower ..."

Her eyes practically pop out of their sockets.

"Separately," I clarify.

Haddie exhales, and I suppress my smile. "Hang your shirt on the towel bar and let the steam help de-wrinkle it. Or I can toss it in on the steam setting in the dryer."

"I'll stick with the shower it will be fine. I have hardly any makeup with me though."

"Don't be that girl, Haddie. Let me see you, and please try to get past the fear of showering with me. Showering with a partner is very sensual, and I don't want to miss out on it." I smile and wink at her.

Her cheeks flush again.

"What did I say to make you blush like that?"

"Nothing, it's dumb."

"If I made you blush, it's definitely not dumb."

"You said 'partner.' You're thinking past today."

I blink and shake my head. Maybe I need coffee. "You're not? Let me be clear, Haddie. I like you. We had a great date. I'm not seeing anyone else. I'd prefer if you didn't either until we know where this is going to take us." I lower my head to hers. "I can count on *one finger* how many women I've invited to breakfast the next day."

"Oh."

"I'm hungry, and I don't want to get hangry. Let's shower and get out of here."

I end up showing her to Sawyer's old room because he has a nicer shower and she doesn't want me displaced from my things. I wish we were showering together, but I jack off to images of her mouth around my cock instead.

It's strange imagining myself with someone other than Belle, but it's also sort of nice. I'm feeling human again, and it's making me realize how disconnected I was from everything. For the longest time, I thought I would be betraying her, but I'm starting to understand how much she would have hated who I'd become.

While I'm getting dressed, there's a knock at my door. "Come in," I call out as I put on my deodorant.

"Hey, sexy, long time no see."

Fuck Rory and her shitty timing. Gritting my teeth, I turn to face her. She grins and rakes her eyes over my chest. I quickly toss on my shirt and grab my keys and wallet.

"Rory, you shouldn't say shit like that."

She laughs. "I've *always* said shit like that to you. It would be odd if I *didn't* say it."

"Yeah, I heard you've been saying lots of things lately. Not cool, Ror."

I push past her and go into the kitchen. The last thing I need is Haddie walking in on something that looks bad. Hell, just Rory being here looks bad.

"About that ... I'm sorry. I was talking to J about the other guy and what's going on, and it just slipped out."

"And what if you let it slip to Sawyer that we fucked, Rory? Then what?"

Haddie enters the room directly behind Rory. Fucking great.

"That won't happen, D. I promise," Rory says before she realizes I'm not looking at her anymore.

My eyes never leave Haddie, but I can tell she's hurt. "Are you ready to go, Haddie?"

Rory looks between us and appears to be remorseful. "I'll let you two get back to your day. I came by to pick up my suitcase. Eli's dad is sick, and I'm flying to Texas to keep him company. I am sorry, Darren, for everything. Jordan has never broken a promise to me, and I don't think this will be the one he starts with."

"Mel's not going?" Eli is her best friend and ex-boyfriend. I'd think she'd be on the first plane.

"She's waiting. She doesn't want to leave Sawyer with all the kids, and since things can go downhill quickly, she'd rather wait. If something worse happens, she can be there longer."

"Yeah, makes sense. Tell Eli if he needs anything …"

Rory nods and leaves the room.

Haddie grabs her purse. "Maybe you should just take me home."

"Breakfast first. Then I'll take you home."

"Bu—"

I raise a brow. "Remember what I said about lack of food and being angry?"

She nods curtly. "Fine."

That gives me an hour to explain exactly what disaster is brewing in the background of my life.

She's quiet on the way to the local diner. I'm glad she's in the car with me and not on her way home in an Uber though. Taking her out is risky. Even though the diner is low key, someone might still spot us. Last night, I wanted to protect her in case our date was a flop. This morning, I don't care if the whole fucking world knows we're together. The only thing I do care about right now is making her understand Rory doesn't mean anything to me romantically.

My favorite waitress greets us with a smile and seats us in the back corner in my usual booth. I'm pretty much invisible where we are—just how I like it.

"Long time no see, sugar. Who's your pretty gal pal?"

Haddie gives her a slight smile. "Wanda, this is my friend Haddie."

"If she's only a friend, you'd better snap her up quick. This one's a catch. Do you want some time to look over the menus?"

I look at Haddie. "Still want to try those banana pancakes?"

"Sure, and a coffee and a water too, please."

"Same." I hand the menus back to Wanda.

When she leaves, I reach across the table and grab Haddie's hand. "I need to talk to you about Rory."

"Is she important to you? She's very pretty."

"Do you remember when I told you I did something that could fuck up my life?"

"Yes, I remember."

"Rory showed up when I was drunk. One thing led to another and we had sex. She's Sawyer and Jordan's sister, and I've always treated her like my little sister too. It's bad, and I hate myself for doing it, but I can't take it back."

She pulls her hands back as Wanda delivers the drinks. While she dresses her coffee, I wait for her to say something.

"Does she want to be with you?"

"No, but even if she did, that isn't what I want. She used me to figure out she was in love with someone else."

"Ouch."

I reach for Haddie's hand again, and she reluctantly gives it to me. "No, not ouch. I can separate sex and feelings. I wish she'd talked to me instead of seducing me."

"Well, she's very pretty."

"She is, and so are you, but Rory's not a threat. I need you to understand she won't interfere with us, but she will always be in my life. Well, until Sawyer finds out and kills me."

She pulls back her hand and sips her coffee. "Do you do that a lot? Drink and then blame your bad decisions on the alcohol?"

I wince. I deserved that.

"I used to when I was younger. It was a rough day, and I wanted to forget and lose myself in nothingness, so I drank a bunch of gin knowing it would have that effect on me. Rory showed up unannounced."

Her expression softens, and she lowers her coffee cup to the table. "What happened to make you want to forget?"

I'm not sure if I want to tell her at all, but I also don't want to lose her.

"Can we talk about that when I take you home? I'd rather not tell you in a public place."

"If that's what you want."

This is the part of getting to know someone new that sucks. I don't know her moods or her tones. I don't know her pissed-off catchphrases. She seems angry but hurt. Maybe I should take it as a good sign. She said she latches on quickly, so if she's hurt, that could mean she likes me as much as I like her.

"I don't think I've asked, but how old are you?"

Her eyes meet mine with a twinkle. "Didn't your dad teach you it's not polite to ask a lady her age, weight, or political stance?"

I lean over the table and kiss the tip of her nose. "My dad taught me to learn everything about the woman I'm interested in so I never miss an important date. If you won't tell me your age, at least tell me your birthday. Throw me an astrological sign, something."

She smiles, and the pressure in my chest disappears. "I turned thirty in February. My birthday is the twenty-ninth."

"Fucking leap day? That's awesome and awful at the same time."

"My dad always jokes about it. He got me a 'happy seventh birthday' card, which he'll do each year until we leap again. He thinks it's hilarious."

I think I'd like her dad. "When do you celebrate?"

"My family celebrates the last day of the month to keep it easy. I like to have a me day on the first of March though. Hair, nails, maybe a massage, and a cupcake."

"You and Mel would get along great. She loves cake, any kind. But Sawyer has a tradition of waking her up on her birthday with a cupcake."

"That's sweet. They sound happy."

"They have their moments, but if I ever wanted to emulate a marriage, it would be theirs. If they fight, they don't sleep until they work it out. They don't leave mad, and they're really good at not being shitty to each other when they're angry."

"Sounds like they've built their marriage on mutual respect. I'm impressed. It's important but hard for a lot of people to achieve."

Wanda sets heaping towers of banana-filled goodness in front of us. "Banana pancakes for two. Let me know if you need a to-go container or anything else."

"Wanda, you know the only place this goes is in my stomach."

She winks at me. "Sugar, your lady friend may need a box."

"I will need a box," Haddie confirms.

"We'll see. I might be able to eat your leftovers too."

"Seriously? No way. You'd pop."

Wanda laughs, which sounds more like a cackle from years of smoking. "Honey, I've seen it before. Those band boys eat half their plates when they come in here, and he scoops up the rest and devours it. This one should've been a country boy."

"Well, leftover pancakes aren't my thing, so you're welcome to whatever is left."

Wanda walks away after leaving a few more napkins for us.

"Same. Cold pancakes just don't hold the same appeal."

Haddie's eyes grow wide as I douse my pancakes in almost half a bottle of syrup. "That is so gross," she says when I pass it to her. I watch as she barely drizzles anything on her golden pancakes.

"That's it? That's all you use?"

She shrugs and cuts into the stack. "I prefer the sweetness of the fruit. Syrup has never really been my thing."

"I bet I can make it your thing if I pour it all over your body and lick it off."

Her mouth drops and her cheeks flush.

"Too much too soon?" I ask with a grin.

She shakes her head. "If you want to lick something off my body, I'm good with that." Her breathy tone kicks my libido into gear.

"Anytime."

She stares at me and absentmindedly takes her first bite. Closing her eyes, she moans appreciatively. Fuck, I'm going to die of blue balls before I get the chance to have her.

"Told you they're good."

"I lied. You can't have them. I'm going to eat them all and then spend the rest of the day at the gym so they don't live on my butt forever."

I take a bite to distract myself from images of her ass.

"I happen to like your derriere, but you can always come over and use my gym if you'd like."

She puts her fork on her plate and takes a sip of water. "Of course, you have a gym. Do you realize we're like different levels of people? I'm this boring girl who would rather sit in my tiny backyard and drink wine and read a book. And you're ..." She looks around and lowers her voice. "You're this megastar with a fucking gym in his house. Do you have an indoor pool too? A bowling alley? Movie theater?"

I reach for her hand. "Breathe, Haddie."

Looking down at her plate, she takes a deep breath and meets my eyes.

"First, you're not boring. I've worked my ass off for what I have, and I'm not ashamed. I'm also happy to share. The pool is in Sawyer's yard because the new studio took up most of my yard. The theater and gym are necessities because leaving the house to do normal things can be more trouble than it's worth. Negative on the bowling alley, but it's a fucking cool idea. I almost regret the studio now." I flash her a grin and squeeze her hand.

"I'm so sorry. This is a lot to take in."

"I understand. If we decide to make a real go of this relationship, it's going to become your life. My house will become our sanctuary unless you're willing to go out and face the masses. At times, you'll have to. I still have obligations like award ceremonies, interviews, and other things that keep the band relevant and bring eyes to the studio and our emerging artists. My life is in the public eye. I can't change it even if I wish I could. I want to be with someone who will attend events with me. I'm tired of going alone."

Haddie lowers her eyes to her plate, and we continue eating in silence. I know that was a lot to throw at her, but it was the opening I needed. She has to understand before we further this relationship. I can't let myself fall for her if she can't handle my life.

chapter 10

Haddie

"You can pull into the driveway and we'll go straight into the back yard. It'll be quicker, and there's less chance of you being recognized by my neighbors."

When we get out of the car and to my gate, Darren inspects it and looks around. Once we're in the back yard, he does the same.

"Problem?"

"Maybe." He shoves his hands in his pockets and follows me to the porch swing. "If the paparazzi become an issue, that's not going to keep them out. I could send someone over to install cameras and locks and do a basic security overhaul ... once we know where we stand, of course."

"Let's worry about that when the time comes. Do you want something to drink?"

His sad eyes meet mine. "No, come sit with me. I need to talk to you."

Once we're seated, I squeeze his hand. "You don't have to tell me anything you don't want to. We have time—"

"Do we?"

"I hope so."

Darren takes a deep breath and slowly releases it. "I want to tell you this, but no one else knows about it. My instincts tell me I can trust you."

"I'll take it to my grave."

"It's about Belle ... and me," he says cautiously.

"Can I interrupt for a second?"

He nods and laces our fingers together.

"Darren, I think we're doing this wrong."

"Doing what wrong?"

"Worrying about discussing our past. Richie and Belle were monumental parts of our lives. We didn't *choose* not to be with them anymore, but we *are* choosing to move on and try again. I think we need to let go of the fear we're going to hurt each other if we talk about them."

"We're just getting to know each other though. Don't you think that's too much too soon?"

Smiling, I respond, "No, because I want to know you, Darren. How can I know who you are if you don't feel free to talk about how you got to where you are? You can't skip over the happy parts your life because you're afraid it'll hurt me. It won't. Maybe sharing our feelings will make it so we don't feel so alone anymore."

"What if it hurts to talk about her?"

"Then don't. I'm just saying don't hold back on account of me. Don't be afraid to talk to me about Belle, and I'll open up to you about Richie." I take a deep breath and lift my eyes to his. "Other people are empathetic for the most part. But there are times ..."

"Tell me, I want to know," he encourages.

"Things that would be stupid to other people. Where his favorite song comes on the radio and I either cry or smile depending on my mood. When I'm having a hard day, and I call his voicemail so I can hear his voice when I'm feeling desperately alone. Or when the wind blows a certain way, and I think it's him saying hi, because the scent of Rosemary from the yard hits me all of a sudden. Nobody I know understands how the little things can throw your world into a tailspin. And yes, I still pay for his phone. Please don't judge me."

"I wouldn't because I understand," he whispers. "Belle's mom cut off her phone, but I have messages, and I listen to them occasionally. Plus, she was in the media so I have other options when I miss her terribly. Cadence gets extra love on those days because when I wrap her in my arms, she's tangible proof Belle was here, if only for a little while."

We're teary-eyed, but I sense we've crossed a boundary of sorts.

"I wish we'd met sooner. I could've used you the day I slipped with Rory."

"Was it one of those days?"

Darren blows out a breath. "It was. Mel and I took the kids to kindergarten registration. Each time one of the kids has a milestone, Mel and I try to connect. Sharing in the same trauma made us close. We wade through the milestones together when we can."

"It's nice you have each other even though it's a sad reason to bond."

He releases my hand and slides his palms against his jeans. "Mel has become a lifeline, and I'll always be grateful she's in our lives." Darren stands and begins pacing.

"Hey, if you don't want to do this, we don't have to. I won't be angry; I promise."

Suddenly, he drops to his knees in front of me and rests his hands on my thighs. The pained expression on his face hurts me deeply. "I'm torn, I made a promise never to tell, but it's killing me not to."

I reach for his chin, and when his eyes meet mine, I caress his face. "I'll be your vault for whatever you need, whenever you need, for as long as you need."

A tear slips from his eye, and I brush it away. He grabs my hand and holds it to his cheek. The intimate moment fills my heart with love for this man I barely know, but I want to, with every fiber of my being.

"The day we enrolled them in school, I went to the beach house and "Miss You All the Time" by O.A.R. came on. The song reminds me so much of Belle, and I took it as a sign. I grabbed a blanket and took a walk. I guess I was trying to connect with her because sometimes, it's like I feel her presence. I know it's silly—"

"It's not silly; it's love."

"It is that for sure. Anyway, I went to our spot—it's uh, where we conceived Cadence." He blushes.

I bring my fingers to his hair and massage his scalp. "So public sex is a thing for you, that's good to know."

He grins before moaning and laying his head in my lap.

"It's a private beach, but I'm not opposed to public sex. Knowing you're doing something carnal around people who have no clue can be a turn-on. We should try it sometime."

I laugh, and he sits up and kisses me quickly before joining me on the swing again. "That would take a committed relationship, and probably a whole lot of alcohol before I'd even consider it."

"We can arrange that, but without the alcohol. The right kind of foreplay can push your boundaries in ways you never imagined."

I'm not sure what kind of foreplay he gives, but I'm looking forward to it. "Sorry, I shouldn't have interrupted. Go on."

"If we can do this and still share them, it will be the best of both worlds. One of my main concerns was how to move on without shame. Are my feelings for Belle supposed to disappear if I fall in love again? Or am I supposed to hide them from a new love? This shit has been tearing me up inside. It's been easier to swear off women. Then I don't feel like I'm betraying Belle."

"I'm always going to love Richie. For everything he was, and everything we were and I'm going to forever be sad about all the things we missed out on, that *he* missed out on. There has to be room for more love, for more life, and a future with someone new. Otherwise, what's the point? Why would we still be here if we're not supposed to be happy? There's no room for shame, Darren. You can love her until your dying breath and also be in love with someone else."

He pulls me into his embrace and we hug for a long time. This man centers me in all the best ways. I hope I'm helping to center him too.

"Belle and I got married in our spot," he says as he releases me. "It wasn't legal, but it was real. It was us. Belle struggled with traditional religion, but she believed in God. She loved me but didn't feel she needed a marriage license to prove it. Being married is important to me ... *was* important to me. The two of us agreed to marry in a spiritual ceremony and have a regular wedding a few months later when we finished touring." He pauses and brushes his hand against my cheek. "Are you still with me?"

I'm captivated by his story and the fact that it's a secret. "Why don't your friends know this?"

"We promised each other we would keep it to ourselves until the wedding. We exchanged vows in July. Five weeks later, she was gone. Our Thanksgiving wedding never happened, and I felt I'd be betraying her trust if I told anyone."

"Why me?" I whisper.

"I've wanted to tell someone for years. I've come close many times, but it never felt right. For you to understand what threw me for a loop the night I fucked Rory and why I turned to alcohol, you had to know the story."

"You could've made something up or told me it was none of my business ..."

Darren laces our fingers together again. "You're right, I could have, but that's not the kind of foundation I want to build a relationship on. I hate secrets. I kept this one with Belle because she needed time and it was supposed to be short-lived. A few years ago, I kept one for Sawyer and Mel, and everyone found out in the end. Secrets are just pauses in time. The truth will come out anyway."

His brow furrows, and I wish I could take away his frustration. "This secret with Rory feels like a ticking time bomb, doesn't it?"

"You nailed it. She showed up when I was missing Belle more than I had in years. I drank to lighten the sadness of the day. Rory showed up drunk and with a plan."

"She took advantage of you."

He shakes his head. "No, she didn't. I just didn't give a fuck about the consequences. She pushed and I gave in. I was a willing participant, and it was enjoyable until I passed out. When I woke up, I was filled with remorse. I'm still regretful."

"So what are you going to do?"

He starts rocking the swing back and forth as he looks out into the yard. "I'm not sure. Rory told Jordan, and that means Allie and Sasha know. I don't think any of them will say anything, but I'm not sure Rory can keep it secret. Deep down, Rory doesn't think it will affect my relationship with Sawyer." Darren puts his arm around my shoulder and pulls me to him.

"And you do."

He snorts. "Friends don't fuck their best friend's sister. Especially not without a conversation about it first. If I were in love with Rory, I think Sawyer could get past it, but it was a one-night stand, and that's all it will ever be. Sawyer is going to hate me."

"Sometimes the people we're closest to are the people who surprise us the most. I wish I had some advice for you, but this is a decision you're going to have to make on your own. I'll be here for you either way. I'm a good sounding board or a shoulder to cry on."

Darren laughs, "I've never been the most sensitive of men. I'm crass and unapologetic and don't give a fuck about what people think of me. It's strange because the past week you haven't seen much of that part of me. I feel like you're not really seeing the real me."

"Considering you asked me if I wanted to fuck in the first two minutes we spoke, I think I see you."

"Ha! You've got a point, but you can't blame me. You were looking right at me, or through me as I know now. Sexy girl, sexy guy ... fucking seemed like an appropriate conclusion. Still does ..."

Darren leans down and kisses me deeply. It's the kind of kiss that makes you weak in the knees and wet between the thighs. It's a kiss filled with desperation, hope, and promise. Sadly, it ends far too soon when his phone rings.

He looks at me apologetically, "I'm sorry."

"Don't be. Life waits for no one."

While Darren takes his call, I open the house and go inside to get us some water. I notice the mail on the floor by the front door and bend down to pick it up.

"Damn, that's a sight I'm not sure I'll ever get tired of seeing."

"Just seeing?" I ask, peeking over my shoulder.

With the determination of an animal after its prey, he's behind me quickly. His hardness presses against my backside and as I straighten up his hand goes to my breast. "Does this feel like I only want to see?" He pushes my hair to the side and kisses the column of my neck. I'm about to drop the mail right back to the floor.

He traces the shell of my ear with his tongue and pinches my nipple. A needy cry escapes my lips, and he hums his approval against my skin. He nips the skin of my neck with his teeth before sucking and kissing away the burn. "Darren," his name is a desperate plea, and he pulls me tighter to him before bringing his mouth back to my ear.

"I'm so fucking hot for you, Haddie. Unfortunately, I have to go." He turns me around and pulls my mouth to his. My lips part and his tongue greets mine fervently, and I lose myself in his kiss while I can. School starts this week, and I may not see him again for a while.

We part reluctantly, "I'll walk you out."

"No, let's not risk it. Come over tomorrow to see my house and the studio. Cadence and Nate are going to church with Belle's mom."

"Are you sure? Maybe you should enjoy your alone time."

Darren kisses the top of my head. "You're cute. I've had enough alone time over the last five years. Besides, I'm sure you'll soon learn that in my life there's not really such a thing. I want to spend more time with you, but right now I have a pressing appointment to take my daughter school clothes shopping. I can't believe this is starting already."

There is something about the smile Darren gets when he talks about Cadence. It's like he's on cloud nine. "You better not keep her waiting any longer. Don't tell her no too often; you only start kindergarten once. Let her have the sparkly shoes and the matching purse, the character backpack and the matching lunch pail. Just draw the line at thongs for kids ... they're so ... wrong."

Darren laughs, and I furrow my brow.

"They're just shoes; flip flops never killed anyone ... I don't think. I'm sure she'll be fine."

Laughter rolls out of me, and I can't stop it. Now he's looking at me like I'm the crazy one. Once I finally contain myself and wipe the tears from my eyes, I explain. "I wasn't talking footwear. I mean butt floss for kids Cadence's age exists. Don't buy it. Well, you can if that's your thing, but I wouldn't recommend it."

His eyes widen in horror. "That's a thing? No ... you're fucking with me."

I cross my heart with my finger.

"That's unbelievably ridiculous and never happening."

"Good. When I was little, it seems like we had superheroes or underwear labeled with the days of the week and little flowers on them. I didn't understand the vast variety of sexier panties and lingerie until much later."

"Damn, it's a shame I have to leave. I'd love to see your collection." He licks his lips, and my heart slams against my chest.

"You'd better go," I manage to spit out and walk him toward the front door.

"Now you're kicking me out?"

"No, I'm being a good ... friend? Date? Whatever, I'm trying not to be the reason you disappoint your little girl. She's waiting for you."

He wraps an arm around my waist, pulling me close. After kissing my cheek, he whispers in my ear, "Date, friend, both sound good. Soon to be my everything ... sounds even better. I'll text you my address be there at eleven am sharp."

Fuck a duck this man has me completely twisted.

"One question before you leave, why is it always sharp with you? Eleven sharp, seven sharp, are you a stickler for being late?"

"Nope," he says pulling his keys from his pocket. "I just don't want to wait one second longer to see you than I have to. Have a good day, Haddie." With a wink and a smile, he's out the door and pulling away before I've had a chance to catch my breath. If he keeps having this effect on me, I'm going to need to start walking around with oxygen.

"You spent the night and didn't have sex? Haddie! Do you know what that means?" Marina and I sit in front of the fire pit drinking piña coladas and catching up on my date.

"That I'm not the kind of woman who puts out on a first date?"

She rolls her eyes. "It means he *likes* you."

"He's a good guy, but we still have things to discuss. Cadence is his world, and—"

"You didn't tell him."

I top off our drinks with the pitcher on the table. "There wasn't a good time."

"Well, I have something else to tell you. I found out a few days ago, but I didn't want you to use it as an excuse not to go out with him." She breaks eye contact with me and looks up at the sky.

"What is it? Is it bad? Is he seeing someone else?"

Marina cracks a grin and looks my way. "Not that I know of, but if that was your first concern, I'm glad I held off and didn't tell you. You like him a lot, don't you?"

I sigh and lean back in my seat. "More than I should for how early it is. Now, spill."

"I got my class roster last week. Cadence Miller and Nathaniel Weston are two of my kindergartners."

This can't be happening.

"Breathe, Haddie. I know it's not ideal, but there are workarounds. Talk to Principal Lewis and explain what's going on. These aren't at-risk kids. Their parents can afford the best therapy in the world."

"You know it's not that easy. They're from single-parent households with a deceased parent. If nothing else, I'd *want* them on my watch list. What if they need testing?"

"And that's a problem how? You don't even know them yet. This isn't a unique issue. You'll just need someone stand in for you if they need services." She pauses and nails me with a glare. "Going out on a few dates with someone who has a kid in our program isn't a reason to ask for reassignment."

"How did you know that's what I was thinking?"

"I always know what you're thinking. Besides, didn't you say there are no immediate plans to meet her in case things don't pan out?"

"I did ..."

"Talk to Lewis and go from there. She's going to tell you the same thing. She fought hard to get you into her school; she's not going to let you go easily."

I down the rest of my drink. "You've got a point. I guess we'll wait and see. I never imagined they were in our district and not going to private school."

Marina refills my glass and tops off hers. "Principal Lewis gave me a letter from Amelia Weston explaining their safety plan and a few other things. She also wants me to let her know if there are any distractions because she doesn't want their kids disrupting the learning cycle of others."

"Wow, that was thoughtful of her."

"It was. Little does she realize, the only thing that will likely distract these kids is their own attention spans. They're five and six years old—snack time and finger paints are the highlights of their day. It's a little intimidating knowing I'll have kids under guard, but hopefully, they'll never need one."

It was surreal to be picked up by a guard even though Darren was there. I know these kids are growing up with them, but still, it's such a different kind of life. "I hope they don't either."

"So ... what's your favorite thing about him so far?"

"The way he loves his daughter. This man would sacrifice anything for that little girl."

Marina eyes me skeptically. "That's a glowing recommendation for someone who hasn't seen them in the same room together."

"I know, but his face lights up when he talks about her. She's all he has left of his ex, and he doesn't take that for granted. Even if I never meet her, I know he will cherish Cadence as long as he lives."

Marina smiles, shakes her head, and smiles again. It's apparent her alcohol has kicked in. "You're falling hard for him."

"No, I'm falling for the *idea* of him. So far, he's everything I could possibly want in a man. It's way too soon to have the talk, but if I keep putting it off, it's only going to lead us down a road of heartache."

"You don't know that for sure."

"I'm pretty sure I do. Enough sappy shit. Let's order some pizza and watch a funny movie."

Darren

After getting Cadence ready for church, I take her over to Sawyer and Mel's. Nate is waiting at the door with Mel, and he's in his church suit, looking more like a mini Noah than I've ever seen.

He holds out his hand for Cadence. "You look pretty, Cady."

"Thank you; I like your tie."

Mel purses her lips until the kids go inside.

"Are they not the cutest thing you've ever seen?" Her eyes sparkle. "Like, where does that even come from? It's not like we teach him that kind of stuff. He should still be in the yard making mud pies, not showing off his swagger."

I chuckle. "Noah and Sawyer are his fathers—nothing that kid *ever* does will surprise me."

"Fair point. Are you really going to tell Veronica you're seeing someone already?"

"That's the plan, and then I'll send her over here for the kids. Think she'll castrate me before or after church?"

Mel snickers. "I think she'll be fine. It's not like she hasn't told you she'd be okay with you dating again."

"Right. Saying it and seeing it are two completely different realities though."

"Mama loves you, Darren."

"Wish me luck."

"Luck, but you won't need it."

The doorbell rings shortly after I get back to my house. When I open the door, Veronica flashes me a beaming smile and greets me with a hug.

"Darren, how are you?"

I motion for her to come inside. She's wearing a purple dress and a matching hat. "I'm good. And you're looking beautiful as always. How are you?"

"I'm wonderful. I woke up still breathing *and* I get to take my precious grandbabies to church. It's going to be a glorious day. Where are the little munchkins?"

"They're at Mel's, but I was hoping we could talk for a few minutes first."

She follows me into the living room and takes a seat. "You've met someone," she says before I even have a chance to sit.

Deciding to stay close, I take a seat on the table right in front of her. "I have."

Blinking rapidly, she reaches for my hands and squeezes them tightly. "I'm so happy for you. Is she a good woman?"

Veronica is an old soul. She's always loved and accepted me, but talking to her about Haddie instead of Belle brings tears to my eyes. "You're not angry?"

"Before I married Marcus, I'd been alone a long time. Belle was my world, but the love of a child is not the same as the love of a partner. When I met Marcus, it was like the sun had risen after an exceedingly long winter. Each day was a bit brighter when he was around. My Belle couldn't have asked for anyone better than you to love her, but it's time for you to let someone in. I know it's what Belle would want for you, and it's what I want for you too."

I reach out and hug her again. "You would've been the best mother-in-law."

She pulls back and smacks me on the shoulder. "You mean I *am* the best mother-in-law. You're my grandbaby's dad and a part of my family. Now, tell me, is she a good woman?"

I clear my throat. "It's new, but I think she is."

Veronica gives me the all-knowing once over she's mastered through the years. "You wouldn't be telling me about her if you were doubtful. What makes her special?"

"Her name is Haddie, and when we met, something about her spoke to me. I needed to know her. I can't explain it, but it's something I've only experienced one other time in my life …"

"When you met my Belle."

I nod. "I know it seems crazy, and I promise I'm being cautious, but when I found out she lost her fiancé too, I couldn't help but think—"

"You've got an angel looking after you. Listen to your heart, Darren. It won't steer you wrong. I told Mel the same thing and look at her now. Life's too short not to be happy."

I swallow the lump in my throat. "Veronica, thank you."

"When you admit to yourself it's more than 'something new,' I want to meet her." Veronica leans forward and kisses my cheek. "If she's going to be part of the family, I want to get to know her."

"You don't have to do that."

"You're like a son to me. I'm invested in your happiness. Besides, if this woman is going to influence my granddaughter's life, I need to know her."

"Deal." Standing, I pull Veronica out of her chair and into a hug. That was easier than I thought it would be.

When we get to the front door, V opens it and pauses before turning back toward me. "If she isn't the one for you, don't let that keep you from trying again. Happiness is emanating from you right now. I've missed your happy face, Darren. It's a beautiful sight. This is what Belle would want for you. Remember that."

Her words sink in as she walks toward Sawyer's. "Hey, V!" I run to her. "Cady doesn't know, and I'm not telling her until I know this is real."

"I figured, but it's good to hear it."

"I'll see you guys after church. Have a nice day."

I find Sawyer sitting in my kitchen when I return.

"I heard my son was hitting on your daughter again," he smirks. "You gonna let that slide?"

I've seen that look many times before when groupies hit on us. It's crazy how times have changed.

"I know I'm supposed to have this protective dad thing going on, but I'm pretty sure Cady isn't the only one that kid has wrapped around his little finger. He's a flawless mixture of you and Noah."

Sawyer laughs. "The teen years are going to be fun."

"Dude, you've got four fucking kids, I've got one. My forties are going to be a breeze compared to yours, and at the rate you and Mel procreate, you'll have six or eight by then."

"Nah, Mel would kill me if I tried to have that many kids. At some point, one of us is going to have to get fixed. Enough about kids … how goes it with the new girl?"

"Not fast enough for me to be worried about getting her pregnant. Besides, you know how I feel about that."

Sawyer shrugs, "Feelings change. How was your date?"

"It was good. It's still early, but I like her and I'm thinking positively for a change. She's coming over today while the kids are at church. I thought I'd show her around the studio."

"Cool, do we get to meet her? You know Mel will be hurt if you don't bring her by. Also, how did it go with V?"

I lean back against the counter. "As long as Haddie's up for it, I'll bring her by. V was amazing; it's no wonder Belle was so special. Cadence and I are lucky to have her in our lives."

Sawyer grabs a bottle of water from the fridge. "You're doing okay then? No regrets?"

"I'll always have regrets, but not about Haddie. You don't have to worry about me, I'm fine."

"Cool. Shawn Lucas is recording today. If your girl is a fan, you should bring her over."

I look up at the clock—it's almost eleven. "I figured he would cancel since Eli's out of town. She doesn't follow celebrities. I'd be surprised if she knows who he is."

"Eli said Shawn's eager to record and see what we have to say about his stuff. Wyatt and J are coming by, and Warren said he would try but no promises."

Warren is our old manager and one of our partners in the studio. He and his husband have been enjoying married life since he retired.

"I'll talk to Haddie and see what she says. With Jordan there, she may be more comfortable since she already knows him. Can you hang out a minute? I need to piss, and Haddie is supposed to be here soon."

"Yup, I've got nothing but time."

After using the restroom, I walk out of my bathroom to find Noelle with her hands pressed against the sliding glass door in my bedroom. She claps excitedly when she sees me, and although I hear the doorbell ring at the same time, Noelle takes first priority.

"Uncle Darren!" she squeals as I open the door and scoop her into my arms. I step outside and make it about ten steps before Mel runs out her back door and looks around frantically with a half-naked twin in her arms.

"I've got her. I'll take her to Sawyer," I call out.

"Daddy! Let's go!" Noelle cries, and Mel's shoulders sag in relief. This is the exact reason they put a big-ass gate around the pool.

"Thank you, Darren!"

Noelle claps my cheeks with her chubby little hands and kisses me. I give Mel a quick thumbs-up as we head back inside, and Noelle copies me. Sawyer and Haddie are talking away as we step inside the house. Sawyer's brows shoot up in surprise when he notices Noelle in my arms.

"I thought you were using the restroom."

"Daddy, I come find you!" Noelle wiggles in my arms and reaches for Sawyer. Haddie flashes me a beautiful smile as I hand Noelle off to her favorite person.

"I was, but we had a runner. I figured I'd let your wife know before she lost her shit."

Mel knocks on the sliding glass door as she balances a twin on each hip. I open it for her, and she steps inside. "I'm so sorry! Noelle, you scared Mommy!"

Noelle giggles in Sawyer's arms as he gives her a disapproving glare. "It's not funny, Noelle. You made Mommy sad."

Noelle's big green eyes fill with tears. "I'm sorry, but I found Daddy."

I take Grey from Mel to ease her load, and she sighs in relief. "Thanks, Darren."

"It's okay, Princess, she's fine. I should've brought her with me." Sawyer closes in on Mel and kisses her tenderly.

"Sorry, Haddie, it can get hectic here sometimes."

I cross the room to her as she looks on with a bemused smile.

"It's okay; I'm used to hectic."

I motion toward Mel and her eyes light up as she realizes who is here.

"You've already met Sawyer, and this is his better half, Amelia. That beauty over there is their daughter Noelle, and this guy is Greyson, and that's his twin, Joey."

Haddie reaches out a hand, and Grey grabs her fingers. "They're all adorable."

"Thanks. They're a handful at times, especially that one," Mel says, pointing at Noelle.

Sawyer shrugs as Noelle kisses his cheek. "Can't help that she's a daddy's girl."

"Mmhm, sure …" Mel replies. "I'm sorry, Haddie, I think I lost my manners when I missed my morning coffee, but it's nice to meet you."

"It's nice to meet you too. All of you," Haddie answers as Grey reaches for her. She takes a step back.

"He won't bite," I tell her softly.

"Well, he might actually," Mel adds with a giggle.

"Oh, well … I just didn't want to assume it was okay. I'm still a stranger and all."

Mel waves off her concern. "Please, any friend of Darren's is a friend of ours, and Grey seems taken with you. He knows a pretty lady when he sees one."

Haddie holds out her arms and Grey practically leaps into them. He settles his head right on her breasts, hands clutching her shirt, and closes his eyes. She's a baby whisperer.

Sawyer and Mel exchange glances as Haddie runs her fingers through Grey's hair.

Sawyer chuckles. "Are you available between midnight and six a.m.? We pay extremely well."

"Kids have always seemed to like me. I'm not sure why, but it helps in my line of work."

Mel pats the seat next to her at the kitchen table, and Haddie joins her.

"Uncle Darren, cookie?"

Mel looks up rapidly. "Only one, Noelle. You still need to eat lunch."

Noelle nods solemnly. "Okay, Mommy."

Sawyer follows me into the pantry as Haddie talks to Mel. I give Noelle a cookie, and Sawyer blocks the exit and grins. "You weren't kidding when you said she looked like that model. She's sweet too. I see why you like her."

"Do you think Mel's really okay?"

His eyes widen and he shakes his head. "Mel's only concern is your happiness. The four of us should go on a date. I'd love to get Mel out of the house all dressed up. She deserves a fun night."

"Okay, I'll see what I can do, but no promises."

We step back into the kitchen where Mel and Haddie are chatting away like old friends. Grey is fast asleep in Haddie's arms, and I'm almost jealous—he's exactly where I'd love to be.

Noelle finishes her cookie and looks at Sawyer. "Daddy, can we have lunch now?"

"Yup, but you have to walk home like a big girl so I can carry Grey, okay?"

"Okay, Daddy! Come on, Mommy, it's time for lunch."

Haddie watches Noelle with an amused expression. I hope she's not at that stage where her biological clock is ticking away—this house is like fuel for needy ovaries.

With extreme caution not to rub against her breasts, Sawyer collects his son flawlessly from Haddie's arms.

"Maybe we'll see you guys later at the studio," Sawyer says as they wave goodbye and walk outside.

I lock the sliding glass door behind them before striding to Haddie, pulling her to a standing position, and crushing my mouth to hers. She parts her lips and sighs, and I swallow her air as if it's my lifeline. At this point, maybe it is.

"I've been wanting to kiss you since I saw you standing in my kitchen. I'm sorry for the unexpected welcome. Noelle is—"

"Adorable. She's entirely too cute for her own good. They're going to have to watch that one; she's going to be a heartbreaker."

I wrap my arms around her and pull her close. "You're okay? I know it's soon to meet the family, but someone is always here; it was bound to happen."

"I'm fine. It was a bit strange meeting Belle's best friend, but she seems nice."

"Mel is great; you'll love her. I'm glad you're here." I give her a brief squeeze.

She looks up at me, and pulls away, tilting her head. "Isn't that weird?"

"Why would it be weird? I'm hoping you'll spend a lot of time here. Do you want a tour of the house?"

"I'd love to see your home, but I think we should talk about something first."

I lean back against the table and cross my arms over my chest. "What's going on?"

"I found out the kids are going to be in Marina's class for kindergarten. I didn't know you guys were in our district, or that the kids were going to my school."

"Is this going to affect your job?"

She sighs. "I'm not sure. It shouldn't yet, especially since I don't even know Nate and Cadence. But if we get closer ..."

I step forward. "*As* we get closer ..."

She blushes. "Right. Once I meet Cadence, I might be able to skate around it and get a backup for her if I need one. Or I may be reassigned."

"Shit, babe, I'm sorry."

Her eyes widen, and I'm a bit surprised at myself for calling her that, but it feels right.

"It is what it is. I just thought you should know. It's not a big deal if what we have between us keeps progressing. I'd just hate to lose my place for nothing."

I reach for her hand and entwine our fingers. "This isn't nothing. I told Belle's mom about us this morning."

She gasps. "Why would you do that? That's ... huge!"

"I don't half-ass anything. When I decide I want something, I go balls to the wall. I trust my instincts because they've never steered me wrong. You're important to me, and I'm not going to hide it. I'm just waiting for you to decide if you can handle my life."

She steps closer, her voice dropping to nearly a whisper. "Your family I can handle. I love that you have so many people who care about you. It's the other stuff ... the press. They're cruel, and I have concerns."

I cup her cheeks in my hand and lock my gaze on hers. "I can't change what may or may not be said about you and us. What I can promise is that I'll be by your side through it all. We'll be a united front, and there's nothing they can say that would change how I feel for you. I want you in my world, and I wish I could make them disappear, but they're always going to be a part of my life."

"You think you'll still feel like that when they talk about your fat girlfriend?"

"Haddie ..."

"I'm not being disparaging. It will be a thing. There will be stories about how the last member of Bastards and Dangerous is dating a plus-size woman. People will talk shit and ask questions. Fat and beauty are not synonymous. People see fat, and it automatically equals ugly."

My blood boils. It's bullshit she has to worry about this.

"The entertainment industry is a fucked-up place. Rumors spread like wildfire, and the public is your judge, jury, and executioner. We don't read the articles, and we don't comment on anything unless we absolutely must. My feelings for you will never falter, and I will always put you first. No one has the right to tell me who to love."

She looks at me with sad eyes. "But you shouldn't have to defend yourself, not because of me."

I hop up on the counter and spread my legs, motioning her to come closer. She steps between them, and I rest my hands on her voluptuous hips. "I'm going to tell you something. The only people who know this information are my band and security team."

She looks at me hesitantly. "Okay ..."

"Do you think people had a problem with my relationship with Belle?"

Her brow furrows. "No, why would they? She seems like she was perfect. I've heard she was funny, sweet, and well-liked. Wait ... you can't mean because she was black?"

Haddie's eyes widen with surprise and perhaps a bit of sadness too. "Belle was all of those things. She was hilarious and full of life, she loved me like no one ever had, and I her. She was a kind, beautiful, smart, well educated, successful, African American woman, full of black girl magic, and she was dating someone the public perceives as a run of the mill, average white man who lucked out with fame. Some of her fans thought I wasn't worthy of her. Although she got less hate from her readers, it was strong. She was a rising star in African American media, and I was the scuzzy, heavily tattooed, drummer of a rock band. A portion of her fans couldn't understand why this USC graduate, who spent her spare time mentoring young black women would lower herself and her standards by dating someone like me."

Haddie's eyes fill with tears. "That's so ... *wrong*. You can't help who you love. And anyone who knows you knows what an amazing man you are."

A single tear escapes her eye, and I brush it away with my thumb. "It *is* wrong, and it always will be. Those people didn't know us, they just knew how they perceived us through the media. Belle eloquently but firmly put the haters back in their place.

"The hate mail I received was disgusting enough to make me want to pack up my wife and daughter and move to a desert island. The ridiculous part was, all those people accused me of betraying my race because they assumed I'm white. The media rarely covers my Mexican heritage, and since my coloring comes from my dad, no one would guess otherwise."

"That's so unfair. How can you talk about it so calmly? I'm so *angry* for you!" Haddie's eyes flare with rage to match the indignation in her tone.

"Anger only gets you so far before you have to step back and think."

She caresses my cheek. "I'm so sorry, Darren."

I bring her hand to my mouth and kiss it, needing to ground myself. "I am too. I'm sorry we live in a world where people are stereotyped by the color of their skin, their religion, or a number on a scale. We have a security firm who goes through our mail, tracks our threats, and keeps lists of people who could pose a threat to us. Do you have any idea how disturbing it is to receive hate mail about your child?"

She shudders, and the look of horror on her face is nothing compared to how it makes me feel inside. "She's an innocent child! I hope to God you found out who those people were and extracted a lethal form of revenge on each and every one of them. Jesus, why would people do that?"

Watching Haddie get worked up over Cadence is just another affirmation she's the right person for me.

"According to them, she's impure and tainted. They send me hate mail about my bastard child and call her the N-word. We received letters from people who offered their condolences after Belle died, but they felt she died because we were traitors to our races. It makes me sick to think about my beautiful daughter growing up in a world where people would threaten her because of her heritage."

Haddie presses her hand against her stomach and looks physically ill. Taking a deep breath, her determined gaze meets mine.

"You'll raise her to become a strong woman, just like Belle would have. You will teach her to rise above the negative with a sharp mind and a grace all her own. Educate her about all parts of her heritage and teach her our differences make us stronger. Remind her every single day she is strong and beautiful, just like her mom. Tell her how proud you are of her and that you know Belle is proud of her too."

I pull her into my arms. Hugging Haddie comforts me, and I've been sorely lacking in that department for the last six years. With a kiss to her cheek, I move my hands back to her hips, and she moves hers to my thighs.

"Thank you for saying all of that. I needed to be reminded I can do this."

"Of course, you can. It's obvious how much you love Cadence. There isn't anyone on this planet who will look out for her the way you will."

I nod and swallow over the lump building in my throat. "Anyway, I guess one saving grace is that after Belle passed away, the letters about her and I ceased. It can be a scary world at times, but typically the threats are harmless even if they're shitty. The letters about Cadence were the worst, but they were also few and far between, to begin with – there haven't been any in about two years."

"Thank God," she whispers.

"The point I'm trying to make is, people are always going to be assholes. I don't live my life for them. I'm living my life for myself and my family. Yes, someone may say some negative things about you, but other people are going to say the most amazing things in return. You already know how I feel about you. I've already introduced you to my family, so this isn't a game to me."

She nods. "Kiss me, Darren."

I trace the seam of her lips with my tongue until she parts them for me. As I bring my hands to her cheeks, I nip her bottom lip, and she whimpers. Our tongues meet and dance together slowly, licking at each other like the flames of a fire, our chemistry fueling the kiss. Each time we kiss, it's with a deeper need than the one before. There is something to be said for the build-up of waiting. Noah was right about anticipation making things better.

When we break apart, she looks up at me with determination. "This isn't a game for me either. The media aspect is going to be my least-favorite part, but if I have you by my side, I'm all in."

"You're sure?"

"I'm as sure as I'm going to be. I wish I could own my figure like other women do, and maybe I will one day, but it's apparent you understand the articles may be hurtful—"

"I understand completely. How about I make you a deal? For each article you see that makes you second-guess yourself, I'll worship your body and make love to you until you no longer doubt how fucking sexy you are to me."

She inhales deeply, and her eyes flare with lust. "That would mean we need to be having sex."

I bring her hand to my aching cock. "I'm ready for that whenever you are."

"Sex with me may be something best done with the lights off."

"Dammit, Haddie—"

She brings her finger to my lips to silence me. "I have scars from the accident, Darren. They're not pretty."

"They won't affect my desire for you."

"You say that now, but—"

I shake my head vehemently. "Scars mean you survived. I know the significance of those scars because I lived it. We walked that journey with Mel, and it was so fucking hard. The two of you have a lot in common. You and I aren't that different either. I'll never be able to shake that night from my conscience."

I blink back my tears and try to push the image from my mind. "You don't need the details. All you need to know is, I understand more than you think. You may hate your scars, and you have every right because you went through a traumatic experience. But don't tell me I have to fuck you in the dark because you're afraid. I will worship every single one of those scars. No matter how ugly you may think they are, they led you here to me, and I'll never fucking take that for granted."

chapter 12

Haddie

The air between us sparks heavily with passion and truth. I suck in a deep lungful of air and exhale. My hands tremble as I reach for his. Darren's raw honesty slams down every doubt or fear I've had about us. Cut from the same cloth, we're survivors of unspeakable trauma. It doesn't matter that we haven't known each other long, something greater than us brought us together for a purpose.

"Take me to your bedroom."

"That wasn't why I said what I did." Sadness masks his features, and I tug his hand and coax him off the counter.

"And I don't want to go there to have sex. I want you to see, to understand, and to still be able to tell me we'll be fine."

He looks at me wearily before pulling me down the hall and pausing at the door. "This isn't going to change anything." He kisses my head and opens the door to a room that's probably bigger than my house. With the push of a button, the shades come down over the sliding glass door, and when I step inside the room, he locks the door behind us.

My hands are shaking, but the only way to do this is to get it over with. I pull my shirt over my head and toss it to the floor. His eyes immediately zone in on my lacy red bra and stay there while I kick off my shoes. He steps closer as I unbutton my jeans.

"Let me." Unzipping my pants, Darren drops to his knees and pulls them down my legs. I lift my feet so he can pull them free, and he caresses my calves and works his hands up my body. Reaching my lower thigh just above my right knee, he comes across the first scar. Halting his movements, he follows the scar with his eyes all the way up to my right hip.

"Get on the bed and lie down, Haddie."

I do as he asks and am almost swallowed by his thick duvet. I'm not sure I've ever felt a more comfortable bed in my life.

Starting at my ankles, Darren gently works his way up my legs again. When he reaches the base of the scar, I jump. "Is it painful?"

"No, it's a bit numb from the nerve damage and trauma. I don't touch it often because it feels different, but you can. It just takes a minute for me to acclimate to the sensation."

This isn't supposed to be sexual, but as he kisses his way up my leg and slides his hand along my inner thigh, it's turning me on. He's being a gentleman and not straying from the inside of my thigh, even though part of me wishes he would.

"Is this the only scar?"

"No, but are you sure you want to see the rest?"

He climbs up my body and kisses me. "There isn't a part of your body I don't want to memorize."

I wore high-waist panties for a reason. They're sexy and lacy but still cover the damage. "You'll need to lower my underwear."

"It's going to be an extreme pleasure."

"I wouldn't be so sure," I caution one last time, preparing him for the worst.

He tugs on my underwear until they're barely covering my mound. As much as I don't want to look, I raise my head to see how badly I repulse him. His expression softens as he sucks in a breath and meets my gaze. "There is nothing about you that is going to scare me away. Do these feel strange too?"

"Sort of. They're a bit ticklish but not as numb."

Darren traces the outer edges of my scars across my abdomen. Almost my entire stomach is affected; some areas are worse than others. One section is bulkier than the rest, almost like layers of scar tissue on top of each other. Some of the smaller ones could almost be mistaken for stretch marks.

Darren hovers over me and places open-mouth kisses everywhere he sees a scar. When he finishes, he climbs on top of me and settles between my legs. I spread my thighs to accommodate him, and he brushes back my hair.

"I'm still here, baby, and I'm not going anywhere."

I wrap my arms around his neck, and he lowers his lips to mine. "You must have fought so damn hard. Can you tell me what happened?"

I release him from my embrace, and he rolls to his side. I turn to face him, and he scoots closer, resting his hand on my hip. I start to pull up my panties, but he stops me.

"Leave them. I want to see."

"Please, you don't need to see my belly flab."

He tugs my lip between his teeth. "I want to see every sexy inch of you, but I understand if it makes you more comfortable." He reaches between us and adjusts them. "I know we've pushed through a lot of boundaries today."

"Thank you."

He lightly traces my breast at the edge of the lace cup. "I'll give you a condensed version and we can go deeper some other time."

"Deal," he says, never breaking eye contact.

"It was raining, and we were on our way home. Richie and I couldn't stop laughing about some drunk guy who sat next to us at the bar. The man spent the whole night plotting ways to get his girlfriend back."

Pausing, I take a deep breath before I continue. "The truck hydroplaned, and my side of the truck hit the center divider, and then we banked off the divider and into a tree. It happened in seconds, but it seemed like hours."

I close my eyes and exhale as I try not to cry. "Richie died on impact with the tree. I was impaled by part of the car and parts of the tree. I was lucky there was a highway patrol car right behind us;

they saw the whole thing happen. If they hadn't been there ..." My eyes meet his and I whisper, "I probably wouldn't have survived."

He squeezes my hand. "I'm so glad you did."

"Me too, but I wasn't at first." I hate admitting that, but I want him to know the truth.

"I had lots of surgeries, pain, post-op infections, secondary procedures, more infections. It could have been worse, but it wasn't a walk in the park. They offered plastic surgery, but it was high risk due to the infections, and I didn't want to go through more pain. There was part of me that felt I deserved to walk around with scars for the rest of my life because Richie died."

"You know it doesn't work like that. It was an accident."

"My logical mind understands that, but my guilt was intense. I witnessed the instant life was taken from someone. That moment was more painful than any of my injuries. He was my world, and then he was gone."

Darren pulls us flush together and holds me. His comfort is exactly what I need.

"Haddie, we're on this journey to find our way together. We're going to make amazing memories along the way, but moving on doesn't mean forgetting."

"What do you think it means?" I ask, tracing a tattoo on his neck.

"Living your best life in their honor. We remember them, we honor them, and we love *for* them."

"I like that," I whisper as I trace Cadence's name on his arm.

"Me too, and I like the thought of doing it with you. Now, as much as I love lying here with you, my cock doesn't understand the art of taking things slowly. Let's go to the studio and see what's going on."

"Okay, sounds good."

Darren leans in for a lingering kiss, and I melt under his touch.

Once I'm dressed, I sit down to put on my shoes, and Darren takes a seat next to me. "I've been known to take things for granted in the past. It's something I've worked hard to change since Cadence was born. In light of that, I want to thank you."

"Thank me for what?"

"For being honest with me. That was brave, Haddie."

Heat washes over my face as he leans in to kiss my cheek.

I wonder if he'll still compliment my honesty when he finds out the one thing I can't seem to talk about.

Once we're outside, Darren shows me around the property.

"If you follow that trail over there," he says, pointing toward Sawyer's yard, "it takes you to a huge treehouse Noah and Sawyer used to play in as kids. Sawyer's house used to belong to his grandparents, but he bought it when they passed away. The path also leads to a gazebo, and eventually to a creek at the end. You can sit out here at night and listen to the frogs and crickets." He reaches for my hand and laces our fingers together.

"They're not worried about the kids playing in a treehouse?"

"Nah, Sawyer had it rebuilt with all the necessary safety precautions. It's a great place for the kids to escape and still be safe. Way better than vegging out in front of the T.V. or playing video games."

We stop in front of a swing set. "I'm sure they get good use out of this too."

"Oh yeah, and the pool. All the kids take swimming lessons, even the twins, but the gate is still a necessity."

I'm surprised at the size of the studio as we approach it. It has its own driveway and quite a bit of parking. I'm a horrible judge of space, but it looks like the size of maybe a six-car garage.

"Wow, this is a literal studio. I don't know why I thought it would be a room or a converted guest house or something."

Darren laughs. "We get that a lot. It allows the artists to enjoy a sense of privacy. This is technically horse property, which is why each street only has four to six houses. Being at the end of the cul-de-sac is perfect, and since Sawyer is my only neighbor, no one protested when we built it."

He steps ahead of me and punches a code into the keypad outside the studio door. When the latch clicks, he opens the door and motions me inside first. I blink at the change in lighting. It's darker but still pleasant.

A toddler playing with trucks on the floor of the reception area looks up when we enter. His eyes shining with excitement, he grabs a truck and runs toward us.

Darren scoops him into his arms. "Brayden, my man. High-five, dude!"

Brayden giggles and slaps palms with Darren.

"Darren!" A petite woman with short purple hair stands from the couch in the corner and gives him a huge hug. "I was hoping I'd get to see you today. It's been a while."

The baby reaches for her, and Darren passes him off and takes my hand. "Anna, this is Haddie. Haddie, this is Wyatt's wife Anna and their youngest son Brayden."

"Hi, Haddie, it's nice to—" She drops her gaze to our linked hands and looks back up at Darren with wide eyes. "Oh my goodness!" She grins and lightly bounces on the balls of her feet. "Are you dating?"

"We are," Darren confirms with a smile.

Brayden reaches for Darren again with a giggle, and Anna passes him back eagerly. Darren releases my hand as she pulls me into a huge hug.

"Haddie, you have no idea how nice it is to meet you." She releases me, squeals, and pulls me back into her hug. "Sorry, I'm a hugger, and you're just a sight for sore eyes."

Anna holds her arms out for a hug. "Put Bray down, Darren; it's your turn again." The baby reaches for me, and Darren passes him to me.

I point to his toy. "Hey, Brayden, that's a cool truck you've got there."

Anna whispers something into Darren's ear and wipes away a tear.

Brayden's chubby cheeks and bright-blue eyes are adorable. When he leans in and kisses me smack on the lips, I'm not sure what to do.

Anna laughs. "He only kisses the pretty girls. Take it as the highest compliment."

"Bray, my man ... why you trying to steal my girl?"

My heart flutters at his words, but it's been a long time since something has felt so right.

Darren turns to Anna. "Is everyone here?"

"Yeah, they just got here and wanted to see Jake playing the guitar. As soon as they've finished feeding his five-year-old ego, we're off to lunch with my parents."

"Cool, I'm going to take Haddie back and show her around. Bring the kids and come by for dinner this week. I'm sure Nate and Cadence will want to talk all about kindergarten."

Anna bites her lip. "Well, I'm going to the school on Monday to see if I can still enroll Jake. We decided private school isn't the path we want to take after all. Since it's not our home district, though, I'm not sure if they'll squeeze him in. Keep your fingers crossed for us."

Darren looks at me and raises a brow. "Do you have any insight?"

"Oh, do you have kids in the school too?" Anna asks excitedly.

"No, but I work there. Tell them your niece and nephew have been placed with Miss Marina for kindergarten. Emphasize the fact you're choosing their school over private school—Principal Lewis loves hearing that. If things haven't changed since last week, there should still be openings for kindergartners."

Anna squeals. "That would be a Godsend. I don't know what I was thinking not enrolling him with his cousins."

"You weren't." Darren shrugs, fighting a grin.

Anna bumps her shoulder against his chest. "Don't be mean to me or I'll tell Mel not to make you sweet potatoes at Thanksgiving, Christmas, Easter, or ..."

"You wouldn't dare."

She arches a perfect brow at him. "Try me."

Darren laughs, reaches for my hand, and kisses the top of her head. "I love you. Come for dinner this week, okay?"

"A day I don't have to cook? You don't have to ask me again. Let me know what day and we'll be there. Haddie, will you be there too?"

"No, I don't plan to meet Cadence for a long while."

Anna blinks slowly as if confused. "Is it because you work at Cadence's school?"

I look to Darren, and he crinkles his nose as if he doesn't like my answer either. I want him to take this question and not make me look like a bitch to his friends.

"No, it's because meeting a child before a relationship is stable and committed isn't a good idea. It's not fair to put her through the pain of losing a bond if Darren and I don't work out."

"Huh." Anna shrugs. "You guys have to do you, so I get it, but I've never known Darren to make a move he wasn't already sure about five steps before he takes it. However it plays out, I hope I'll be seeing more of you, Haddie. Meeting you made my day."

"It was nice meeting you too."

Darren motions to me to step into the inner studio and leads the way until we're about halfway down the hall. He opens the door to a room where a little boy is playing guitar as people watch from the couches.

I look around and notice all the kid-sized equipment—guitars, drums, miniature keyboards, even a small piano. There are other instruments like maracas, tambourines, harmonicas, bongos, and ukuleles. He could run an entire music program here. Then again, with all the kids they have, that might be what they're doing.

The little boy playing is talented for his age.

"That's Jake, Wyatt and Anna's oldest," Darren whispers in my ear.

"He's flawless," I whisper back, and he nods.

When the song is over, everyone claps as Jake puts the guitar on its stand. "Dad, I'm starving can we eat now?"

The man next to him smiles. "Yes, we can eat. Go say hi to Uncle Darren and then tell your mom to pack up Bray."

The little boy runs up to Darren with a smile and high-fives him. "Did you hear that, Uncle D? I got it right this time!"

"We told you all that practice would pay off. Too bad Nate and Cadence weren't here to play with you."

"Yeah, Uncle Sawyer said they went to church with Grandma V. I was supposed to go, but we had to go shopping for school." Jake scrunches his eyes and looks at Darren holding my hand.

Shit.

He looks back up at me. "Who are you?"

I bump Darren with my shoulder. He turns to me, and I raise a brow to encourage him to answer.

Darren takes the hint. "Jake, this is Haddie."

His dad comes closer with a huge smile on his face while Sawyer talks to the men on the couch.

Jake looks up at me. "Are you a singer too?"

"No, I'm afraid I don't sing very well, but I used to play the piano when I was a little girl."

"That's cool. That's what I want to learn next. Do you think you can teach me?"

Wyatt laughs and places his hands on Jake's shoulders. "It's not polite to ask big favors of people we don't know well. Don't worry, we'll find you a great teacher. Go tell your mom we're almost ready."

"Okay, Dad. See you later, Uncle D!"

Jake runs from the room, and Wyatt extends his hand to me. "I've heard a lot about you, Haddie. I'm Wyatt."

I take his hand. "It's nice to meet you. Your son is very talented."

"Thank you. I hate to meet and run, but we need to feed the kids. I hope to see you again soon, Haddie." Wyatt pats Darren on the shoulder and leaves.

Sawyer stands, and the two men follow. "Now that Jake has finished showing you his skills, how about we take this to the studio and lay down some tracks?"

Darren and I step aside and then follow them down the hall to the last door.

One of the men whistles. "This is impressive. No wonder Shawn and Eli have been singing your praises."

Darren releases my hand and steps forward. "Good to see you again, Ryder."

"You too, man. It's been too long."

They do the whole man-hug-back-slap thing before Darren swings his gaze toward me.

"This is my girlfriend, Haddie Davidson."

Sawyer's eyes widen, and my heart stutters again. I try to recover quickly as Ryder smiles at me.

"Ryder Stone. It's nice to meet you, Haddie." He holds out his hand to me, and I shake it as Darren places his arm around my waist possessively.

His friend steps up and holds out his hand next. "Shawn Lucas. It's a pleasure to meet you. Are you a musician too?"

I shake my head and release his hand. "No, I'm a psychologist."

"She's a professional," Ryder says to Shawn, and I tilt my head in curiosity.

Shawn grins at me. "Sorry, sometimes it's surreal when women don't get excited when they recognize us. When it happens, Ryder and I tend to speculate as to why."

Sawyer laughs. "Darren and I used to do that too, but we would place bets on whether they were faking or they really didn't care who we were."

I look at Darren, and he blushes and shrugs awkwardly. "We were young and dumb, what can I say?"

"I'm a bit of an enigma," I reply. "I like music. If you tell me some of your songs or your band, I might recognize it, but I don't follow gossip or celebrities with the exception of David Beckham. I could be standing next to one of the most famous musicians in the world and not have a clue who they are."

Sawyer snorts. "For those of you not in on the joke, that's how she met Darren."

We all have a good laugh, and the four of them excuse themselves for a minute to check out the inside of the studio. My heart fills with pride as I take in all the awards and platinum and gold records hanging on the walls.

Darren has accomplished so much at such a young age. I know things were cut short because of the accident, but it seems like they lived a lifetime of dreams in the time they had.

"Impressive, isn't it?"

I turn my head to find Mel smiling at me. "It's incredible. They should all be so proud."

"They are when they allow themselves to be. It's hard for them to have so much and still be missing one of the key people who helped make them who they are."

"I'm sorry for your loss. Darren talks fondly of Noah and Belle all the time."

Mel motions to the couch, and we take a seat. Watching the men through the glass wall as they talk animatedly brings a smile to her face.

"Earlier, I wanted to talk more and tell you I'm happy for you two. It's not easy finding someone who understands the gravity of your loss. Darren has had a rough time since Belle left us. I hope the two of you heal each other the way Sawyer and I have," she says sincerely.

"Belle was your best friend?"

"More like my sister. When my parents died, and then my grandma, Veronica treated me like her own. She pretty much did before, but that solidified it. You'll like her when you meet her. She's amazing."

I rub my hands against my jeans—just *thinking* about meeting Belle's mom freaks me out.

Mel reaches across and grabs my hand. "We're not ordinary people. This family fights for each other. We push through the difficult issues and make sure our own are taken care of."

"It's a lot to take in. I come from a small family."

Mel smiles. "Me too. I judged them before I met them, but I try not to do that to people now. I could've missed out on knowing these amazing men. They're special. They are hands-down the nicest, most caring people I've ever had the privilege of knowing."

"How did you find your footing?"

"It wasn't as difficult as you'd think. They're patient and loving, and they're excellent at bringing you into the fold. I won't lie, they're also overwhelming and at times overbearing. They talk through everything and give sound advice. When this family pulls you in, embrace it. I promise it will be the best thing you've ever done for yourself."

Darren waves at me through the window, and I wave back. Mel watches us closely, almost as if she's assessing our every move.

"Does it bother you he's dating again, Mel?"

"I'm ecstatic. Darren is my brother now and one of my best friends. I know how you must feel, though, so don't be afraid to ask questions or just talk to me."

She looks at her husband like a lovesick puppy, and when he blows her a kiss, she doubles over in laughter. "Sorry," she says, catching her breath, "it's an inside joke. Wyatt and Anna blow kisses all the time, and they all make fun of them. When Sawyer is feeling silly, he'll do it just to see my reaction. It makes me laugh every time."

"Oh, gotcha. Mel, do you know why Darren called me his girlfriend when he introduced me to those guys?"

Mel sighs. "Do you want the truth?"

"Nothing but."

"I think he was staking a claim. Letting his alpha side out. If he didn't mean it or want it, he wouldn't have said it. The guys know what they want, they go for it, and they get it."

Taking a deep breath, I exhale slowly. "I see."

"Haddie, if you like Darren *half* as much as he likes you, lean into that feeling and go with it. Fear holds us back, but somehow life always brings us full circle to what was meant to be. 'The only way out, is through.' From the day Noah died until the day I married Sawyer, their mom drilled that into my head." Turning sideways, she lifts her shirt and reveals the text tattooed up the side of her body. "It became such a big part of me, I made it permanent."

"It's so hard though."

She nods. "Saying goodbye to the past and diving headfirst into the future is scary. Perhaps I'm biased, but Darren is special. He doesn't love easily, so if he's falling for you, there must be something special about you as well."

"Princess, are you causing trouble?" Sawyer leans against the doorframe and stares at Amelia like she's his entire world.

"Only the best kind," she replies with an innocent smile.

Something hits me in the feels like a tidal wave. I want what they have—desperately.

chapter 13

Darren

"Did I freak you out back there? Is that why you're so quiet?"

Haddie has been silent since we left the studio. I open the sliding glass door, and she follows me into the living room. Once we're comfortable on the couch, she turns to me.

"I'm confused. Is that what you want?"

"What do you mean?"

"You told them I was your girlfriend and acted kind of jealous when they looked at me. Do you want to be exclusive?"

"Would it scare you away if I said yes?"

She flashes me a beautiful smile. "No, but I still want to take this slowly."

Moving to sit across from her on the coffee table, I reach for her hands. "I'm willing to go as slowly as you'd like, but ..."

"It's about what Anna said, isn't it? About Cadence?"

"I think there's another aspect we neglected to consider. You've met most of my family, nephews and niece included. It's not exactly fair to Cadence, and if Jake says something to her, I don't want her to be confused or have hurt feelings."

Haddie sighs softly as she laces our fingers together. "Either way, it's a risk, but I agree we should've thought ahead when it came to the kids. I don't ever want to be the cause of your daughter's pain."

I move quickly from the table to the floor and drop to my knees. I pull her mouth to mine and devour her like a starving man. The flavor of her intoxicates me, and I want so much more. I want to dip my tongue between her thighs and taste and tease her until she explodes on my tongue. I'll never get tired of kissing Haddie, but we still need to talk, and we're running out of time.

I pull myself away from her and take a deep breath. "Thank you for thinking of Cadence first."

"I'd hope anyone would think of a child first and foremost. I think you should warm her up to the idea though. Let her adjust to school before you talk about how she would feel if you dated. She probably doesn't even understand what it means."

I mull over her words. The kids are six; they don't have any clue what dating is. We need to have an important conversation before she meets my daughter, but now is not the time. We've covered too much emotional shit today to add anything else to the mix.

"Agreed." I kiss her hand. "And as much as I'd love to spend more of the day with you, they're going to be home from church soon."

She sighs. "It's okay. I need to go home and get ready for work tomorrow. First day jitters and all."

"Me too. If you see Mel bawling and me tearing up tomorrow, just ignore us."

"You're pretty hard to ignore, but I'll do my best to try. The moms are going to love you and Sawyer. I bet we see less pajamas and frazzled women this year."

Her lustful gaze is an aphrodisiac straight to my cock.

I tilt my head and look at her curiously. "Are you the jealous type?"

"I'm not sure. I've never been that way before, but I imagine seeing women throw themselves at you won't make me feel great."

"Yeah, about that ... I have to be nice, friendly, and open to conversation. If you see it and it bothers you, talk to me about it and remind yourself it's not flirting. Treat it like business. I'm a lot of things, but one thing I'll never be is a cheater."

"I'll keep that in mind."

I stand and pull her to her feet. "I'm glad you came over today."

"Me too, even though I had to show you my scars."

"Your scars only enhance your beauty. Don't let anyone ever tell you differently."

She inhales sharply, and I kiss her, hoping to drive my point home. When we break apart, I walk her to her car.

"I'll call you later after I get Cadence down. Well … I'll try. This is the first night she and Nate are sleeping separately. I'm not sure how it will go, but if I can't call, I'll at least text."

"Enjoy your night," she replies as I close her car door for her.

I wave as she pulls out of my driveway and Veronica pulls into Sawyer and Mel's drive. That was close.

"Daddy, are you almost done?" Cadence squirms on the chair, and if she could hold still for five more seconds, I'd be finished with her hair.

Thank God for Veronica and Mel. Without their help, she'd look like a ragamuffin all the time. It took a few weeks to get it down, but now I can do her hair just as well as they can.

"Hold still and count to ten."

As she counts, I yawn. Last night was a long one. Sleeping alone was not easy for her, but once she finally fell asleep, she was down for the count.

"All done, Cady. Let's get your backpack and your lunch and go see if Nate is ready."

She jumps off her chair and dashes out of the room. I don't remember much about my first day of school, but I'm pretty sure I was never excited about it. Belle's genes are shining through. Thinking of her puts me in a solemn mood. Last time, I screwed up and fucked Rory, but I'm determined to have a better outlook on things this go-around.

"Daddy, come on!" Cadence impatiently calls out from the front door.

The moment she sees me, she throws it open and runs to Sawyer's house. Mac and Ryan are waiting by the SUVs to drive us. We aren't sure if it will get a little crazy, but the plan is to park a block over and walk up. If there's an issue, they'll come get us.

Mel, Sawyer, and the kids are all outside, and Mel swipes at her tears as she takes photos. My phone vibrates, and when I see the text notification, I smile.

Haddie: Are you crying yet?

I'm not, but Mel is. I'm a bit melancholy, but Cady is happy.

I snap a few pictures of her and Nate and debate on sending them for about half a second. If Haddie is going to be part of my world, I should be able to share moments like these with her. I send the photos, and she replies instantly.

Haddie: They're adorable, and Cadence's hair is gorgeous.

Thanks. My hairstyling skills are better now than they were three years ago.

Haddie: You did her hair? High-five. That's impressive.

She's my little girl; there isn't anything I wouldn't do for her. Maybe I'll see you soon?

Haddie: Maybe only a glimpse across campus. Text me if you need me to sneak you some tissues.

Have a good first day. I'll talk to you soon.

After tucking my phone in my pocket, I take the travel mug of coffee Sawyer offers me.

"Thanks."

"No problem. If Cadence was as hard to put down as Nate was last night, you're going to need it."

"She finally fell asleep around midnight. I'm hoping tonight will be smoother."

Mel poses the kids with boards that have their school and year information on them.

"Nate went down about the same time," he points to Mel, "but that one spent an extra hour reminiscing and freaking out."

She flashes him a death glare. "It's an important day, and ..."
Mel swipes away more tears, "we're blessed to be here for it."

Sawyer and I exchange glassy-eyed looks and pretend not to
notice we're feeling it too.

"Daddy, I want to go to school too." Noelle peeks up at Sawyer
with expressive eyes.

"You get to go to preschool next year, and you can go with us
to drop off Nate and Cady, but you can't stay at his school. You're
still too little, sweetheart."

Her bottom lip wobbles. "But I will miss them."

Sawyer places his hand over his heart before he scoops her up
into his arms. "I will miss them too, but we can draw them pictures
and call Grandma to come make some cookies with us. Will that
make you happy?"

She nods and throws her arms around Sawyer's neck. Mel
snaps a shot of it and shrugs when I catch her. "Dads are hot. I'm
not apologizing."

"Is *my* dad hot?" Cady asks, and Sawyer snorts.

Mel suppresses a giggle. "He is, and your mommy used to say
it all the time. But hot isn't really a nice word to use. Your mom
would say he was very good-looking."

"Liar," Sawyer says under the guise of a cough, and Mel grins
at her victory.

"Then I won't say the not-nice word." Cadence turns around
and walks directly to Nate. "Nate, you're very good-looking."

The three of us exchange shocked expressions. Cadence isn't
dumb, none of our kids are, but damn, I did not expect her to pick
up on that context.

Nate smiles and simply answers, "Thanks." As often as he calls
her pretty, I think he understands as well.

Sawyer recovers first. "Pile in, everyone. It's time for school!"

We arrive early enough to easily find parking spots around the
corner. Mac walks in front, and Ryan stays with the cars. Mel
pushes the twins in a stroller, Sawyer carries Noelle, and Nate and
Cadence follow excitedly behind Mac.

Anna's car is parked in the lot, and I hope she's able to get Jake in with the kids.

Only two other parents are waiting outside the classroom when we arrive. I stand by the stroller so Mel can take more photos, and as the minutes pass, a buzz begins. At first, it's stolen glances and then whispers. Sawyer and I exchange knowing looks.

"Big day, huh?" I say to the mom standing to my right.

"You're talking to me?" She looks behind her and then back at me. "Oh, I guess you are. Hi! I'm Cara, my daughter Athena is in Miss Marina's class. And you're Darren. Gosh, you know that already ... why are you here?" She smacks her head lightly. "Ignore that, please ... I'm just a bit ..."

"Surprised?" I fill in with a smile.

She laughs and puts her hand on my shoulder. "Yes, I'm surprised."

I take a step forward with the stroller, and her hand falls off. "It's okay, we get that a lot. Our kids are in Miss Marina's class too."

I catch sight of Sawyer walking around with Noelle and meeting parents. Dude sure knows how to work his magic. My phone buzzes and I pull it from my pocket. "Excuse me. It was nice meeting you, Cara. I'm sure I'll see you again soon."

She wanders to a group of moms off to the side and squeals.

"Hello?"

"I forgot something from in my car. Imagine my surprise when I walk out and see quite the fuss."

I turn around with the stroller and see Haddie in the lot with her trunk open. "I wouldn't know; I'm completely distracted by the most breathtaking woman right now."

"I'm jealous," she says softly. "You asked me if I would be and I didn't know. Now I do. I'm pretty sure you guys have already been crowned DILFs of the school."

I laugh. "As long as I'm the dad you'd like to—"

"Shh," she squeaks out through her laughter. "Don't say that there, or you'll have a very specific target assigned to you. When *they* know *you* know, the shameless flirting will never end."

"Well, we wouldn't want that, would we?"

"Never. I have to go, but you seem to be doing great. Keep your head up. You've got this."

"Haddie … thanks. I needed that today."

"You're welcome."

A few seconds later, Anna and Wyatt join us with their kids. Anna and Mel hug excitedly when they announce Jake is in the same class. The classroom doors open, and most of the kids and parents start moving inside.

Cadence's eyes are locked on the parking lot, and Nate and Jake flank her like matching protectors. We all notice at the same time and look to see what in the world is so fascinating.

A man pulls a tiny wheelchair from the back of a car, and a woman lifts a little girl from the back seat. We all watch as they make her comfortable in her chair. She's a tiny little thing wearing a pink dress, a big white hair bow, and glasses.

The parents seem apprehensive as they make their way to the curb where we're all gathered. The second they roll onto the sidewalk, Cadence steps in front of them.

"Hi, I'm Cadence, and this is Jake and Nate. Are you in Miss Marina's class too?"

The dad looks us over, surprise etched on his face—he seems to be aware of who we are—and the mom openly cries, but the little girl flashes the biggest smile.

"I am. My name is Heather."

Cady returns her smile. "Cool, maybe we can sit together. Let's go inside and see the classroom!"

My heart damn near explodes, and the second a tear slips down my cheek, Wyatt tosses his arm over my shoulder. "I would love to give you credit for that, but if that wasn't a sign from Belle that she's guiding that girl, I don't know what is."

"You took the words right out of my mouth. I'm so proud of those kids."

Heather's dad wheels her into the classroom, followed by our kids, and the rest of us pull up the rear.

Someone taps my shoulder before I enter the class. I turn around, and Heather's mom engulfs me in a hug, tears streaming down her face. "I was going to home school her because kids can be so cruel. Thank you. Your daughter just gave her a memory she will never forget. None of us will."

She quickly releases me and rushes in to catch up to her family. I meet up with everyone and listen as Marina talks about what they're going to do today. When she dismisses the parents, our kids smile and wave goodbye. I'll take that over the tear fest freakouts some of the kids are having any day.

Maybe I would've worried more about leaving, but my mind is at ease knowing Marina is Haddie's best friend. Hell, the fact Haddie is in the office takes a huge weight off my shoulders.

Haddie may not be here with me now, but I know if I need her, she's only a phone call away. As far as milestone days go, this one is by far the best yet.

chapter 14

Darren

"Daddy, will your girlfriend like me?"

For the last three weeks, I've been trying to ease Cadence into the idea of me dating. For the most part, she seems to be amenable to the idea. Times like today, I can tell she's worried about what it means.

"Cady, she's going to *love* you. If I didn't think so, she wouldn't be my girlfriend."

"Will you kiss her like Uncle Sawyer kisses Auntie Mel?"

This kid ...

"When grownups like someone the way I like my girlfriend, they often kiss and hug."

She looks up from the page she's coloring, "Will she be my new mommy?"

Damn, right in the gut with that one. I finish cutting up her apple and take a seat at the table with her.

"Do you want a new mommy, Cady?"

She puts down her crayon and looks up at me. "Is it okay to have two mommies like Nate has two daddies?"

Have I failed her? I've been against dating for so long, I never thought of all the concerns she might have.

"It's more than okay. Sometimes mommies and daddies go to heaven and people get a bonus parent."

"What's that?"

I hold out my arms and she climbs into my lap. "It's what Uncle Sawyer is to Nate. He loves Nate just as much as Uncle Noah would've."

This is a big conversation to have with a six-year-old, but I might as well have it now because Cadence is too smart for her own good.

"Sometimes, parents don't get along anymore and kids end up with two sets of parents. And there are kids who have two dads or two moms who love each other very much."

Cady jumps off my lap and looks up at me. "Like Uncle Mac and Tyler?"

"Yup, exactly, and there are kids who only have one or the other, like you and me."

"Will you love her more than you love me?"

"Nope, it doesn't work like that."

"Then how *does* it work?" She moves over to the counter and grabs her apple.

I can't explain how I'd murder someone to keep her safe and that loving her is different than loving a partner, so I try to keep it simple.

"You love all your aunts and uncles, right?"

She nods as she chews.

"Do you love any of them more than the others?"

"No, but Auntie Mel is my favorite."

I hold back my laughter. "Maybe you shouldn't say that to the rest of them. We don't want to hurt anyone's feelings, okay?"

"Okay, Daddy."

"You love them all the same though. That's how love works, Cady. We can love lots of people for the role they play in our lives. I will never love someone more than you, but I may love people as much as I love you. Does that make sense?"

"Yes, it makes sense," she says after she finishes her apple. "Can she come to the movies with us on Sunday when we take Nate?"

"I'll ask her if she wants to come with us. She's a little scared to meet you."

Cady giggles. "I'm not scary!"

"She's nervous you might not like her. I think that would make her sad."

"I'll be her friend if she's nice."

Oh, Belle, she becomes more and more like you every day.

The doorbell rings and Cadence takes off running. "It's Grandma V time!"

I follow her, and she grabs her suitcase by the front door.

"Grandma V!" she squeals, when I open the door.

Veronica crouches down for a hug. "Now that's what I call a greeting. Are you ready to go get Nate for our weekend?"

"Yup. My daddy has a girlfriend, and if she's nice to me, I'll be nice to her, but he won't love her more than me."

Veronica flashes one of her special smiles reserved for Cadence. I've always imagined it's the same smile she gave Belle. "Of course, he won't love her more. Now, we'd better get going before the groceries get hot. Go put your bag in the car."

Cadence gives me a hug and a kiss before running out to the car, and Veronica side-eyes me. "Darren, it's been nearly a month now. Less talk, more action. You're confusing her, and if she's asking questions, she's worried. Put those fears to rest and introduce them already."

"I'm working on it. She wants Haddie to go to the movies with us on Sunday."

"That sounds like a lovely idea. There is never going to be a right time. Rip off the bandage. You'll be glad you did. See you after church on Sunday."

"Thanks, Veronica. Enjoy your weekend."

Haddie is supposed to come by tonight. Most of the time, things between us are great, but there's been some underlying tension lately. Some of it can be attributed to sexual frustration.

She's not ready yet, and I'm happy to go at her speed. There's also something important I need to discuss with her, but it never feels like the right time.

We talk multiple times a day, and we've spent the last three weekends together. She's slept in my arms, laughed at my jokes, and cooked meals for us. I'm in love with her, which complicates things. I've been following the plan and getting Cadence ready to meet her because I want to integrate Haddie into our world. When it comes down to putting our plans into action, I'm hesitant, and I think Haddie senses it.

I pull out my phone and send her a text.

Come over when you're ready. I can't wait to see you.

She texts back about thirty minutes later.

Haddie: Sorry, I had an IEP that ran late. I'll be over in about an hour, if that works?

Sure. Sawyer asked about going out Saturday night. Would you be up for that?

Haddie: Can we talk about it tonight? It's not really a great time right now.

Okay, see you soon.

My body drips with sweat as I leave the studio. Fuck, I miss playing every night. The adrenaline high, the crowds, the motherfucking music—it was my life for so long, it's hard to believe it's over. I still can't bring myself to play our music though. Bastards and Dangerous without Noah isn't right. Someone approached us a few months ago and wanted us to play with Noah's hologram. I don't think I've ever seen Sawyer so pissed.

My phone rings. *Shit. I'm late.* I start walking faster and answer it. "Hey are you here?"

"I've been waiting for about five minutes, but I figured you were probably in the studio."

I open the sliding glass door and close it behind me. "Two seconds. I'm almost there." Opening the front door, I smile. "I'm sorry for making you wait."

Haddie rakes her gaze over my body and as she steps inside. "It's okay, this was worth it."

"Me being hot and sweaty?"

"Oh yeah, you look pretty hot." She bites her lip.

I pull off my shirt and step closer. "Hot as in sexy, or hot as in heat?"

Her breath hitches. "Both."

I lean forward and give her a quick kiss. "Let me shower. Otherwise, I'm going to start doing things I may not be able to stop."

She steps back, and her body language shifts—she's no longer relaxed and enjoying the view. "A shower is a good idea. When you come out, put some clothes on. We need to talk."

"Haddie, is everything all right?"

"Sure," she answers distractedly. "We'll talk when you're finished."

As I shower, I think about us. There's no denying I've fallen hard for her. We're at the point in our relationship where some difficult choices have to be made. We talked briefly about being exclusive, but it hasn't been mentioned since. Haddie still hasn't been in public with me except for our breakfast at the diner.

While I get dressed, I firm my resolve—we have to talk about kids. Haddie is five years younger than me, and her career revolves around children. She probably wants a house full of them, which poses a huge problem. I don't want more children—ever. Cadence is it for me

One of the biggest things that held me back from relationships over the years was fear. Belle's death crushed me. I can't handle the idea of losing someone else, and I can't raise another child by myself. I refuse to drown in survivor's guilt again.

Cadence and Nate are proof that even though God took Belle and Noah, he left the best parts of them here with us. I know they're here for a greater purpose. Although it might destroy us, it's time I tell her the truth. We're growing too close to keep it from her any longer. If she wants a baby someday, I'm going to have to end things. It's non-negotiable.

When I enter the living room, she stops pacing and flashes me a weak smile.

"We need to talk," we say in unison.

"You go first," she says, sounding relieved as she leans back against the couch. She digs her fingers into the fabric like she's holding on for dear life. Maybe she is.

"I'm not sure how to say this other than to just come out with it. Why don't we sit?"

She shakes her head. "I'd rather stand, if you don't mind."

I take a deep breath. "Haddie, I want this more than I've wanted anything in a long time. For the first time in years, I want to be with someone ... with you ... and I know you understand how big of a step that is."

Haddie nods her head solemnly, but her normally bright eyes dim. I move to step closer but stop myself. This is going to be hard enough.

"The thing is ... I don't ever want to have another child."

Her eyes widen before her expression falls. Haddie lets herself slide down the back of the couch until she's sitting on the floor and covers her face with her hands and sobs. With each anguished cry she releases, my gut tightens until I can't take it anymore and I sit beside her and pull her into my embrace. What was I thinking letting this go on so long?

"I'm so fucking sorry. I should've told you sooner. I didn't mean to hurt you, but this is a deal-breaker for me. We have to talk about it before ... it gets harder to say ... goodbye." I'm barely able to speak the words over the lump in my throat. I don't want to lose her—I just found her.

She finally looks up at me, and I brush away her tears. "It's not that. Darren ..." She pauses to catch her breath.

"Take your time, gorgeous."

Haddie leans into my shoulder, our heads touching, and regains her typical calm demeanor. Eventually, she scoots back a bit and turns to face me.

D. Kelly

"I've been keeping something from you as well. I justified a thousand reasons not to tell you. I told myself this was a fleeting moment in time. You're sexy and famous, and I'm just—"

"Beautiful. Haddie, you leave me fucking breathless. I wish you understood how much."

The redness that flushes her cheeks brings a smile to my face, and I lean forward to kiss her briefly. Damn, I wish she could see herself the way I do.

"Thank you," she replies softly. "I guess I wasn't the only one feeling things shift between us. The truth is, the car accident didn't just steal my fiancé; it stole my ability to have kids."

She pauses and my heart drops. I can't imagine her suffering though that alone.

"I'm sorry, Haddie."

"Thank you. I didn't think I'd move on after Richie. Once we started dating and I understood how important Cadence is to you, and how amazing you are with her, I've felt so inadequate."

"You could *never* be inadequate."

Knowing she can't have kids flips a switch inside me. Haddie would be an amazing mother and deserves to have babies. Even though I don't want them for myself, I'd give anything to make it possible for her, even if it means I'd have to let her go.

"But don't you see?" Her eyes light up. "You don't want more kids. You have no idea how much of a relief that is. I don't have to worry about letting you down. You have Cadence, and I have my students."

Damn. This isn't at all what I expected, but I still can't help wanting to fix this for her.

"Is there a procedure you can have to help? Maybe you can freeze your eggs and hire a surrogate?"

Haddie shakes her head. "There was a lot of internal damage. They removed my uterus. Fortunately, I was able to keep my ovaries but now there are lots of adhesions. On the plus side no more monthly periods."

In a way I'm not surprised. Haddie's scars are pretty intense and sometimes she still has pain. She tries hard to hide it but I've caught her wincing a few times with certain movements.

"What about adoption?" I ask, needing to know why she's so accepting of her fate. If it's a money issue I'll help her.

"There's nothing wrong with adoption – it's a beautiful thing for everyone involved. If we're laying all our cards on the table, I've never wanted to have kids. I love children but I've never had the desire to have one of my own."

Fuck

"If you never wanted kids then why would you want to be with me? Cadence and I come as a pair, you know that, right?"

Haddie places her hand over my heart. "You're an incredible father Darren. Being Cadence's dad is a huge part of who you are and I … love that about you. I love kids and even though I don't want biological children that doesn't mean I wouldn't be happy having stepkids in my life. You guys have a great family structure, Cady looks up to Mel as if she were her mom already."

I caress her cheek and rest my head against hers. "There is more than enough room in Cadence's heart to love you too. If you want her to."

"I'm scared I'll hurt her if this doesn't work out."

I brush my lips against hers. "Then stop acting like we're going to fall apart. You were on board when we talked about being exclusive. Ever since then, you refuse to go out in public, and you talk like we're about to implode."

"Darren, I was terrified not being able to give you babies was going to be a deal breaker. I was just trying to protect my heart and yours."

"It's too late for that. If we're past all the secrets—"

"We are."

"Then you have to become part of my world. All of it. No more dancing around the hard stuff. Sunday, we take Cady and Nate to the movies. The two most important ladies in my life need to meet. You're my girlfriend, Haddie, not my dirty little secret."

"Okay, on one condition," she whispers as my lips hover over hers.

"Name it."

"Don't break my heart, Darren. I won't survive it a second time."

Fear, anger, possessiveness, lust, and need swirl around inside me like a tornado. I hate everything she's been through because I know how hard it is to fight through the pain. As my mouth crashes down over hers and our tongues meet, all I want to do is prove to her how much I care. It's as if I hear Noah's voice whispering in my head that fate brought us together—Haddie and I are meant to be.

She grips my shirt in her fists as I caress her curves. With a groan, I pull back and stand, bringing her with me.

"Bedroom, Haddie, now." I pull her behind me, determined to make it to my room in record time and never more thankful Cadence is with V tonight.

I close the door behind us and push her up against it. Growling, I lower my lips to her neck and kiss a path to the shell of her ear.

"There's no fucking way I'll ever break your heart. If I did, mine would break right along with it. I'm never going through that again. Are you still all in, Haddie? After tonight, there's no turning back."

The rise and fall of her chest speeds up as I take her earlobe between my teeth. She moans softly and drops her mouth to my neck. Haddie blazes a trail of slow, decadent kisses against my skin, sending a flame of desire straight to my cock. When her mouth meets mine once again, her words are so full of heat, I'm surprised they don't catch fire.

"I'm all in, Darren. Falling in love with a rock star is by far the scariest thing I've ever done though."

"I love you, and I know you're scared, but we're taking this leap together. From here on out, it's you and me."

She slides her hand inside my shirt and explores my body as I press myself against her.

"I love you too. It's crazy how fast it happened, but nothing has felt this right in a long time. You brought me back to life."

Haddie pulls off my shirt and throws it aside. "So many tattoos," she says, tracing my ink with her fingers.

"Does that bother you?"

"Not a single bit. They've never been my thing, but they add to your sex appeal."

I laugh and pull her shirt over her head, tossing it next to mine. "Do you ever think about getting any?" I tease her nipples with the tips of my fingers and admire her breasts.

"I've never thought about it before," she hisses as I flick her taut nipple.

"We could get couples tattoos one day."

Her eyes widen. "Have you ever done that with someone?"

"Nope, you'd be my first."

Lowering my mouth to her chest, I flick her nipple with my tongue through the silky material of her bra. She arches toward me and weaves her fingers through my hair.

"When we have a … significant event where it would be appropriate, maybe we can."

I lift my head and trace the exposed skin of her breast near her heart. "My name would look pretty good right here, don't you think?" I ask, with a smirk.

She looks at the same spot over my heart which is already filled with ink. "I'm not sure that would be fair. You don't get my heart if I can't have yours."

"Babe, it's already yours." I crash my lips against hers and reach behind her to flick open her bra. She whimpers as our tongues meet, and I make quick work removing her bra.

She unbuttons and unzips my pants before pulling away from our kiss with a gasp. "You're not wearing boxers."

I take off my pants so she can have the full view. "I was hoping we'd end up right where we are." I bring her hand to my dick, and she wraps her fingers around me.

"Fuck, Haddie."

Lifting her eyes to mine, she strokes me and swipes my pre-cum with the tip of her finger before bringing it to her mouth.

Instead of sucking it, she sticks out her tongue and licks it like an ice cream cone. Groaning, I push her hand away.

"You have far too many clothes on. It's not fair you get to taste me and I can't return the pleasure. Strip."

Her eyes widen as I take a step back. When I reach for my cock and stroke myself, she shimmies out of her pants and moves to the bed and crooks her finger at me in a come-hither motion.

I shake my head. "Underwear too. Take them off, lie down, spread your legs, and let me feast on you."

She sucks in a breath, stands, hooks her thumbs into the sides of her panties, and pauses. I know this is a huge step for her, so I take a few steps closer. I swipe my thumb through my pre-cum and bring it to her lips, and she sucks me into her mouth. Our bodies are now flush, my cock pressing into her belly, and when she sucks my thumb deeper, I can't hold back my frustrated groan.

"I love you—every beautiful inch—and I've seen your scars. I didn't run then and I'm not going to run now. But so help me, Haddie, if I have to stand here a minute longer and smell your arousal without knowing what it tastes like, I will bring you to the brink of orgasm again and again and never actually give you one. At least, not tonight."

Her nostrils flare as she blinks repeatedly. I expect her to come back at me, but she surprises me by removing her underwear instead. Before she has a chance to get back on the bed, I slip my hand between her thighs. She gasps as I slide my fingers over her clit and into her pussy.

She digs her fingers into my shoulders and cries out against my neck. "Darren, please," she begs, and my cock twitches.

"Please what, baby? What do you need?"

"You, always you."

I guide her to the bed and climb in next to her. "I'm not going anywhere," I say, brushing her hair away from her face. Our lips meet, and we kiss until we're both breathless before I begin moving down her body.

Her curves feel like perfection in the palms of my hands. As I slide my hands over the swell of her hips, my cock jerks at the thought of holding on to them as she rides me. I shift her hip and let my hand trail over the globe of her ass. When I imagine spreading her apart and taking her from behind, I can't suppress my groan. But as my lips meet her pussy for the first time, all I can think about is how she'll sound when she explodes in my mouth.

Haddie hisses and arches her body off the bed when I flick her clit with my tongue. I could ease her into this more, but I've been waiting a month to hear her scream my name. With each stroke of my tongue, she pushes against me, eager for more. I lick and suck my way to her entrance and enter her with my tongue as I pinch her clit.

"Oh God!" she screams, and I groan as I devour her essence.

Pausing, I pull back. "Not even close. I want to hear *my* name on your lips, Haddie – *mine*."

She grips my hair and bucks against my face as I dip my tongue back inside her. Haddie fucking my face is exactly what I wanted. I press against her hardened nub, and she comes with a force I'm not sure I've experienced before.

"Darren!"

She mutters incoherently and thrashes against me as I lick and suck my way through every pulse of her release. She sighs and relaxes as her orgasm subsides. I kiss my way up her body, paying extra special attention to her scars. There isn't a single part of her body that's off limits to me.

As I make my way up to her breasts, she rubs my shoulders. Pushing her tits together, I take my time learning what type of breast play turns her on.

She squirms beneath me. "Darren, please ..."

I move to her mouth and kiss her lips. "Please what?"

"Fuck me," she says, eyes blazing.

"Now that would be my pleasure. Did you go over my test results?"

We emailed our test results to each other last week but never talked about them.

"I did. Did you go over mine?"

"I did, but that doesn't mean we don't have to use a condom, Haddie. It's up to you. I want you to be comfortable with this choice."

She bites her bottom lip. "Have you been with others without protection?"

"Only Belle, and you?"

"No one."

"Not even ..."

She shakes her head. "We were extremely cautious. I didn't want kids, and back then, it was still possible."

"Let me grab a condom. We don't have to decide this right now."

Haddie wraps her arms around my neck and pulls my mouth to hers. "Don't. I want this with you. It feels like this is the way it's supposed to be."

"You're sure?"

She answers by kissing me and spreading her thighs wider. Our tongues meet, and I slip my hand between us to guide myself to her opening. When the head of my cock presses against her, she whimpers.

"Are you okay?"

"Yes. Give me more, Darren. Please ..."

I push into her slowly, groaning as her body adjusts and welcomes me. She's so tight and wet. I cup her cheek and lower my mouth to hers as I push all the way in.

"You're incredible," I whisper.

Our tongues meet slowly, and I match the rhythm with my hips. I want us to enjoy every second of this moment. Soon, our kiss turns frantic as Haddie meets me thrust for thrust. I raise her leg over my shoulder and angle her to take me deeper as her cries fuel my desire. She laces the fingers of my free hand with hers, and I slam into her hard. Each time we connect, her pussy becomes wetter and her walls clench me tighter.

I'm barely holding back my orgasm when she screams my name again.

"Darren, yes!"

"Fuck!" I shout as my body jerks violently through my release. Haddie laughs as I collapse on top of her.

"I'm sorry," I mumble into her glorious tits.

"I'm not. That was amazing."

I roll to the side and pull her into my arms. "It was pretty damn fantastic. Give me thirty and I'll be ready to go again."

"Thirty minutes, huh?"

"Woman, I haven't had sex in … damn, seven months. That's my second-longest drought since high school."

"What was the … right, never mind."

And then it hits me. "Hey, I'm sorry. I feel like an ass. Are you okay?" I lace our fingers together and kiss her hand.

She sighs and scoots closer to me. "I'm fine. I waited a long time so I'd be ready. I've got no regrets. I never thought I'd be lucky enough to fall in love with the first guy after Richie, but I'm glad it happened this way."

"Can I take you to dinner?"

She laughs and kisses me. "You are so random sometimes."

"I'm hungry. Hunger depletes brain cells, it's a fact."

She arches a brow. "Is it?"

"If it's not, it should be."

"Do you mind if we order in?"

If this is about her not wanting to go out with me …

"Oh my God, Darren. Stop with whatever you're thinking. I've got sex hair, need a shower, and have nothing here to fix myself up."

"We can change that. Let's go shopping tomorrow."

She sits up and pulls the duvet over her. "What in the world are you talking about?"

"Spend the weekend with me. All weekend. No more trips to your house to get ready or grab clothes. I've got more than enough space. Take over my bathroom, take over my closet, I'm not even sure I keep anything in my dresser – take it."

"I think you're right. I think your brain cells are depleting at a rapid pace and you need food ASAP. If you're still thinking crazy after dinner, we'll talk about this."

I get up and head toward the kitchen for take-out menus.
When I open the door, Haddie yells, "You're naked!"
"It's my house. I can freeball if I want to," I call back to her,
and the sound of her laughter follows me.

chapter 15

Haddie

"*Now* can we discuss going shopping tomorrow?" Darren asks as he opens a bottle of wine.

We took showers, ate dinner, and are now getting comfortable in front of the fire.

I turn toward him with a smile. "You *do* realize I'm a grown woman with a job, right?"

"Yes, and I'm very proud of you, but of my favorite things to do is make people happy. Taking you shopping is going to make my day." His eyes light up.

"What are you thinking, and can you explain why it's going to make you happy?"

He grabs my wine glass and sets both glasses on the coffee table.

"I want more of you in my life. I'd also prefer to spoil you when it's my idea to go shopping."

I could get lost in the depths of his eyes, especially when he's being vulnerable. "Okay, what things are going to cost money?"

"Haddie, I want you to have a second set of anything you need here. Extra clothes, toiletries, books, glasses ... Wait, *do* you wear glasses?"

"Contacts and glasses."

He groans. "I bet you look sexy as fuck when you wear your glasses."

I laugh. "Go on."

"Well, shoes and lingerie ... Seriously, so much lingerie. I'm hard even thinking about it. But also simple things like your favorite coffee or ice cream. I want you in my home more, and I'd like you to be comfortable while you're here."

"And why is it going to make you happy?"

"How could having you around more not make me happy?"

And how can I not love that answer? I lean over and kiss him, and he pulls me onto his lap until I'm straddling him. I start to move off, but he clamps his hands down on my hips.

"Oh no, this is where I want you, can't you tell?" He pulls me flush to his groin and groans. "We should get naked and you should ride me right here."

"First we need to finish talking ..."

He nips my neck. "You can talk right here."

"I have money. Richie left me everything—his restaurant fund, his life insurance, and there was a hefty payout from the car insurance. You don't have to buy me things in order to spend more time with me. You just need to ask me to do it."

Darren tugs on my bottom lip with his teeth and then kisses me. I'm pretty sure if I were dying, his kiss would bring me back faster than CPR. This man connects with my soul on a level I'm not sure Richie did. It seems like I fell in love with Richie a little bit each day, but with Darren, I fell all at once.

When we break apart, he caresses my cheek. "I'm happy Richie took care of you, Haddie, but now it's my turn. I *need* you to let me take care of you too."

Tears spring to my eyes.

Darren's eyes widen. "I'm sorry, I didn't mean to—"

"No, stop ... thank you." I lean forward and kiss him again. "You're right. I have to figure out the line between 'he's a rich and famous rock star who can have anything and anyone he wants' and 'this man loves you and wants to do nice things for you.' It's a lot to process."

"I'm just Darren when it's us. Think of me as some random guy with a shitload of tattoos. My hobbies include spending time with my girlfriend, doting on my daughter, and making sure my family is taken care of. My after-dark hobbies include feasting on your pussy, fucking you until you scream my name, bringing you to multiple orgasms, and falling asleep with you in my arms."

Well hell ...

"Do you have a driver tonight?"

He cocks his head and grins. "I've only had about three sips of wine. I can drive us. What are you thinking?"

"I'd like to go home and pack a bag for the next couple of days. We can go shopping tomorrow, but I need to bridge the gap between then and now. Then I want to come back here and get started on the after-dark activities."

"Sounds good to me. Let's go."

"Shower with me."

I pause and look up from my duffel bag. "We just showered before dinner."

Darren steps behind me and meets my gaze in the mirror. Making a show of licking his lips, he lowers his mouth to my neck and licks a path to that sweet spot below my ear. "We did, and now I want to get you dirty in the shower, clean you off, and get you dirty all over again." Darren squeezes my ass and his eyes flare. He brings his arms around my breasts and squeezes my nipples.

"You don't play fair."

"I never claimed to. Strip while I start the shower."

When he releases me, I stop unpacking and watch as he shucks his clothes on the way to the shower.

He looks over his shoulder and shakes his head. "Less watching, more stripping. The real fun can't start until you're as naked as me."

I strip, and he beckons me closer. He steps into the shower and holds out his hand for me. Accepting his offer, I step inside and wrap my fingers around his hard cock as water rains down on us from multiple showerheads.

"Haddie … fuck yeah," he groans as I stroke him.

I take a step back and sit on the shower bench, putting his dick level with my mouth. Darren steps closer and places one hand on the wall behind me.

I circle the tip of his cock with my tongue, and he hisses. "You don't have to do this," he says as his dick jerks against my lips.

"And you have no idea how long I've *wanted* to do this." I reply before taking his length deep down my throat.

"Oh my fuck," he growls and brings his free hand to the top of my head.

Blowjobs have always been one of my favorite sex acts. I've missed this almost as much as sex itself. He pulls my hair, and I moan around his length.

"Damn, Haddie … you're going to make me come."

I tighten my grip on the base of his cock and redouble my efforts. Looking up, I meet his gaze as he fucks my mouth and cries out his release. I swallow again and again, milking every drop he gives me. Gently, he pulls out of my mouth and helps me to my feet. Caging me against the wall, Darren kisses me as if his life depends on it.

He slides his hand between my legs and dips two fingers into my pussy. I cry out as he thrusts a few times before pulling one out and sliding it to my ass. "Whoa," I hiss.

He flashes me a cocky smirk. "If you hate it, I'll stop." Darren continues finger fucking me, and when I nod, he uses his other hand to rub my clit. Dropping his lips to mine, our tongues meet as his finger enters my ass.

I cry out into his mouth as he continues thrusting into me and circling my sweet spot. He pushes a little deeper into my ass and wiggles his finger. My orgasm hits with a blinding quickness, and my knees are like jelly. Darren presses against me, keeping me between him and the wall. As I come down from my release, he slowly removes his fingers.

"Holy shit," I pant breathlessly. "That was …"

"Pretty fucking good, right?"

He chuckles against my skin and pulls me back under the spray. He slides his hands down my backside and cups my ass. "One day, I want to fuck you here too."

"Your dick is a lot bigger than that finger. Would you let me do the same to you?"

"I've never given much thought to pegging, but if you want to try, I'm game."

Laughing, I flip around in his arms and reach for the soap over his shoulder. "Maybe we can revisit that conversation another time."

We take turns soaping each other up and washing each other's hair.

"We should get out. We're wasting so much water."

Darren begins rinsing the conditioner from my hair. "I've got a reclaimed water system. Whatever we're using will be reused."

"Wow, that's really cool."

"Do you want one? I can have one put in at your house when we update your security."

Once he finishes my hair, he turns off the water and steps out and grabs a towel for him and two for me.

"No, you don't need to spend that kind of money. It's just me. Wait, were you serious about updating my yard and stuff? I thought that was a worst-case-scenario thing."

He steps up behind me. "I want you safe, Haddie. When the news breaks about us, you're going to be a hot-ticket item. I could hire guards instead."

"No guards, Darren. I need to be me."

"Then you have to have security. It's one or the other, but you're lucky I'm not forcing both. A few years ago, I would've."

I move to put on my underwear, but he stops me. "Sleep naked with me."

"Do you always sleep naked?"

He grins. "Whenever there aren't kids in the house. Try it. If you don't like it, you can sleep in your underwear."

"Okay, but just for you. I've never liked sleeping naked."

Darren reaches for my brush. "May I?"

"You want to brush my hair?"

"I'm pretty awesome at it. Don't you like it when someone brushes your hair?" He steps behind me and pulls the towel from my head.

"I love it." My shoulders relax as he squeezes the towel around my hair.

"I know you think I'm overreacting about things, but I promise I'm not. Did I ever tell you Noah had a stalker?"

"I think you briefly touched on it."

Once my hair is finished, he lowers my towel and begins drying me.

"You know, I can do that myself."

Darren smirks. "What's the fun in that?"

After we're both dry, he takes my hand and leads me back to his bed and turns off the lights. "Noah's stalker almost killed him and Mel. It was a wake-up call for all of us, especially Sawyer. She got to them while we had security on high alert. We had extra guards, failsafe protocols, and she still managed to get through it."

We lie side by side, facing each other, and I bring my hand to his cheek. "That's crazy. I'm sorry."

Darren rests his hand on my hip. "My point is, you have nothing protecting you right now. Unless you're ready to move in with me, we have to fix that. I can't risk losing someone else."

I exhale softly. "Okay, do whatever you need to. Let me know how much it is—"

"Absolutely not. This issue comes to our relationship because of who I am. I'll pay for it."

"Fine, but no reclaimed water system. I mean it. And as far as moving in with you … it's way too soon. You should ask me again later on though."

"You'd consider it?"

"I'd consider a lot of things when it comes to you."

He laughs. "Like pegging me?"

"If that's really something you want, consider it done."

He laughs again and pulls me into his arms. "We're going to have an incredible sex life, and we'll figure out what we do and don't want as we go."

"Does it bother you that I'm not as … experienced?"

"Does it bother you that I am?" he counters.

"No, because you wouldn't be who you are without the experiences you've had. Good or bad."

He kisses me and nips my lip before pulling away. "Thank you. I know it's old-fashioned, but I like that you haven't been as adventurous as I have. I'd never ask your number—"

"Six, and that includes you."

"Jesus," he groans and buries his head in my chest.

"Why are you hiding in my breasts?"

"Your breasts are extremely comfortable, and I'm not hiding; I'm thinking."

"About?"

"What an asshole I am for being happy your number is so low. How excited I am because I know I can corrupt you sexually, give you new experiences, and enjoy every fucking minute of it. But what if I'm too overwhelming for you?"

I push him away. "Are you trying to say I can't keep up with you? That I'm too vanilla for you?"

"Fuck no … that sounded bad. I'm very sexual, Haddie. There isn't anything about sex that I don't like. I'm excited to explore every aspect of it with you."

I take a cleansing breath and calm my anxiety. "This is a closed relationship, right?"

He pulls me close and presses his hardness against me. "Most definitely, but if you want to try a threesome, I'd be open to that as long as it's not a long-term situation."

"The only kind of threesome I'd be interested in would be with two men."

"We can do that if you want," he replies without hesitation.

I choke on my own saliva and cough. "Are you serious? You'd willingly be with me and another guy?"

"If it turned you on, without a doubt."

"What if I wanted him to be with you too?"

Darren slips his fingers between my legs. "You're wet."

"Answer the question."

"I've been with a man before. It wasn't horrible."

"Do you consider yourself bi?"

"Nope, I did it for her. Watching me with someone else turned her on and that turned me on. Sex isn't only for my pleasure." He pushes his fingers deeper and crooks them against my g-spot.

"Ahh ..."

Darren flicks my nipple with his tongue. "See, we're just talking about it and you're drenched. Is it the idea of us with another man turning you on? Or is it my dirty talk?"

"Dirty talk ..."

He removes his hand. "Turn over."

I do as he asks. He scoots close behind me and slides his cock down the seam of my ass, leaving a trail of wetness behind.

"This ass is going to be mine." Darren pulls my leg back over his hip and presses his cock inside me, filling me completely.

"Oh God," I whimper, and he nips at my neck.

"Nope, still me, Haddie."

"You're so deep." I grip the sheets in my fists as he slowly and meticulously fucks me.

"What if we watched people at a club? I could fuck you while we watch from behind privacy glass, or I could eat your pussy as someone else is feasted upon. Maybe they'll be blindfolded or receiving punishment. Would you want me to spank you? Slap that voluptuous ass while I fuck you from behind?"

I can't catch my breath. His mouth is in complete control of my body right now.

"Darren, please."

He thrusts faster, deeper, and harder, sending me to the point of no return. When he grips my hip and slams into me, I shatter completely.

"Darren!"

He comes on a roar, and it's everything I never knew I needed to hear during sex. I clench around him tighter, riding the waves of our shared orgasm.

When we're both spent, he pulls out and lies behind me with his arms around my waist. "That was hot. You've got some kink inside of you, and I'm going to have a blast helping you explore it."

"What if I'm pure vanilla?"

He kisses the back of my neck. "As long as you're fucking me and I'm the one you come home to, you can be as kinky or as vanilla as you want. I love sex, but I love you more. I can talk to you about all the dirty, sexy, and depraved things you want *if* it turns you on. But if you never want to do any of those things, we don't have to."

"In other words, you just want to make me happy?"

"Happy and sexually satisfied. Both are equally important in any relationship."

"Relationship ..."

Darren entwines our fingers. "Is it strange to think about?"

"No, the opposite. That word has taunted me for years, but with you, I wouldn't want anything less. Thank you for bringing me back to life."

He releases my hand and pulls the duvet over us. Curling up against my backside, he whispers in my ear, "I should be the one thanking you. Goodnight, Haddie."

"Night, Darren."

chapter 16

Darren

"Are you sure you're ready to do this?" Haddie paces the floor anxiously.

"Baby, I'm sure. Cady and Nate are going to love you. Stop worrying."

She throws her hands up in the air. "Aren't you worried? If she doesn't like me, this is it, Darren. We can't be together if she hates me."

I cross the room and wrap my arms around her. "She's going to love you. Maybe not at first because kids don't typically work that way, but she will. We'll figure it out, Haddie, because there is no way my little girl isn't going to love you as much as I do. It's not possible." The doorbell rings and I reach for her hand. "Come on, it's now or never."

She takes my hand and grips it tightly. I wish I could take away her fear, but I've got a feeling this goes far deeper than just meeting Cadence. Her whole life is about to change.

I pause on the way to the door. "If you don't think you can do this and be part of our lives … if that's why you're scared, speak up."

Haddie leans forward and kisses me. "That is not what this is about. Open the door, Darren."

I open the door to V and her husband Marcus. Looking over their shoulder, I find the kids playing in the yard behind them. V looks down to where Haddie's hand and mine are laced together and smiles. "It's about damn time."

V hugs me, forcing me to let go of Haddie, and whispers in my ear, "I'm proud of you, Belle would be too. This is a big step."

I swallow over the lump in my throat as she steps to the side and Marcus shakes my hand. "Good to see you, Darren."

"You too, Marcus."

V jumps right in with Haddie. "I'm Veronica, and you must be Haddie. I've heard a lot about you and it's very nice to finally meet you."

Veronica pulls Haddie in for a hug. Haddie quickly swipes at her tears as V pulls away, and V nods as if she knows a secret.

"It's nice to meet you, Veronica," Haddie answers softly.

Veronica reaches out and squeezes her hand. "This is a happy day; no tears are necessary. God has a plan and this is part of it. Be good to each other and to my grandbaby." The "don't fuck with my grandchild" message is clear.

"You know I always am," I reply firmly.

Marcus chuckles. "Come on, V, stop intimidating them and let's go get some food. I'm starving and you promised you'd cook a Sunday dinner feast if I went to church."

V points at Marcus. "Do you two hear him? I have to bribe him to give God some of his time one day a week."

"I call it an enticing incentive."

"Incentive, my ass," she mumbles. "We'll see you later. After all, if Marcus doesn't eat soon, he might wither away and die. Then he'll at least be grateful he went to church today."

We all laugh as they walk toward the car and say their goodbyes to the kids.

"Oh God, this is it. I think I'm going to be sick."

I turn toward Haddie and put my hands on her shoulders. "Breath, babe, this is going to be fine. I promise."

"Daddy! Are we going to the movies now?" Cadence runs inside with Nate hot on her heels. They both look up at Haddie and back to me. "Are we in trouble?"

I release Haddie's shoulders and turn to the kids. "No, why would you be in trouble?"

They point at Haddie as Cadence says, "Isn't she from our school? She works in the office."

"Yeah, but she's Miss Marina's friend too," Nate adds.

"Oh yeah, she is. You're Miss Marina's best friend, right?" Cadence looks up at her with her big brown eyes.

"Yes, I'm Miss Marina's best friend, and I also work in the office at your school. The kids at school call me Miss Haddie, but you can call me Haddie when we're not at school."

I crouch down to eye level with the kids. "Do you guys remember when I told you I have a new girlfriend?"

"Yes," they reply in unison.

"Haddie is my girlfriend." I pause as Cadence looks between us and Nate looks at Cadence. "Do you guys have any questions?"

"Is she nice?" Nate asks, taking the lead.

Haddie kneels next to me. "I try to always be nice. Being nice is a lot easier than being mean."

"Do you love her yet?" Cadence locks eyes with me.

"I love her very much. We talked about this before, but if you have feelings you want to discuss, we can talk about anything you'd like."

Cadence cocks her head to the side and assesses Haddie and me. "Does she make you happy? Grandma Karen said when grownups fall in love, they should always be happy."

Sawyer's mom Karen fills these kids with a lot of knowledge about grownups. She's raised some pretty incredible kids so I think it's all part of her process.

"Haddie makes me very happy."

Cadence nods, steps forward, and hugs Haddie. "My dad is sad a lot because he misses my mommy in heaven. Thank you for making him happier."

Tears fill my eyes, and as soon as Cadence releases Haddie, I swoop her into my arms. "I love you, Cady, so very much."

She giggles in my arms. "I know, Daddy, I'm your number-one girl." She looks over her shoulder. "Haddie, do you like ice cream? Daddy said we're getting ice cream after the movie."

"I do like ice cream," Haddie answers with a smile.

"Me too. Me and Cady get the kind that makes our tongues blue!" Nate tells her excitedly, and I put Cadence down.

Before long, the kids bombard Haddie with all kinds of questions about movie snacks, drinks, and her favorite children's movie.

I'm not sure I realized how worried I was about Cadence accepting Haddie, but my heart feels a lot lighter now that we've completed the introductions.

Once we're all in the car and pull out of the gates, I know we're in trouble. There are a couple of reporters camped outside of the exits.

"Is that what I think it is?" Haddie asks.

"Just ignore them," Nate tells her. "We do."

I grab my phone and call Mac. "What's going on, Darren?"

"We just left the house to take the kids to the movies and I think we've got a few tails."

"All right, you know the drill. Same theater as usual, right?"

"Yup, see you soon."

After I hang up, I make another call. "Sawyer, hi."

"Hey, I thought you were going to the movies."

"We are, and we've got friends. Any idea why they were hanging outside the house?"

Sawyer groans. "Eli is back in town. I'm sure they think he's coming out here. Do you want me to meet you guys?"

"Nah, Mac's on his way."

"What about Haddie?"

I flash her an encouraging smile. "She's with us."

"Hi, Dad!" Nate yells.

"Hi, Uncle Sawyer!" Cady screams.

Sawyer laughs. "Hello, everyone, have fun at the movies. Haddie, I know it's hard, but try to breathe. It won't be horrible if you don't freak out."

"I told her to ignore them, Dad."

"Good job, Nate. Okay, have fun and call if you need anything."

After Sawyer hangs up, I reach over and squeeze Haddie's thigh. She flashes me a forced smile.

Mac meets us in the parking structure of the theater with Ryan in tow. Three reporters may have followed us, but when we leave the theater, there's going to be a lot more once they figure out I have a new woman in my life.

We're not even out of the structure before the camera flashes start going off.

"Is this your new girlfriend, Darren?"

"Is it true the last eligible member of Bastards and Dangerous is off the market?"

"Would Belle be supportive of this?"

The last one makes me want to fuck a reporter up, but Mac clamps his hand down on my shoulder. Even Haddie gasps, but Ryan is doing a great job of keeping the kids occupied. These motherfuckers …

Mac already called ahead to the theater and talked to their security team about keeping the reporters out. None of them will be getting into the theater while we're here. Haddie takes the kids to the snack bar with Ryan and loads them up with junk.

"Give me your keys," Mac orders. "Ryan can take your car after the movie while the rest of you ride with me."

What else can I do?

"We promised the kids ice cream. Can you send Ryan to pick up all their favorites and extra toppings? If this is anything like it was when Mel and Sawyer started dating, I don't want the kids exposed to it any longer than necessary."

"Sure thing," he says, pocketing my keys. "What about school tomorrow? Want me to go too?"

"You don't think—" I check myself when as he raises a brow. "Yes, to be on the safe side. I know it's going to be boring."

"It's my job, Darren, and protecting these kids is my number-one priority these days."

I clap him on the shoulder. "Thanks, Mac."

We meet up with Haddie and the kids and take our seats. Mac and Ryan flank each kid and Haddie and I sit next to each other. I reach for her hand and bring it to my lips. "I'm sorry," I whisper in her ear. "This is going to get worse before it gets better, but my promises still stand. I love you."

She leans over and kisses my cheek. "And I love you."

Her words help take the edge off the lingering anger from that reporter. No matter how hard I try to focus on the movie, I can't. I'm terrified once we step outside, Haddie is going to decide she can't do this—I wouldn't blame her either.

Mac leaves the second the movie ends to pull the car around, but the rest of us stay put until the theater is empty. The kids talk about the film excitedly and do a good job of bringing Haddie into the conversation.

My phone and Ryan's go off at the same time.

Mac: 25 to 30 paps

It's not as horrible as it could be but that probably means they're camped out at home too. Fuck.

"Ryan, carry Nate. I'll take Cady."

"You got it."

"I'm not a baby, Daddy," Cady pouts.

"I know you aren't, but there are a lot of reporters outside and they sometimes forget their boundaries. Remember when we talked to you guys about boundaries?"

They both nod.

"Good. Pretend we're superheroes flying you to your car, okay?"

"Okay, but we still get ice cream, right?" she asks.

"Yes, but Uncle Ryan is going to pick it up and bring it home so we can have an ice cream party with Noelle, Uncle Sawyer, and Auntie Mel."

Both kids cheer. I know they've got a good life overall, but it fucking blows not to be able to take the kids for ice cream when I want to.

I reach for Haddie's hand and hold it tightly as we exit the theater. Mac is at the curb, door open, and we make a mad dash for the car. Ryan gets Nate inside then grabs Cadence from me. The flashes from the cameras and the reporters screaming their questions is insane. I could pull Haddie into my arms and kiss her now—tell them about us and get it over with—but I can't without talking to her first. I know it won't be more than an hour before her name is splashed everywhere—if it isn't already.

When I was with Belle, this was easy. She was the media; she made the announcements. I let my publicist go years ago, but maybe I need to hire a new one. I stand behind Haddie as she climbs into the car. Ryan closes the door as soon as I jump in behind her, and Mac takes off the moment the kids are snapped into their seats.

"Daddy, that was crazy! Why were there so many of them?"

I take a deep breath. "People are curious about Haddie. When someone famous starts dating someone new, the fans want to know all about it. Until they learn everything they want to know, we might have to deal with that a lot more than usual."

"Haddie," Cadence says, "are you famous too?"

Haddie turns and faces her. "No, sweetie, I'm just a normal person with a normal job."

"Okay, good," she replies on an exhale.

I look at my daughter and raise a brow. "Cady bear, why did you want to know?"

"Because that was a lot of people. If Haddie's not famous too, they'll go away like they always do."

"Remember when we went to Disneyland?" Nate pipes up, and I groan.

"Those were fans." Cady points out matter of factly.

172

"Doesn't matter, they were crazy!" Nate's animated tone cracks me up.

Haddie smiles. "Care to share?"

"Sawyer, Wyatt, and I thought it would be fun to take the kids to Disneyland on a rainy day when it wasn't so busy. It turned out they had some kind of sorority and fraternity day event. For the most part, everyone was cool, but at least fifty kids followed us around all day with their cell phones."

"How did you get them to stop?"

Cadence and Nate laugh and shout in unison, "Balloons, churros, ice cream, free tickets!" The two of them break into a giggle fit with the memory.

"Seriously?" Haddie asks, sounding amused.

I shrug. "We bribed them with food and told them we'd give them free tickets for both parks if they left us alone until the end of the day. In order to collect, they had to meet us at a specific time and place. Worked like a charm, and it was totally something Noah would have done. It felt like he was there with us in spirit."

"Daddy Noah liked making people happy," Nate says proudly.

"He sure did, buddy. Your dad was one of the best people I ever knew. You're pretty awesome all because of him."

Nate shakes his head. "And because of Mommy and my dad."

Cadence looks at Haddie. "Haddie, are you going to marry my dad now?"

Haddie's eyes widen as she looks at me for guidance.

I shrug. "Answer her."

"When your dad and I get to know each other better, we might talk about it in the future. If we stay in love a long time and he asked me to marry him, we would talk about it then."

Cady huffs. "But would you say yes?"

"I can't see why I wouldn't."

"Okay." Cady turns to Nate and begins babbling about the movie again.

I lean close to Haddie and speak softly, "Couldn't help but notice that wasn't a no."

She whispers, "You seem happy about that."

"I'd be lucky to have that honor one day. Besides, after today …"

Haddie leans her head against mine. "I'm a little scared, but I'm trusting that we're stronger than whatever comes next."

As Mac pulls up to the house, reporters hover around the gates like vultures. There must be just as many here as there were at the theater. This is ridiculous.

"I'm going to go through the studio entrance so I can pull around back and avoid them," Mac says as he turns into the drive.

"Sounds like a good plan."

Sawyer is walking to the studio when we pull in. The kids and Mac hop out and follow Sawyer inside while I stay in the car with Haddie.

I reach behind her head and pull her mouth to mine. Her lips part and our tongues meet. She whimpers as we kiss and I feel it straight in my soul. After today, the two of us desperately need to connect on a deeper level. As we part, she sighs.

"It's like you knew how much I needed that."

With a grin, I reply, "Only because I did too. There's something else I need from you, and please don't argue with me."

"Why would I argue with you?"

I pull a tendril of her hair between my fingers. "I'd do anything to protect you, Haddie. I don't want anything to happen to even a single strand of hair on your head."

She tilts her head and narrows her eyes. "Okay …"

"I can get a security team to your house tomorrow, but for tonight you need to stay here."

She leans back in her seat. "Don't you think you're overreacting? Surely, no one knows who I am."

I release a sigh and pull out my phone. "I'd be willing to bet you a thousand dollars that if I type your name into the search bar right now, photos of the two of us will pop up. Even if we don't, the people who are here will follow you home if and when you try to leave."

She blinks rapidly. "I-I'm … fuck, I don't know what to say."

"I think we need to call Sam."

Haddie looks at me quizzically. "Remind me again who that is?"

"Sam Owen Stevenson, he owns SOS Media and *Slammed Magazine*. We need to give a statement, tell our story. It will be personable and relatable if it comes from us. This will die down, and things will go back to normal sooner rather than later."

She pulls her phone from her purse as it starts sounding off alerts. "Messages from my mom and Marina. We've gone viral. Oh God ... my parents didn't know I was dating again. Now they want to know why I didn't tell them."

"Why didn't you?"

She sighs loudly. "They're beyond overprotective since my accident. I wasn't ready to let them in yet, not until we talked about the kid situation and I knew we'd be okay."

"I understand. Stay tonight so we can talk about this. Would you like to invite your parents over for dinner?"

"You'd do that? Let them come here and grill you?"

I open the door, hop out of the car, and hold out my hand for her. "For the girl I'm going to marry one day? Absolutely. We can invite my parents too."

"You're not going to let me live down that marriage thing, are you?"

I chuckle. "Cady was looking out for her old man. Remind me to buy her something special."

Hand in hand, we walk toward the house.

"I like the parent idea, but let's wait a few weeks and let things die down a bit. My parents will need to get used to the idea that I'm dating a rock star."

"Will it be a problem?"

"No, they know they can't control who I date. If they could, I'd be married to Jeremy Goldstein. He's a dentist and very attractive—according to my mother—and he has a nice nest egg."

I laugh as we step into the house. "And your opinion of Jeremy?"

"He's all of the above, but he's also condescending, a big know it all, loves to talk about aliens, and he's gay. His parents have no clue. They think he's going to bring home a nice girl one day. Either that or they're in denial."

"Hey, what's wrong with aliens? Have you ever been to Roswell?"

Haddie's eyes grow wide and she backs away from me. "Oh God, is this your fatal flaw? The one thing I can't get past?"

I laugh so hard I'm nearly crying. "I'm joking, Haddie."

"You're a jerk!" She shoves me, and I pull her close.

"Maybe, but I'm your jerk."

"Hm, I definitely love the sound of that."

chapter 17

Darren

It's been almost a week since the news broke about Haddie and me. As she feared, there are quite a few websites slamming the hell out of her because she's plus-size. They're slamming me too, but I couldn't care less what they say about me. Sam is coming over today to interview us and set the record straight about all of this.

We were able to install the security system at Haddie's house, but she's been staying here because the paps haven't left her street. Thankfully, they stay away from the school. Between the police patrols and our increased security, not to mention the risk of being accused of something inappropriate with a minor, I think they realize it's better to stay away.

"Haddie, can you help me brush my hair?"

I stand and head to the bathroom. "I'll do your hair, Cady."

"No, I want Haddie to do it. Please?"

Haddie has been watching me with Cadence all week. She has our routines down to a T, but still, she's not Haddie's responsibility.

Haddie nods at me. "Sure, give me just a second."

Cadence flashes her a beaming smile. "Thank you!"

"You don't have to do this."

Haddie kisses me on the cheek. "It's not a big deal. She wants some girl time. Relax, this is a good thing. She wants to bond with me."

"Okay, have fun."

Cadence has been bonding with Haddie this week. She's read stories to her, helped cook dinner, even asked her to give her a bath. I know how much Cady adores Mel, but if this past week is any indication, she's needed a woman in her life more than I ever realized.

I'm sad I didn't acknowledge her needs sooner but also excited that she's so accepting of her.

For now, Haddie's school principal is monitoring the situation, but she doesn't see any reason why they would need to reassign her.

The doorbell rings, and when I open the door, Mel and Sam are on the porch.

"Come on in. Where's Warren?"

Sam gives me a quick hug. "In the studio with Sawyer. He said he'd missed his roots."

"That sounds about right."

Mel looks around as we step into the living room. "Where's Cady?"

"She asked Haddie to do her hair today."

Her eyes light up as she smiles. "That's awesome."

"Grandpa Sam!" Cadence squeals and runs to Sam so fast she practically knocks him off his feet.

He scoops her up and spins her in a circle. "If it isn't my beautiful princess. We've missed you. When are you coming to visit?"

"Whenever you want, except for tonight. We're spending the night with Grandma Karen and Grandpa Owen. Tomorrow, we're going to the zoo!"

Sam carefully lowers her to the floor. "That sounds exciting. We should plan a trip to Sea World."

"Yes! I'm so down!"

We all laugh at her enthusiasm.

I crouch down to her level. "Give me a hug. Be good for your grandparents and tell them thank you."

She wraps her arms around me, and I breathe her in, wishing I could keep her this small forever. "I will, Daddy."

Cady runs to Haddie and gives her a huge hug. "Thank you for doing my hair. I'll see you when I get home!"

Mel covers her heart with her hand and whispers in my ear, "My heart might burst with joy. She loves her already."

"It's amazing isn't it?" I whisper, and she nods.

"Come on, Auntie Mel, let's go show Nate how Haddie did my hair!"

Mel snickers and follows her out the door.

"And so it begins," Haddie says softly.

"Indeed," Sam concurs.

"Both of you can kiss my ass."

Sam laughs. "Another decade, another place, and I might have taken you up on that."

Haddie giggles. "Should we put that on the list of wishes along with the—"

I cover her mouth with my hand, and she licks it. "Be good and save the private things for the bedroom."

"Well, color me intrigued." Sam eyes us with interest.

"Sam, you haven't met my girlfriend yet. Haddie, this is my good friend Sam."

"It's nice to meet you," Haddie says with a smile.

"Likewise," Sam replies.

We walk toward the living room, and Haddie continues chatting. "I'm a little confused. How are you Cadence's grandpa?"

Sam chuckles. "It's an honorary title. Those little munchkins have more than enough aunts and uncles. Warren and I thought they could use another set of grandpas instead."

We all get comfortable in the living room. I sit next to Haddie on the sofa, and Sam sits across from us in a chair. I brought some drinks in earlier along with some snacks in case Sam was hungry.

"All right, you both know why I'm here. I've put together a list of questions for you guys. Some of them might be a bit inquisitive, but feel free to pass on anything you might be uncomfortable with. The goal is to give your fans a look into your world and, hopefully, decrease some of the paparazzi."

I squeeze Haddie's thigh. "Are you ready for this?"

She bites her lip. "As much as I can be."

Sam turns on the recorder. "Okay, let's get started. Darren, it's been over six years since the accident. Is this your first time dating?"

"Yes."

"Do you mind if I ask why now?"

"I'm not sure it's a thing where how much time has passed is a factor. It's more of a moment-in-time scenario. When I met Belle, I knew she and I were meant to be. I can't explain it, but we both felt it." I look at Haddie, and she nods her encouragement.

"It was the same with Haddie. Only this time, we bonded over our mutual grief of losing a significant other."

Sam takes a deep breath. "You lost someone as well?"

"Yes," Haddie answers softly before regaining her confidence. "My fiancé and I were in a bad accident. He passed away and I almost didn't make it. It had been a few years, but I was trying to figure out a way to say goodbye to him the night Darren and I met."

Sam leans forward and eyes us seriously. "Are you in love?"

"Yes," we answer in unison.

"Darren, you're a single dad. How is your daughter dealing with this?"

"Haddie is a child psychologist. We worked together for weeks to prepare Cadence for the meeting and how to handle it whether it went well or not. My daughter is the most important person in my life, and it's my responsibility to be sure she continues to feel loved and valued."

Haddie rubs my shoulder. "Cadence has been very accepting of me. We're building a relationship day by day. At some point, we may have issues. I think that's to be expected in any situation where a father brings a new woman into the home. Cadence's happiness will always be my number-one priority as well."

Sam flashes us a beaming smile. "Are there wedding bells in your future?"

Haddie shakes her head and points at me to answer. "When we're both ready. We know time waits for no one, and the people we love can be gone in a flash. But we also know the fear of losing someone is not an excuse to skip the important steps."

Sam taps his pen. "What do you consider important steps, Haddie?"

"Giving Cadence time to get to know me and understand she's important to me too."

I bring her hand to my mouth and kiss it. "God, I love you."

She blushes, and I turn to Sam as he continues to observe us. "Enjoying the firsts. Like today, my daughter asked Haddie to do her hair. Most people think that's simple, but this is the first time Cadence has indicated she's accepting Haddie in a mother-type role. You see, these aren't just firsts as a couple, these are firsts as a family. The first time Cadence hugs Haddie or includes her in her prayers are milestones that are just as important as our anniversary or other firsts couples have."

Unshed tears swim in Sam's eyes.

"There have been some unkind headlines since the news of your relationship has broken. Do you have anything you want to say about that?"

Haddie shakes her head, but I'm not about to be quiet. "When I became famous, I loved it. The support of the fans, playing music I loved, touring with my brothers—it was all a dream come true. A month or so into the fame, we started dealing with the media. For some reason, most media outlets like to focus on the negative— stories about our failures, potential paternity suits, possible drug and alcohol abuse allegations—you get my drift. It's like they forgot we're people with families, lives, jobs, and feelings, just like anyone else."

"Darren—" Haddie interrupts.

I meet her eyes. "I need to get this out."

"Okay," she answers softly.

"I don't care if people question my love for a plus-size woman just like I didn't care when I was criticized for an interracial relationship with Belle. All the media does with these articles is breed hate and make the people second-guess their own physical attributes. It doesn't take a lot to make someone feel bad about themselves. When you question a few extra pounds on someone, how do you think a reader who is larger than the person you're shaming feels?"

"So you think the media is bullying people?"

I lean forward. "I think the media has a responsibility to highlight positivity. If they don't, maybe their sponsors ought to rethink who they give their money to. Writing an article about an assumption doesn't do anything. Your readers can look at photos and make their own observations. The articles aren't going to affect us. All they do is affect your readers and determine what kind of following you're going to get. We know who we are, and we're confident in our relationship."

"It seems like you care a lot about the self-esteem of others. What do you do to combat self-esteem issues with your daughter?"

"Daily affirmations. It's our favorite part of the morning. I know I'm laying the groundwork for the rest of her life. No one will ever have an easy time making my daughter feel less than anything."

Sam looks to Haddie. "What about you, Haddie? Do you have any thoughts on the articles?"

"Well, they're not great. Darren has helped me understand they will find some way to ostracize me regardless of my size. They'll dig up a secret in my past or an unflattering photo—if they can make it look bad, they will. I'm a good person, I help children for a living, and I'm in love with a man who is quickly becoming my best friend. I've stopped looking at the articles; they no longer have power over me."

"That's wonderful." Sam sits back in his chair and steeples his fingers. "What is the purpose of this interview? If you've gotten past the articles, why did you want to talk?"

I lean forward. "It's a media frenzy out there. Haddie isn't famous, she's a normal person just like most of your readers. We're hoping by coming forward and answering questions, the press will back off and give us enough breathing room to drive into our driveways for a change. We're not an exciting story; we're just two people who happened to find happiness with each other."

"Thank you both for sitting with me today. The two of you seem to have found something very special. It's obvious how much you love one another. I expect an invitation to that wedding once you've had enough firsts to merit one."

Sam turns off the recorder and puts it away. "I meant what I said. The two of you better put me in the front row. You know how much I love weddings, Darren."

"You'll be one of the first on the list. Thanks for doing this, Sam."

"Are you kidding? It was the highlight of my week. I'm a sucker for a good love story and for putting assholes in their place. That line about the sponsors pulling their funding? Epic. People will be talking about that for weeks. I'll clean this up and get it ready for publication on Monday. Did you email me a photo?"

"We did, it should be in your inbox."

"Perfect! Let me go find Warren and then we'll all grab some dinner. I've already reserved a private room with a backdoor entry. We'll be golden."

I snicker. "You're a gay man who said backdoor entry. Sorry, I'm still twelve at heart and that shit was funny."

Sam shrugs and grins. "I'll let it slide because I love you."

Haddie giggles as Sam heads off to find Warren.

"Are you okay?" I lower my lips to hers, and she kisses me back before answering.

"I'm better than I thought I would be. Thank you for what you said."

"I meant every word. You're the one sticking around through all the bullshit. I should be thanking you."

She slides her hands up the back of my shirt, and I step closer to her. "You're worth it. But if you want to fuck me while you talk dirty to me later, I wouldn't be opposed."

"Deal."

At a little after three in the morning, my phone rings and someone is pounding on my front door.

"What's going on?" Haddie mumbles groggily.

"I'm not sure." I look at my phone and answer it. "Is everything okay?"

"Go answer your door. Hurry, it's Eli and Jordan," Mel whispers over the line.

"What's wrong?"

I grab a pair of shorts from the floor and pull them on.

"Dammit, Darren, I don't think I can fix this. Answer the door, please."

She ends the call, and Haddie sits up. I bend over and kiss her quickly. "Jordan and Eli are here. Maybe you should put on some clothes and come out."

"Okay, is everything all right?"

I sigh. "I'm not sure."

When I open the door, Eli falls into my arms and smells like he drowned in a vat of gin. My stomach roils at the nauseatingly familiar scent. "What in the world is going on, J?"

Jordan closes the door behind him. "It's not good, D. Remember when I said you should have talked to Sawyer about Rory?"

Eli looks up at me. "I'm sorry, Darren, I fucked up. I was so pissed at Rory, and I told Sawyer what happened with the two of you."

My heart stops and the world stills. Jordan and Haddie call out my name, but I'm stuck in a time warp. "What happened?" I finally manage to gasp.

Jordan pulls Eli off of me. "He was drinking at the bar, they fought, and you know how it goes when you drink gin. For some reason, Eli thought calling Sawyer would screw over Rory. He didn't think about what it was going to do to you. We called Mel. She was supposed to get Sawyer's phone and try to delete the message ..."

Sawyer bursts through my front door and wraps his hands around my neck before throwing me to the ground. Haddie screams, and flashes start flashing. I hear the door slam shut, but all I see is the rage in Sawyer's eyes.

"Let go of him! You're going to kill him! Sawyer!" Haddie cries.

I refuse to fight back. I deserve whatever Sawyer wants to do to me.

"Is it true?" he screams, releasing his hands long enough for me to choke out a response.

"Yes."

"You motherfucker!"

Before he wraps his hands around my neck again, Jordan tackles him. "Sawyer, enough!"

I scoot back against the wall and try to catch my breath.

Sawyer looks at me with tears streaming down his cheeks. "We had *one* rule, *one* promise our whole lives. *No one* fucks my sister!"

"I fucked your sister," Eli slurs.

"You don't count, you weren't one of us."

"I fucked your wife too," Eli adds, and Sawyer lurches toward him.

"Eli, stop while you're ahead," Jordan chastises.

"Haddie, can you put him in the guestroom?" I plead. "Go sleep it off Eli.".

I watch until they disappear from sight and then turn to Sawyer. "I'm sorry, man. I fucked up."

"Damn straight you fucked up. I can't even fucking look at you right now."

Jordan looks between us and shakes his head. "Darren, tell him what happened."

"No, it doesn't matter. I knew better."

"*You* knew?" Sawyer snaps at J.

"Yeah, but I promised Rory I wouldn't say anything."

"Un-fucking-believable! You covered for him? My own damn brother!"

Jordan gets in Sawyer's face. "Fuck you, Sawyer. I covered for our *sister*! Rory isn't so fucking innocent in this whole damn situation."

I stand and pull him away from Sawyer. "Jordan, leave Rory out of this."

"Why are you protecting my sister, Darren? Do you still want to fuck her?"

Mac and Mel walk right in and all I see behind them are flashes from the cameras. Fucking paparazzi and their telephoto lenses.

"It was one time, Sawyer. It was a huge mistake and it will never happen again."

Sawyer steps closer. "Why? I know now, you might as well keep going."

"Because I'm not in love with your fucking sister, Sawyer! I've *never* been in love with her. Apparently, that was the whole fucking problem!"

"Darren, it's okay, calm down." Haddie pulls my arm and locks her eyes on mine. "You're both having a rough night. Why don't we all go to our separate corners and talk over coffee in the morning?"

Mel nods. "I think that's a great idea." She reaches for Sawyer, but he pulls away.

"Fuck that. I don't need to have coffee with him to discuss anything. I know all I need to know. Our friendship is over. Sell your house and the studio. There's no coming back from this."

Sawyer storms out, and Jordan follows.

"He doesn't mean that, Darren. He's just angry," Mel says as she hugs me.

"Nah, he does, but I deserve it. It never should have happened. I'm so fucking sorry, but I can't take it back."

Tears slip down my cheeks, and Mel wipes away her own.

"Sawyer doesn't get to be angry for long. Not over this, not after what we did. I will be over for coffee in the morning because I'd like the whole story from Eli *and* you."

Mel leaves through the back door, and Mac levels me with his "I'm on duty, don't fuck with me" gaze. "Best case scenario, the paparazzi only heard Sawyer yelling. Worst case, they heard it, they recorded it, and it's already live on the net. Do you know where Rory is? She's going to need coverage."

"Last I heard she was in Texas or Tennessee, wherever the fuck Eli just came back from. You probably want to call her. I can't do it for you, sorry."

"It's okay. Ryan is with Mel and Sawyer. I'm going to stay here. You two go to bed and I'll lock up and deal with the Rory situation. We'll do damage control in the morning."

Haddie laces her arm through mine and leads me back to the bedroom. "Good night, Mac," she calls over her shoulder.

"Night, guys."

We lie down and she wraps her arms around me. "It's going to be okay, Darren. It will all work out."

"Fuck, Haddie, you don't get it." Tears stream down my cheeks. I'm pissed and I'm scared.

"What, baby? Tell me what's bothering you."

I pull her flush to my skin. "I don't want to lose you."

"Hey," she locks her eyes on mine, "that's not going to happen."

"The press is going to run with the story. I fucked Rory Weston. If they heard everything, they'll report it as breaking news, like I cheated on you. Your friends and family—"

"Will listen to me when I tell them it's not true. We had a deal, Darren. We're going to weather these ridiculous media storms together. *We* know the truth, and I'm sure Rory will back it up. She runs Noah's foundation so she'll have to put out a press release if it gets that far."

"I'm so sorry."

"Shhh. I'm more concerned about Sawyer and you. How serious do you think he was?"

I blink hard to try to stop the tears. "I've never heard Sawyer say anything he didn't mean. He's not that kind of person."

"We all had too much alcohol tonight at dinner. I think you're both emotional from it. Let's sleep and deal with it all tomorrow." She kisses the top of my head. "I love you."

"I love you too." I hope to God it's enough to keep her around.

Haddie

"I'm going to get dressed and make some coffee. Come join us when you're feeling up to it, okay?" I lean down and kiss Darren's cheek.

"Thank you. I'm so exhausted, but I'll be there soon."

Neither of us got much sleep. Darren tossed and turned through the night. A shower helps, and once I'm dressed, I head into the kitchen.

"Morning," Mac says, looking up from his laptop.

"Good morning," I reply as I make a cup of coffee before sitting across from him at the table. "How bad is it?"

"Do you want me to sugarcoat it?"

I take a sip and shake my head. "Not on your life."

He flips his computer around and pushes it toward me. "Each open tab is a different disaster. Browse at your own risk. Sam wants you to call him. He needs to ask you a few follow-up questions he thinks may help Darren."

"Okay, can you get me his number?"

Mac slides a slip of paper across the table with Sam's information on it. "Wyatt and Anna are next door with Mel and Sawyer. They'll be here soon."

"Is Sawyer coming?"

Mac shakes his head. "The stubborn is strong with that one."

"Fuck, why does my head feel like it's in the baggage area of a 747?" Eli groans as he stumbles into the kitchen.

I'm trying hard to school my expression, but damn, Eli Watts was a teenage fantasy for anyone attracted to the sexy, boy band type. Even fucked up and hung over, he's an attractive man.

He pulls out a chair and slumps down at the table, and I get up to make him a cup of coffee. "Eli, do you take cream or sugar?"

"No, just strong and black."

Mac snickers. "I'm already taken, and you're too much drama for me."

Eli lifts his head and starts to laugh but grabs his head and flips Mac the bird instead. "Even if you were my type, I'm pretty sure Tyler would kick my ass or die trying if I wanted you."

"He's been training with me at the gym. I'm not sure your pretty-boy face would survive the fallout."

I hand Eli his coffee, and he eyes me cautiously.

"I'm Haddie, Darren's girlfriend. Sorry we had to meet under these circumstances."

Eli shakes my hand. "Eli Watts, thanks for the coffee and for … putting me to bed last night?"

I nod, and he groans. "Oh shit …"

Mac nails him with a steely glare. "Mmhm you can say that again. You fucked up everything, Watts. Rory is fucking pissed at you too."

Eli sets his cup on the table. "I didn't mean it. Rory just … fuck! That woman pushes every button I have and keeps pushing. When she doesn't get her way, she throws a fucking dagger and … fuck … I'm so sorry." He hangs his head.

I gasp at the headlines as I open the tabs on the computer, and Eli's sullen gaze meets mine.

"Can you tell me what it says?"

"Which one?" I ask. "They're all equally awful."

"All of them, please," he mutters as he brings the coffee cup to his mouth.

"Rory Weston and Darren Miller — The Affair and the Fallout"

"Darren Cheats on Haddie — Is the Plus-size Beauty Too Much for Him?"

"Sawyer Weston and Darren Miller Come to Blows! Click for photos"

"Bastards and Dangerous on the Brink of Fallout — A Legacy in Shambles"

"Where's Wyatt? Rumor Has It the Band Split Long Before the Epic Fight"

"Rory Weston — Young, Hot, and Sleeping with Darren Miller. Click for details"

"Weston Brothers Records Circling the Drain Already"

My heart lurches when I open the next tab. "Ugh, there's a photo of Sawyer choking Darren. The caption is 'You screwed my sister — we're through' and the article is speculating Sawyer and Darren are in a relationship."

"Jesus ..." Eli says under his breath.

Mel and Anna come in through the sliding glass door with bags under their eyes and matching expressions of defeat.

Mel pours coffee for herself and Anna and starts a new pot. Anna makes the rounds giving everyone a kiss on the cheek, including me.

She sits next to me and rests her hand on mine. "How are you doing, Haddie?"

"I'm fine."

Anna arches a brow and cracks a small smile. "You're not, but you're good under pressure. You fit right in. We'll help you through this. No matter what happens between Darren and Sawyer, you guys are family."

"What's going on at your house?" Mac asks Mel when she takes a seat.

"Sawyer is so angry and can't see past it. Wyatt is trying to talk some sense into him. Ryan asked Aria to come over because she has such a calming effect on Sawyer, but that didn't work. He won't even hear me right now, but I think it's because he knows I'm right, and ultimately, this isn't his business."

Eli groans. "I'm sorry, guys … really. I'm never drinking gin again."

"That's what I said," Darren kisses the top of my head and pulls up a seat next to me, "right after I hooked up with Rory. While what you did sucks, I know how Rory can push people to do things they normally wouldn't."

"Darren," Anna says, "why didn't you tell us what happened with Rory sooner? Maybe we could've—"

"That's exactly why. Rory made me promise when I started freaking out about it. She swore she'd keep it a secret. Every time I thought about coming clean, all I could think of was Sawyer's reaction. When Jordan confessed Rory told him about us, I knew I was on borrowed time. I wasn't ready to lose Sawyer. Hell, I'm still not. Last night seems like a bad dream."

Anna looks at me. "Did you know about it, Haddie? Or were you blindsided?"

"I knew. I could be wrong, but I think I know everything. Darren and I chose to be transparent with each other from the beginning."

Darren clears his throat. "Actually, there's something else I want to tell you guys. Another secret I already told Haddie. It's about Belle and me."

I grab Sam's number and stand. "I'm going to let you guys talk about this alone."

He reaches for my hand. "Stay, babe, it's okay."

I bend down and kiss his cheek. "This might get emotional, and I think your friends should feel free to say and ask what they need to right now. I don't want anyone to worry about my feelings and hold back. I'll be back soon."

"I love you," he says softly.

"I know," I answer with a smile.

"Aren't they so cute, you guys? Aww, I'm so happy for you, Darren." Anna says, her voice trailing behind me as I walk down the hall.

I grab my sunglasses and cell phone from Darren's bedroom and go into the back yard. Taking a seat in a comfortable chaise, I dial Sam.

"Hello," Sam answers.

"Hi, Sam, this is Haddie."

"Haddie, how are you doing today? Had I known there was going to be so much excitement last night, I might have insisted on staying after all."

"I'm fine. I'm worried about Darren and Sawyer though. It's all over the internet." I take a deep breath and try to center myself. I wish I were home in my back yard for this conversation.

"I'm hoping I can help you put out some of those fires. Would you mind answering a couple of questions for me?"

"I'll do whatever I can if you think it will help."

"Wonderful. Did you know about Darren and Rory?"

"Yes. What happened between them was a one-time thing, and ..." My voice trails off as I try to decide if I should say anything else.

"And what, Haddie?"

"I'm not sure it's relevant, so you may not want to print this. I think it was something they both needed. Rory needed to close some doors in her past in order to move on. And Darren had been so lost without Belle, I think he just needed something to make him feel again. He loves Rory and all the Westons; they're his family. Crossing that boundary was something he never thought he'd do. He and Rory made peace with everything, and I think they grew from what happened, but there's been a part of him that's been lost ever since."

There's a short pause before Sam replies. "And why do you think that is?"

"It's hard keeping secrets from the people you love most. His fear of losing his best friends has been constant torture. He knew how this would play out if it ever came to light. Darren put his life back together after his night with Rory. He's let himself love again and find a certain level of happiness. No matter how happy you are, if fear is holding you back, you're never going to achieve complete happiness."

"So Darren and Rory are only friends?"

"They're good friends, practically siblings, and they know their places in each other's lives."

Sam clears his throat. "All this happened before you two began dating?"

"Yes, about six months before we even met."

"There's a video … it's really more audio than anything … of you screaming that Sawyer was going to kill Darren. Can you clarify that?"

I lean back in the chair and close my eyes. "I'm sure Sawyer wasn't intentionally trying to hurt Darren, but it was scary. Maybe more so because I knew how fearful Darren was of Sawyer's reaction when the secret came out. I had hoped he was overexaggerating."

"The two of them have been through a lot together over the years. They were always close, but when we lost Belle and Noah, everything changed. They became fathers together. Both of them are stubborn and determined, but they're brothers. This will blow over with time."

"I hope so."

"One more question and I'll let you go. Does what happened last night change your opinion of Darren or Sawyer?"

I release a sigh. "Yes, but not in the way you might think. Their friendship is unique. I'm confident they can get past this. If not, they're going to grieve all over again but this time for someone who is still here."

"We're not going to let it get that far. I'm hoping to have the article out tomorrow. Thanks for your help, Haddie. If you need anything, keep my number and call me anytime."

"Thanks, Sam, have a good day."

"You too, Haddie."

"I've never been this angry before." The voice startles me and I open my eyes to find Sawyer about five feet away from me. "Is he okay? Physically?" He looks off in the distance as though he's deep in thought.

"He seems to be."

Sawyer shoves his hands in his pocket and turns toward me. "Rory and I were never particularly close. She was Noah's shadow growing up, and I was Diane's. After Noah died, Rory and I had a massive falling out. Eventually, we got past it and bridged the gap between us. She always had a major crush on Darren."

He sighs. "It used to worry me. There was more to it than just her crushing on her brothers' best friend. I knew it wasn't a harmless crush that Rory would let go. But Darren is older and more mature than her. I trusted him to never cross that boundary. I don't think it was too much to ask."

"Sometimes," I interject, "the people we trust the most do the things that hurt us the most. It wouldn't cause so much pain if we didn't love them. I can't tell you how to feel, but I know Darren has struggled with this for a long time. I don't think I'd be here if he hadn't done what he did. I understand it's a bad thing for you, but it's a good thing in the end for Darren and me."

He kicks a rock and exhales as he rubs his temples. "I'm happy you two have each other. I've done some really fucked-up shit to the people I love. Knowing how it feels isn't good. I don't know how to look at him without feeling rage and anger. She's my sister."

"What about Eli? He said he's been with Rory *and* Mel. How is that different?"

Sawyer motions to the foot of my lounger. "May I?"

"Sure."

He sits facing me. "Eli and Mel were first loves and now they're best friends. Mel introduced Eli and Rory, and they dated for a while. I guess the difference is that I got to know Eli as the guy dating my sister. He didn't break any friend codes."

"Did you mean what you said last night? About selling the house and the studio?"

Sawyer runs his hand through his hair. "In the moment, yes, but even if Darren and I have issues, it's not fair to do that to Nate and Cady. Right now, I just need some time."

"I think that's fair."

"Why are you outside?"

"Sam had some follow-up questions and Darren needed to confess something to his friends, something he couldn't hold onto after last night. I thought it best to give them privacy."

Sawyer groans "Another fucking secret?"

"Yes, but I'm sure Mel will fill you in, and it doesn't have anything to do with anyone but him. In a way, it ties in with Rory, but in the abstract."

The two of us sit in silence for a few moments before he finally stands. "I'm sorry about last night. Everything is a big mess and I know I have to own my part in that. I didn't mean to scare you though. That wasn't right."

The sliding glass door opens and Mel steps outside with tears streaming down her face. I feel like such an outsider right now.

Sawyer's mood shifts to concern immediately. "Princess, are you okay?"

"I'm fine." She sits and pulls me into a hug. "Thank you," she says through a sob, and Sawyer flashes me a quizzical gaze over her shoulder.

"What did I do?"

"You loved him back. You listened to him when he felt like he didn't have a voice, and you gave Darren the courage to tell his secret. I wish I'd known sooner. Belle kept the things most important to her close to her heart until she was ready to let the world in on her happiness. It's only because of you that he shared that beautiful story with us."

I shake my head. "No, he would've told you all in his own time."

"Mel what is going on?" Sawyer asks as he paces the yard.

"Nothing you need to worry about. I'll tell you later if you calm down a bit."

"Fine," he mutters. "I'll see you inside."

Mel finally releases me from her grasp and wipes away her tears. "It took me a long time to understand and recognize love. Belle, Noah, and even Sawyer had a lot of patience with me. I was literally the romance author who didn't believe in happily ever afters, at least not for myself." She snickers and half rolls her eyes before looking back at me. "Now that I see it, I can't unsee it. If that makes sense. One day, that man is going to ask you to marry him. I hope you say yes because I can't think of anyone else I'd rather have join our family than you."

"Mel, it's way too early to even think about all of that."

"Hm, maybe for you but a girl can hope. I know this is going to sound odd but Belle would have loved you."

That's high praise coming from her best friend.

"It's hard."

She nods, "Trust me, I get it. Sawyer and I stumbled and fucked up so many times. There are days where I still can't believe we managed to get over ourselves long enough to lean into our love for each other. It was hard, and there was a lot of guilt and shame. There are days we're still filled with it."

"What do you do to move past it?"

"We love each other harder when it happens. Our code has become, 'I need to be loved harder today.' When those words are said, we know one of us has been triggered. Maybe it's a memory or us missing them, but whatever it may be … we talk it out. Since Belle, Darren has been closed off, but with you, he talks it out. That's how I know you're the one for him."

Mel stands, and I follow.

"Now, I'm going to go home, pour myself a few mimosas, and toast to Belle and Darren. A wedding of the heart deserves to be celebrated, and this celebration is long overdue. Tell Darren I'll keep working on Sawyer."

"I will. Enjoy your mimosas."

"I absolutely will."

Everyone is still gathered around the table when I rejoin the group. Darren stands and takes my hand. "I need to talk to you."

"Okay …"

He pulls me behind him until we get to the bedroom and closes the door behind us.

"What's going –"

He crashes his mouth over mine, and I part my lips, allowing him entrance. Our tongues meet, but it's not enough. Roaming my body with his hands, he hits just about every erogenous zone within reach. We part breathlessly.

"What was that all about?" I gasp, trying to catch my breath.

"Us. You leave the room for fifteen fucking minutes and I miss you like you've been gone for hours."

I run my fingers through his hair. "I feel the same way. It's crazy, isn't it?"

"It's amazing. I thought I'd never have this again, and I do because of you."

My heart fills with his confession. "How did it go?"

He smiles. "It was sad, but they were happy to know. I felt sort of silly telling them after all this time like it's a huge deal."

"Hey, it *is* a huge deal, and it always will be. You married the love of your life in secret. That's major, Darren."

"It is," he laces our fingers together, "but she was *one* of the loves of my life. Someone recently taught me it's possible to have more than one.

"Is that so?"

"Yup. How did it go with Sam?"

"It was fine. He said the article will be out tomorrow. I talked to Sawyer too."

Darren steps away and crosses his arms. "Yeah? What did he have to say?"

"He's angry, but he doesn't want you to sell the those or the studio. I think he just needs time, Darren."

"Whatever. I can't worry about it. He won't come around before he's ready."

I step closer and peel his arms away from his chest before kissing him again. "Everything will turn out fine. You need to have a little faith."

"I'll try, but Wyatt is waiting for me in the studio. Keep Anna and Eli company?"

"Sure."

Darren steps out through the sliding glass door and walks toward the studio with his head down and shoulders slumped. He's playing strong for me, but he's far from okay.

chapter 19

Haddie

It's been three months since Darren and Sawyer's fight, and a lot has changed. Darren and I have become a lot closer, as have Cadence and I. She's stolen a piece of my heart I never even knew was up for grabs.

After their fight, the media frenzy grew tenfold. Sam's article helped people understand us, and now the fans in our corner are calling us Harren. It's absolutely ridiculous, but it would have been worse if they started calling us Daddie.

Due to the influx in media, I've only spent a couple of nights at my house, and Darren stayed with me each time. We've basically been inseparable. He misses Sawyer terribly. Sawyer asks about Darren all the time— I know he's coming around. Rory handed him his ass when she heard what he did. They no longer speak. She said when Sawyer forgives Darren, she'll forgive him, and not a second sooner.

I just finished getting ready for work and wander down the hall to check on Cadence's progress.

Darren is finishing her hair and they're going over her *affirmations. I've only caught the tail end of them once because I'm always getting ready at the same time. I pause outside the door and peek in.

"Who are you?" Darren asks.

"Cadence Melody Miller."

"What are you?"

"I'm strong, I'm smart, and I'm happy."

"Do you make fun of people?"

"No."

"What do you do if someone makes fun of you?"

"I walk it off."

"Who do you hate?"

"No one. There's no room for hate, only love."

"Who loves you the most?"

Cadence giggles. "You do, Daddy."

"And who do I love the most?"

"Me, Mommy, and Haddie."

Darren pauses and moves in front of her. "Haddie, huh?"

"You said you loved her, so we should add her."

Darren hugs her, and I step away from the door and blink away my tears. I hadn't realized how much Cadence's acceptance would mean to me until this very moment.

I go back to the kitchen and pour some coffee into a to-go mug. There's a knock at the sliding glass door.

"Morning, Haddie!" Nate says as I open the door for him.

I wish I had his kind of energy in the morning. "Good morning, Nate."

"I brought Cady a Pop-Tart. Can she have one?"

"Daddy, can I have one?" Cadence pleads as she runs toward Nate with a huge smile.

Darren sighs. "Yes, you can. Thank you for sharing, Nate. I know your dad doesn't like to share his toaster pastries."

Nate giggles. "Mom told him if he eats them, he has to offer them to us too. She said, 'fair is fair.'"

"And that worked?"

Nate shakes his head. "Nope, but Mom thinks it did. I promised Dad I wouldn't tell on him since it's his favorite snack."

I lean closer to Darren and whisper, "Am I missing something?"

"Sawyer loves two things as much as he loves Mel and the kids: Pop-Tarts and his mom's chocolate chip cookies. He would have a major meltdown on the road if we ran out. It was so bad, Wyatt and I started keeping extras on our bus just in case."

"That's hilarious."

"Yeah, I miss those days," he says sadly.

"Go talk to him."

He shakes his head. "No way. I apologized, so the ball is in his court." He looks over at the kids as they finish their food. "Go brush your teeth again."

They run off to the bathroom, and he pulls me close. "I saw you peeking in the bathroom."

"I just wanted to see the two of you together in the morning."

Darren nuzzles my neck and kisses me below the ear. "Mmhm, and that's why you got all teary-eyed and ran away?"

I sigh and lean into his touch. "You're not playing fair. Stop getting me all worked up when I have to leave for work with the kids."

"You didn't answer me."

"I don't know what to say. I'm honored that she's including me, and I can't even begin to describe how happy it made me to hear her say it. But her recognizing your love for me isn't the same as me earning hers. I know it takes time though."

He drops a kiss on my lips before pulling away. "I'm not sure she would have added you at all if she didn't feel it too. We'll get there."

"I know, and I'm willing to wait as long as it takes. You two are the most important people in my life."

"Haddie," Darren looks me in the eyes, "move in with us."

It's still so soon. I'm here more often than not but making it official is such a big step.

"Can I think about it?"

His expression falls, but he schools it quickly. "For as long as you need."

"We're ready!" the kids yell as they run down the hall from the bathroom.

"All right, let's meet Mac at the car and get to school. Remember, I'm going to be observing your class today."

Cadence nods. "Right, but that doesn't mean we're in trouble; it just means you're doing your job."

"Exactly."

Cadence and Nate hug Darren, and I give him a kiss while the kids groan about us being gross.

"Your parents kiss all the time, Nate." Darren laughs. "You should be used to this by now."

Nate shrugs. "I know, but they're my parents. You're my uncle; it's totally different."

I laugh at his six-year-old logic. "We'll see you this afternoon."

"Have a good day, you guys."

When we arrive, I take the kids to class and head to my office. The morning passes in a flash, and after two back-to-back meetings, I finally grab my bag and go to Marina's class.

I love the kindergarten classes. Maybe it's because their rooms are separate from the rest of the school and they have their own private playground. They still have an imaginative play area inside the class and get to have naptime. Plus, the indoor restrooms are pretty convenient though definitely not for grownups.

Marina lets me in after I knock, and I'm overwhelmed by the scent of finger paints. Cadence, Nate, Jake, and Heather all look up and wave. They've all become good friends. I set up my things at an extra desk at the back of the classroom and pull out my phone.

Darren: Meeting with Wyatt and Sawyer to discuss studio business. Wish me luck.

Good luck, but you don't need it. Everything will be fine.

After tucking my phone into my pocket, I walk around the room and look at some of their paintings. They're a mix of houses and families, trees and flowers, and the unrecognizable.

My breath catches as I pass by Cadence. This beautiful little girl is coming out of her shell in unexpected ways today. I keep walking even though I want to hug her. I'm pretty sure her picture is of Darren and I on either side of her, each of us holding one of her hands. Up in the sky by the sun is a woman with angel wings.

I'm so tempted to sneak a photo and send it to Darren when the kids go to lunch.

The school bell sounds, and I pause and look up at the clock.

It's not lunch time yet.

When it sounds again and again in the longer tone succession, I know we're in trouble. Immediately, Marina and I jump into action. I flip off the lights and begin counting kids. Marina tells the kids to walk single file toward me when the PA system clicks on.

"Students and staff, this is *not* a drill. You are to shelter in place immediately and remain where you are until you are given the all clear. We are not in imminent danger at this time. The police are in pursuit of an armed robber in the area. Do not open your doors under any circumstances. Follow all protocols and stay safe."

My phone rings right after the announcement.

"Haddie, this is Principal Lewis. Where are you?"

"I'm in Miss Marina's class for observation."

She exhales loudly. "Okay, good. Kindergarten is actually a great place for you to be. Make sure to use the emergency snacks and juices. This could take a few hours."

"I'll remind Marina."

"Call if anything happens."

"Will do," I reply as Marina's phone rings.

While Marina gives her head count to the office, I prop open the restroom doors and usher the kids in to wash hands and remove their smocks.

Cady tugs on my hand. "Haddie, are we going to die? I'm scared."

I crouch down to her level and hug her, protocols be damned. "We're going to be fine, sweetie. I'm not going to let anything happen to you guys."

Her bottom lip wobbles. "Promise?"

Nate finishes washing his hands and joins us while Jake helps Heather.

"I promise, and I know Belle and Noah are looking down on you too."

My phone buzzes with the schoolwide text alert system. Darren is going to lose his shit, but I can't message him now.

"Come on," I encourage Cady with a smile, "let's help everyone get washed up and then we'll get some snacks."

Marina and I get the kids paint free and settled in the imagination station. There's plenty of space in here because it's where they nap but it's also away from all the doors and windows.

Marina snaps her fingers once and then holds them up her signal for silence. "Listen, please. I know this can be scary, but Miss Haddie and I are going to be here with you until Principal Lewis says otherwise. This is just like the drill we practiced last month. We have to stay inside until the police say it's okay to come out. Does anyone have any questions?"

Some of the kids are anxious, but for the most part they seem fine and no one asks any questions.

My phone vibrates like crazy, and Marina nods for me to deal with it when I pull it from my pocket.

Darren: Are you guys okay? What is going on?

Darren: Haddie, call me please.

Darren: We're on our way to the school.

Darren: Please text me back. I need to know you're okay.

We're fine. You can't get near the school. I'm with the kids in Marina's room.

Darren: Thank God, how are they?

We're all okay. They're a little frightened, but this is a scary situation. Hopefully, it will be over soon.

Darren: Mac and Ryan are still parked in their usual spot. They're keeping an eye out.

Gotta go, text later.

After putting away my phone, I help Marina pass out snacks and juice. Some of them brought lunches, but we'll hold off on those in case we need them later.

We're trained at least once a year on active shooter drills and protocols, sometimes twice. I hate that they announce what is happening on the PA system. I understand why they have to, but the little ones have a harder time processing what is going on than the older children do.

Fortunately, in our case, we should be safe. Unless the shooter was already hiding on campus. Between the police and the kids' security team, I highly doubt anyone will try to hurt us. At least that's my hope.

"How about story time?" Marina asks softly. "We can pull out our nap supplies and relax. What do you guys say?"

The kids jump into action pulling out their comfort items, and I give Marina a thumbs-up.

Cady looks up at me with her big brown eyes, "Can we lay by you, Haddie?"

I look at Marina for approval and she nods.

I make eye contact with the four kids. "Yep, get comfortable."

Marina helps Heather, and for the first time, I realize her aide isn't here.

"Where's Becky?"

"She was on her lunch break. Lewis said she was in the office when she called."

"I'll send her a photo. Actually, why don't I send one to Lewis so she can see things are under control here? One less thing for her to worry about."

"Yes," Marina says enthusiastically, "I think that's a great idea. In fact, I have a parent-only social media page. I'll upload one with a quick note."

I take the photo and send a copy to Darren.

Darren: I love you so fucking much. Thank you for taking care of our babies.

I'll protect them with my life. Always. I love you, too.

Before Marina finishes the story, all the kids are asleep.

"That never happens," she whispers.

"Well, if I could choose sleep or fear, I'd pick sleep too. It probably helps that the lights are out."

We sigh in unison and she moves her chair closer to mine. "I hate this part of the job. We'd give our lives for these kids at any given time, but why do things like this keep happening?"

I look down at the kids and then at her. "The world isn't always a kind place, no matter how much we wish it were. The program I work for has psychologists all over the district who will help them process and cope when things get hard."

"You're going to be busy for a while after today."

Thinking about how many of these kids may end up with residual fear tears me up inside. "Probably, but at least I'm here and can help."

"That's true, and I'm really glad you were with me today. Having you by my side helps keep me grounded."

"Me too. If I'd been sitting in my office, I'd be just as freaked out as Darren is right now."

She looks at me and smiles. "You're in love with both of them."

"I definitely am."

We fall into silence, and Marina interacts with the parents who have commented on her post. I think about this morning and how sweet Cadence and Darren were, how my heart felt like it was going to burst after hearing her add me to her affirmations, and how Darren asked me to move in with them.

Jesus, what did I even need to think about? I know it's fast, and I keep reminding myself to slow down but why? I pull out my phone and text him, not wanting to wait another second.

You asked me a question this morning.

Darren: I did. An important one.

My answer is yes.

Darren: It's about time.

Where are you?

Darren: At the end of the block with every other parent from the school waiting for the police to remove the barricades and let us in.

You're an amazing father.

Darren: I might never let her out of my sight again.

You will

Darren: How can you be so sure?

Because you love her enough to let her grow.

D. Kelly

Darren: Will you be by my side?
As if you could get rid of me.

Darren

"Hey." Sawyer walks up to me with his hands in his pockets. We've been waiting with all the parents, but our security detail keeps us buffered from them. It sucks, but with all the paparazzi lately, it's a necessity.

"What's up?"

"Haddie send you more updates?"

"Yeah, they're fine. Plus, you saw the class page; they've got things under control."

Sawyer nods and then claps me on the shoulder before pulling me into a hug. "I'm sorry, Darren. I shouldn't have judged. I realized ... if something ever happened to Mel, I'd probably do a lot of shit I'd never had done otherwise. That's what I was going to tell you in the meeting, but now, I just feel like a massive asshole."

"Well, you've been a massive dick your entire life," I grin, "so it's not really that much of a surprise."

Sawyer laughs.

I pat him on the back before releasing him. "You're forgiven, as long as you can forgive me and put the Rory stuff in the past where it belongs."

"On one condition."

"What's that?"

He shakes his head. "You *never* share those details with me."

"Yeah, that will never be an issue. I'm not dissing your sister, but that's a night I wish I could scrub from my memory."

We turn back toward the school, and Sawyer nudges my shoulder. "What's going on with you and Haddie?"

"She's moving in with us. I'll have to figure out how to tell Cady, but Haddie's been there almost every night anyway."

"That's great. I'm happy for you guys. Cady won't care; she loves Haddie."

I look at Sawyer. "Why would you say that?"

"Because she told us."

My brow furrows. "What?"

Sawyer takes a step back and tilts his head. "You didn't know?"

"Nope. What did she say?"

"You know I suck at this word-for-word shit. Mel asked how things were going at your house, and Nate and Cady were making fun of you and Haddie for kissing."

I snicker, thinking about how they were this morning. "Sorry, they're quite the pair. Go on."

"Cady told Mel you loved Haddie and Mel pulled one of those 'Oh, that's so sweet. How does that make you feel?' moves. Cady was super nonchalant and said she was happy because she loved her too."

Damn. "Why didn't Mel tell me?"

Sawyer shrugs. "You'll have to ask her. She probably figured you knew."

"When was it?"

"Hm, maybe a week or two ago?" Sawyer looks over his shoulder and waves Mel over to us. "Princess, when did Cady tell you she loved Haddie?"

Mel looks at me and grins. "Last week."

"Why didn't you tell Darren?"

She places her hand on my shoulder, "Because Cady said Haddie's birthday is coming up and she made her a card to tell her herself. I thought it would be a nice surprise for both of you."

"Sorry, man, I didn't realize it was a surprise," Sawyer says sheepishly.

"You're forgiven. See how easy that was? Next time you want to stop talking to someone, remember this."

Sawyer pats my shoulder and nods.

The police step up to the barricade, and one brings a megaphone up to his mouth.

"The threat has been cleared and the suspect is in custody. Thank you for your patience. If you'd like to check on your children or take them home, you need to go to the office, in a calm manner, and wait your turn to check them out through the proper channels."

Before any parents can take two steps, Mac and Ryan walk into the office to check out our kids. They both have full rights to take all three of them at any given time.

We head straight for the kindergarten and wait another ten torturous minutes for the doors to open and for Haddie to escort them out.

"Daddy!" Cadence screams as she runs into my arms. Nothing has ever felt better.

I hug her tightly and breathe her in. "I'm so glad you're okay."

"Haddie kept us safe. She promised she wouldn't let anything happen to us."

Haddie stands by the door and blinks back her tears.

I smile and wink. "Is that so?"

"Yup, and we had snacks and stories and naps with the lights off. It was only scary for a little while."

"Daddy, I can walk now," Cadence says with a giggle, and I put her down so I can hug Haddie.

"Thank you," I whisper in her ear.

"You're welcome," she says, hugging me tightly.

"Are you coming home with us?"

"No, I'll probably be here late tonight. I'll text you later and let you know what's going on."

I'm disappointed, but I understand. The students are going to need her more than usual today.

"Okay, we'll see you later. I'm glad you're safe."

Her eyes light up at my confession.

"Don't be so surprised, Haddie. You're a huge part of my world, you know."

She squeezes my hand and steps back inside the classroom. A few minutes later, she sends me a text.

Haddie: It's been a long time since someone has loved me like you do. You're a big part of my world too.

I can't wait until you get home tonight.

Haddie: Why is that?

So I can show you exactly how much I adore you ... all of you.

Haddie: What did I say about getting me worked up?

Incentive to come home as fast as you can.

After dinner, I run Haddie a bath and open a bottle of her favorite wine for her before leaving her alone to decompress.

Cadence has a hard time falling asleep, but once I'm sure she's out, I join Haddie in the bathroom. Her eyes are closed and she's covered in bubbles in my giant bathtub. It's the size of a small hot tub—room to relax and more than enough room to fuck.

"You look comfortable."

"Mmm," she hums. "This is exactly what I needed."

"Can I join you?"

She cracks open an eye. "Do you need to ask?"

She watches my every move as I strip down and licks her lips at the sight of my cock as it springs free from my pants.

"I think we should turn on the jets."

"Whatever makes you happy, Darren."

She sips her wine but sets it down quickly as I step up to the tub. Haddie reaches for my thigh and pulls me close before wrapping her lips around the tip of my dick.

"Fuck, babe," I hiss as I slowly move in and out of her mouth a few times before finally backing away and joining her. "Your mouth is a fucking treasure."

She giggles. "So is your cock."

"True story," I smirk.

I straddle her body as I lower my mouth to hers. She slides her hands up my back as we kiss, and my cock jerks against her stomach. I cup her cheeks and deepen our kiss. There's no rush tonight. I want her to understand how much she means to me.

She reaches for my cock, but I pull her hand away gently.

"Darren, I want to make you feel good."

"I'm fine. I want to take care of *you* and help you release some tension. You had a rough day."

She sighs against my lips. "So did you. You must have been so worried about the kids."

"I was worried about *all* of you. Did you mean it? Are you moving in? Or were you reacting to the moment? I'd understand if you were."

I sit next to her and pull her body between my legs. She leans against me, and I kiss the top of her head and lower my hands to her breasts. As I caress, massage, and play with her nipples, she moans and sighs and relaxes into my touch. When I pause, she tilts her head and looks back at me.

"The only moment I'm living in is now. I don't know what to do with my house; I can't give it up. Not because I doubt us—"

"Because your grandpa left it to you."

She pulls my fingers back to her nipples, and I grin. I love that Haddie knows what she wants and has no problem directing me to what she needs.

"Exactly, but we can ... ahhh ..." She loses her speech as I pinch her nipple.

I slide my free hand between her thighs to her sweet spot. "We can what?"

She hisses. "Talk about it later. Oh God, Darren, yes." She writhes against my body trying to match the dance my finger is doing on her clit.

I suck the skin of her neck into my mouth and then flick her earlobe with my tongue.

"Enough, Darren ... I'm about to ..."

"Oh, I know you're about to come. I want to hear my name fall from your lips when you do."

Haddie pulls my hand away and flips around to straddle me. "I want you to come with me, inside me. I want to feel you fill me."

She lifts herself onto her knees, and I position myself at her entrance. Haddie lowers herself slowly, and I hiss as she takes me inch by inch.

"Fuck," I groan when I'm buried to the hilt inside her.

Haddie throws her arms around my neck, and I bring my thumb to her clit as she begins to move. She grinds her hips slowly but with purpose, each thrust bringing her pleasure. I drop my hands to her hips and hold on to them.

"Darren, I'm so close ..."

"Ride me, baby. Take what you need and I'll follow." I'm barely holding on as it is. There is nothing fucking sexier than a woman chasing her desire.

The water sloshes over the side of the tub, and she chants my name again and again as she races toward her pleasure.

"Darren!" she screams as she comes.

Dropping her mouth to mine, she kisses deeply me as her walls pulse around me until I find my release and hug her body closer to mine. Our hearts beat against each other in a frenzy.

"That was so fucking hot." Placing my hand on the back of her head, I pull her to my chest as our breathing slows.

She laughs. "And you never even turned on the jets."

"Next time we'll see what that added stimulation will do to you."

"I can only imagine."

We lie together for a few moments before taking a shower to rinse off the sex and the bubbles. As we're drying off, she looks up at me.

"I was thinking maybe I could rent my house out for now."

"As like a security blanket?" I reach for my boxers and pull them on.

"That sounds awful, like you think I don't have faith in us. Nothing could be further from the truth."

I step behind her and squeeze her ass. "Then what's the truth?"

Haddie finishes putting on her pajamas before answering. "The house *is* sentimental to me," she says as we head into the bedroom.

"Okay …"

When we crawl under the duvet, she sighs softly. "I was thinking maybe it would be a good starter place for Cadence when she grows up."

My heart stutters in my chest. "You'd give your house to Cadence?"

"If she wanted it. I know it's not fancy or anything, but the yard is pretty spectacular, and I feel like I found myself in that house. I wanted to be on my own, on my terms. It's just an idea. I'm sure we could do something else with it."

"Haddie … I love the idea." Pulling her close, I kiss her softly. "Even more so, I love that you'd be willing to give my little girl something so important to you. Why?"

"Isn't it obvious?"

"I don't want to assume anything."

Haddie traces her fingers across the skin over my heart. "I love her just as much as I love her father. I love when she asks me to do her hair in the morning. Or when she wants my opinion on her outfits. The look on her face when she learns a new drum solo and she has to show me right that instant. But it's also kind of scary."

"How is loving Cadence scary?"

"During the lockdown, she looked up at me with the saddest expression and asked if we were going to die."

"Why didn't you tell me?"

"I didn't want to worry you. But in that instant, I knew I would have thrown myself in front of a thousand gunmen if it meant saving her. I've always known I would protect any of the kids in the school. It's my job. But with her and your nephews, it was so much deeper than obligation."

I kiss her again. "Because you love them."

She takes a deep breath and releases it slowly. "More than I ever thought possible."

"Haddie ..." I pause as I try to put my thoughts into words. This can make or break us. "Does this change how you feel about wanting kids?"

"No, but it alters my perception of family."

"How so?"

She runs her fingers through my hair and it feels so good.

"Too many movies maybe? I always thought stepparents were more evil or distant in the lives of their stepchildren. In my line of work, a lot of the stepparents haven't been the cream of the crop."

"So you thought you'd be an evil stepmom?"

She rests her head on my shoulder. "More like resigned to accept a title. I figured I'd be fine watching from a distance, but I'm not okay with that. I need to be in the front row for everything. I'm going to cheer her on in whatever she does. I *have* to be more to her than just some woman her dad loves."

There's a knock at the bedroom door, and I jump up to answer it.

"Daddy, I'm scared. Can I sleep with you guys tonight?"

Except for when she's sick, this is a first. Haddie pats the bed next to her, and Cadence climbs into the middle of the bed and cuddles up next to her. Huh.

Haddie runs her fingers through Cadence's hair and she snuggles in closer to her. "I had a dream that the bad man got us."

"Shh, it was just a dream. You're here and you're safe with your daddy and me."

I reach out and rub Cady's back.

"Goodnight, Daddy. I love you," she says through a yawn.

I kiss the back of her head. "I love you too."

"Goodnight, Haddie. I love you."

Haddie's eyes glass over, but she leans forward and kisses Cadence's forehead. "I love you too, munchkin."

I pull the blanket up over us and turn on my side. There is no better feeling in the world than the one I have right now. Maybe this isn't the life I thought I'd be living seven years ago, but it's one I'm proud to have.

I reach over Cadence and lace my fingers through Haddie's.

"Goodnight, Haddie. I love you."

She squeezes my hand, and I wonder if she's testing her reality as much as I am.

"Goodnight, Darren. I love you too."

epilogue

Darren

One year later

"Daddy! You should see Haddie. She looks so pretty."

Cadence runs into the room wearing her flower girl dress and red ribbons in her hair.

"I'm sure she looks just as pretty as you do. How are you feeling? Are you still okay with all of this?"

She looks me straight in the eye. "You worry too much."

It takes all my self-restraint not to laugh. "Is that so?"

She nods. "Yup, I love Haddie. I'm glad she's going to be my second mom."

My heart aches just a smidge. Cadence is almost eight and will enter the second grade soon. Her baby face is gone, replaced by the beginnings of the pre-teen who will soon inhabit her body. My beautiful baby girl is going to be an adult before I can blink.

"Why are you looking at me like that?"

I chuckle. "Sorry, munchkin, I was just thinking about how much you look like your mom."

Cadence smiles. "Mommy was very pretty."

"She was, and I'm sure she's one of the prettiest angels in heaven."

"Hey, Uncle Darren," Nate says as he walks into the room with Sawyer behind him. "My mom is throwing up again."

Sawyer laughs, "Nice ice breaker, Nate. Why don't you and Cady go sit down before you mess up your clothes."

"Okay, Dad."

Nate's tux matches Sawyer's. He's not in the wedding, but he's officially Cadence's date, or so I've heard.

"Did Mel come?"

Sawyer nods. "Oh yeah, she said she wasn't going to miss this for the world. She was okay until she heard Anna vomit, and then it was over."

"I still can't believe they're both pregnant at the same time *again*."

"Me either. Wyatt and I are vasectomy bound. They're both done and blaming us."

I laugh and pat his shoulder. "Never worrying about birth control again will be more than worth it."

Wyatt and Jordan enter the room with Jake and Sebastian. The three of them are my best men, and Marina is Haddie's maid of honor while Mel and Anna are bridesmaids. At first, Haddie refused to ask them, but Mel and Anna ended up asking her if they could be in the wedding. Haddie was worried about Mel, and so was I, but Amelia Weston is nothing if not persistent. She insisted this is how Belle would want it, and I'm pretty sure she's right.

Wyatt pulls me in for a hug. "Man, it's the end of an era. You're the last man down."

Jordan steps forward and hugs me after Wyatt. "I never thought the day would come when all of Bastards and Dangerous were married off."

"It's a sad day for all the fangirls who were holding out hope for you," Sawyer quips.

"Yeah, now they're just hoping one of us will have …" I pause and look around the room for the kids before lowering my voice "… an affair."

"Isn't that a sad truth?" Wyatt says. "Like, how awful must your life be to wish for something like that?"

"Well," Sawyer hedges, "sad or not, we've all seen it. We've traveled with bands and partied with bands filled with cheaters. It's easier to name the ones who don't cheat than the ones who do."

"It's true, but I'm not a cheater, so let's take some celebratory shots of tequila and get this wedding started right."

Jordan moves quickly to the bar cart in the corner of the room but pauses as he passes the kids. "Why don't you guys carefully walk to the bridal suite and see if there is anything Haddie needs you guys to do. Don't mess up your clothes on the way."

The kids leave in an excited rush, and Jordan pours our shots and passes them around.

I lift mine in the air. "For everyone who couldn't be here with us today."

Noah.

Belle.

Richie.

"And for all the blessings they gave us when they were," Sawyer adds softly.

Wyatt clinks my glass. "To Darren and Haddie,"

"May your love last till the end of time," Jordan finishes, and we all take our shots.

The sun has set and the outside lights are on and setting the mood.

"Daddy, Grandmother says it's time now," Cadence squeals as she pops her head into the room.

"Let's do this," the guys say in unison as they clap me on the shoulder and we walk outside.

"My baby," my mom cries as she kisses me on the cheek.

"You look gorgeous, Mom. Looking pretty good there yourself, Pop."

My dad hugs me briefly. "Well you know you got your looks from your old man. Better take your place. Mom is giving you the look."

Sure enough, my grandmother is staring at me and taps her finger on her watch.

"You look beautiful, Grandmother." I kiss her cheek as the guys take their places.

"Thank you, Darren, you look very dapper. Now take your place so we can start in a timely manner."

There's the woman I know and love. I step up to the front of the aisle and take a deep breath.

Sawyer leans over and whispers in my ear, "It's different when it's you in the spotlight, isn't it?"

"Yes, but it's a good kind of different, you know?"

He chuckles. "I know. I'd marry Mel every day if it were an option. That woman is my entire world."

Wyatt snorts and scoots in. "Remember how he used to make fun of me about Anna? How he used to call me whipped?"

Jordan leans in. "Looks like we all belong to that club now. You should be proud, Wyatt. You knew you had a good thing a decade before any of us had a clue. Showoff."

The music begins to play, indicating everyone needs to take their places.

Sawyer claps my shoulder one more time. "You got this, D," he whispers.

My dad walks my mom down the aisle to their seats, and my grandfather escorts Haddie's mom immediately behind them.

Anna is next, followed by Mel. They look stunning in their sleek, red dresses. They both recovered quickly; you'd never know they weren't feeling well.

Marina follows, looking just as gorgeous.

My heart begins to race the closer we get to Haddie. Brayden is the ring bearer and he's such a little ham. He smiles the whole way down the aisle and high-fives Wyatt before taking his spot.

When Cadence steps out, I flash back in time to Sawyer and Mel's wedding and can't believe how the time has flown. She's beautiful, and when she finishes dropping her petals, she steps forward and hugs me so completely I'm nearly in tears.

"I love you, Daddy," she whispers as she takes her place with the women.

"I love you too, Cady." I don't whisper, and the sound of our guests aww-ing carries through the yard. Mel flashes me a thumbs-up and I return it with a smile.

The music changes, and everyone stands. Haddie and her father appear, and I can't catch my breath. One of the things that shocked me most was that although she wanted a formal wedding, she wanted a non-traditional gown.

Haddie's wedding dress is black, form-fitting, and strapless. She holds a bouquet of red roses, and her hair cascades around her shoulders in big, bouncy curls. She's fucking stunning. Her lips are painted bright-red like the night we met, and her red heels complete the look—she could be a pin-up girl.

She smiles as she walks with her dad, but her gaze is locked on mine. It takes all my self-control not to pull her from her him and kiss her under the moonlit sky.

Her dad places her hand in mine with tears in his eyes. One day, that will be me with Cadence. "Take care of her."

"Always."

Much to the dismay of my family and hers, Haddie found a non-denominational minister ordained online to perform the ceremony. It was a fucking brilliant idea.

I lean forward and kiss her cheek. She blushes, and I whisper in her ear, "I love you."

Haddie squeezes my fingers before releasing my hand and mouths the words back to me. Cadence steps in and takes Haddie's bouquet and passes it to Marina.

"Welcome, everyone!" the minister begins. "Darren and Haddie are thrilled you could all join them this evening."

She pauses, and Haddie smiles at me. This has to be the most formal, non-traditional wedding ever.

"Our universe is an incredible force filled with many souls. On occasion, we're lucky enough to find the soul meant for us. And when we're truly lucky, we find love more than one time. Darren and Haddie were both blessed to know great love before they found each other."

I'm sure my family is freaking out at this new-age minister, but Haddie and I think she's great.

"Darren and Haddie want to send a reminder out to the universe that although they're moving on, love never dies. Cadence, would you be so kind as to retrieve the butterflies?"

Cadence nods excitedly and brings a small birdcage with two monarch butterflies to Haddie and me.

"In many cultures, butterflies represent the soul. Monarch butterflies specifically are believed to represent transition and new life, spiritual evolvement, and guardian angels. Some say orange butterflies represent love. Tonight, Darren and Haddie are going to release two monarch butterflies out into the world with the hope that Richie and Belle can feel their love. While Darren and Haddie are moving on with new love for each other, Richie and Belle will always have a place in their lives. They are gone from this earth but never from their hearts."

Haddie and I hold the cage in the best amount of light, and when Cadence looks up at us, we nod as she opens the lid and the majestic butterflies fly free into the night sky.

Haddie blinks back her tears as I swallow over the newly formed lump in my throat. I close the lid, and Cadence takes the cage and moves it off to the side. Mel, Anna, and Marina shed silent tears at our gesture.

"Darren and Haddie have chosen to say their own vows. Darren, whenever you're ready."

The minister takes a step back, and I take one forward and reach for Haddie's hands.

"Haddie, you came into my world at a time when I was lost. Although our first few sentences may have not been the most eloquent, they opened the door to a life I never thought I'd have. We shared similar nightmares, and we discovered kindred spirits within each other."

A tear slips from her eye.

"You're sexy, brilliant, honest, and one of the most compassionate people I've ever met. You stepped into my life and made me want more for myself and for Cadence. Because of you, I understood a mother's love could be more than the stories we told and photos and videos we shared. That it was okay for us to let someone in to help with the skinned knees and to give hugs after bad dreams. I learned through my daughter's happiness it was okay for someone new to help pick out clothes, cheer on her accomplishments, and love her as completely as I do. You've taught me I'm not taking anything away but instead adding another mother to her heart."

Tears stream down Haddie's cheeks, and I want to wipe them away but I have to finish.

"Haddie Davidson, you are my everything. With you by my side, the world makes sense. I can't imagine my life without you, and I pray I'll *never* have to. I want to spend the rest of my days making you happy, seeing you smile, and loving you so completely that you'll always look at me as you are right now. You are my salvation, Haddie. I'm in love with you. Will you do me the honor of becoming my wife?"

"Yes," she cries through a sob as she nods.

Sawyer hands me her rings, and I slide them on her finger as a huge weight lifts from my chest. This time, the universe gave me the opportunity to do it right.

The minister steps forward.

"Before Haddie says her vows, Cadence Miller would like to talk to her."

Haddie looks at me with wide eyes, and I smile. Cadence and I worked on this part together; it was important to her. I lift Cadence into my arms so Haddie doesn't have to crouch down in her dress.

"Haddie, thank you for making our family complete again. I know you're going to be my stepmom now, but since my mommy is in heaven, I wanted to know if I can call you mom."

As her tears fall faster, Haddie reaches out and hugs Cady in my arms. "Oh, sweetie, of course. I'd be honored."

Cadence hugs her back and kisses her cheek. "I love you, but now it's your turn."

Haddie returns her kiss. "I love you too, so very much."

Cadence smiles from ear to ear as she steps back in front of Mel. Mel and Anna couldn't reel in their pregnancy hormones if they tried right now. They're both a sobbing mess, but they did have a heads-up and made sure to have tissues.

"Whenever you're ready, Haddie," the minister says as Haddie swipes at her cheeks with a handkerchief.

"Oh man," she says, inhaling deeply. "You couldn't have warned me?"

"Where would the surprise be in that? Breathe, baby, we have all the time in the world."

She looks out at the crowd. Sam passes Warren a tissue—Warren plays tough, but he's the biggest sap out of all of us. I'm pretty sure even my grandmother is dabbing away a few tears.

Haddie takes another deep breath and reaches for my hands.

"The night we met, I thought you were crazy and conceited. Who demands to know if they've been recognized? Obviously, I had no clue who you were, but I'm always going to be happy you aren't the kind of person who gives up easily."

I smile at the memory of our first meeting. I'm glad I didn't give up either.

"There was something about you that told me I needed to know you better. Perhaps it was the way you looked at me. No one has ever looked at me the way you do. It's difficult to describe, but it's like adoration, desire, love, and intrigue all in one glance. It is the best feeling in the world when you look at me that way. Someone who can put that much emotion into a look was someone I had to know."

I flash her "the look," and her hands tremble in mine as her lips tip up into the briefest of smirks. She knows exactly what I'm doing.

"Considering our shared histories, I know the universe brought us together that night for a greater purpose. We were meant to end up here together. We stumbled a bit as we fell in love. I think it was not only expected, considering our pasts, but necessary. With every stumble, we granted each other grace and forgiveness. And since we both understand loss more than we'd like, we held on tighter during the difficult times because that's when we needed each other the most. I promise you'll feel my love even more during the hard times. The two of us are a team, but the three of us are a family. I vow my love and devotion not only to you today but to Cadence as well. Our adventures are only getting started, but I promise to cherish each one and never to take a single memory for granted."

Haddie pauses, and Marina hands her my ring. She holds it up I her trembling hand. I lock my eyes on hers and hope she knows there's nothing to fear.

"Darren Miller, will you be my husband?"

"Yes." Because I'm me and can't hold back, I answer the way I really want to. "Fuck yes!"

As she slides the ring onto my finger, I pull her face to mine and kiss her. I make it short as the crowd chuckles, but fuck, I needed that fix.

The minister steps forward again.

"By the power vested in me by the State of California, I now pronounce you husband and wife. You may kiss your bride … again."

The music begins to play, and this time I kiss Haddie deeply and without one single fuck of who is watching me stick my tongue in her mouth.

When we break apart, the first thing I hear is Cadence. "Auntie Mel, is Nate going to kiss me like that one day?"

My mouth drops, and Mel flashes me a smile as Haddie politely pushes my mouth closed. "Relax, husband. If she loves him even half as much as I love you, they're going to have an amazing story to tell."

I groan and pull her into my arms again, forgetting all about Cadence and Nate for now. "Mrs. Miller, can we go home now? I'm ready to strip you out of that dress with my teeth. What do you say, wife?"

"I say your grandmother would probably kill us in our sleep if we leave before we dance and cut the cake, but after that, I'm all yours."

"I love the sound of that."

As Haddie and I make our way up the aisle and toward the reception area, everyone claps and cheers. We're supposed to meet up with the photographers for some more pictures, but I pull Haddie off to the side of the house near the rose garden instead.

"Darren, we're going to throw off the schedule."

I wrap my arms around her waist and kiss her cheek. "Do you care?"

"Not really," she answers softly.

"I want us to enjoy our night, but I also wanted to pause and check in. Including Belle and Richie was a bit unorthodox, and I know it was hard for both of us. Are you okay?"

She cups my cheeks and kisses me. "I'm better than I thought I would be. I will never forget Richie, but my heart is in your hands now, Darren, not his. You're my husband, and I'm never going to treat that lightly. I'm looking forward to making new memories with my new family. The past will still be there, but the pain will ease with time. I know it's different for you, and that's okay because I'm going to love you through it."

"I only had Belle for a year from start to finish, but in that year, I swear I loved her enough for a lifetime. At times, I wonder if I'd have moved on sooner if I hadn't been blessed with Cady. Because of Cadence, Belle will never be in my past, but when I talk to her, it's about Cady and you—the love of my life. She would love you, and I know she'd be happy you're Cadence's mom.

"You're my wife now, Haddie, and even though it's hard for me to describe my love for you," I cup the back of her head and tilt her face to look into her eyes, "I'm excited to show you how much I love you every day in the most creative ways. Words are inadequate most of the time anyway." I lick the column of her neck from her collarbone to her ear, and she whimpers. "That whimper means you're needy for my cock."

She hisses, and I run my hand over the curve of her ass and pull her to my groin. "My dick is pretty fucking ready for you too. If I wasn't worried about one of the kids finding us, I'd push you up against the wall, hike up your dress, and fuck you slow and deep."

"Darren ..."

"I'd bring you to the edge of orgasm, but I wouldn't let you come. We'd finish our night with you desperate for release, and when we get to the hotel, I'd push you against the wall, drop to my knees, and feast on your pussy until you come all over my face."

She closes her eyes and inhales deeply. "Why are you doing this to me?"

I dip my tongue into her mouth and taste her thoroughly before stepping away. "Because when we get to Paris, I'm going to recreate that exact scenario. Be ready, Haddie. Our adventures are only beginning."

Haddie and I dance the night away. Our first dance is to "Spend My Life with You" by Eric Benet and Tamia. We take it all the way back and teach the kids the electric slide. Veronica took the lead on that; she's better at it than all of us combined. My grandmother even lets me spin her around for a few songs. While Haddie mingles with a few of her co-workers, I step off to the side to grab a drink and soak it all in.

It's been nine years since we took off on our last tour. Our lives have changed dramatically since that day. We're no longer young men figuring out who we were. Now we're raising a whole new generation of kids who will be there soon enough. We may be the grownups, but we're always going to be brothers first. I miss Noah more than ever tonight. It has hit me hard enough that I'm considering finally pulling out that video he left me and watching it. But not tonight. Whatever Noah has to say will make me cry like a baby. Maybe when we get back from Paris.

Haddie joins me and leans her head on my shoulder. "You doing okay over here?"

"I'm perfect. Just thinking about how grown up we all are now compared to our rock star days."

Haddie laughs. "You say that as if those days are in the past. Have you looked around tonight? This is a pretty big rock star wedding. There are celebrities here people would kill to meet. Marina's been drooling over the lead singer of Collateral Damage all night. At least he's single."

"This is tame compared to what it used to be."

"Do you miss it?"

I wrap my arm around her waist. "I miss making new music with my brothers."

"Do you think watching Noah's video may help you with that dilemma? Either by figuring out a way to make new music, or helping you let that dream go and focus on something new?"

It's like she can read my mind.

"I was just thinking about watching it when we get back from our trip. Speaking of, have we danced enough? Had enough cake?"

Haddie laughs. "Come on, can you ever have enough cake?"

"Good point. What if I told you I had Mac put two pieces in the car with our luggage?"

"Post-sex snack?"

I lower my voice so only she can hear. "During-sex feast. I'm dying to lick frosting from all your erogenous zones."

"Darren …"

"Yes?" I flash her a devious smile.

"You win. Let's go say our farewells."

We say our goodbyes fairly quickly, but when Sawyer and Mel bring Cadence out to the car, I almost break down. I've never been apart from her for more than a few days. Haddie and I are going to be gone for three weeks.

I crouch down and pull her into my arms. "I'm going to miss you so much."

"I'll miss you too, but Uncle Sawyer said we can Skype whenever I miss you guys."

"That sounds like a good plan."

Sawyer pats my shoulder. "She'll be fine, Darren. We won't let anything happen to her. You have our word."

"I love you, Daddy. Have fun!"

Cadence releases me and turns to Haddie and hugs her. "Will you bring me a pretty doll? And some candy? But don't forget something for Nate and Jake and Heather ..."

Haddie laughs. "I've got the list, sweetie. I won't let you down."

"I know you won't, Mom, I'm just reminding you. I love you. Have fun!"

All night I held it back, but hearing her call Haddie "mom" finally does me in. I'm blaming it on the alcohol. We wave as we hop in the car, and Haddie wipes my cheeks as Mac pulls out of the driveway.

"Will you ever get used to it? Or is it going to make you cry each time?"

"Why aren't you crying?"

Haddie flashes me a beaming smile. "It's one of the best things I've ever heard. She makes me incredibly happy."

"And that's why it's making me cry. I know we were meant for each other and you were meant to fill this role in our lives. I'm completely blissed out knowing everything is as it should be."

"We're quite the pair, Mr. Miller."

"I wouldn't have it any other way, Mrs. Miller."

Sometimes, life is wicked and unkind. It puts us through the worst kind of torment, and the only thing we can do is fight to see another day. But when we least expect it, we're given incredible people to walk beside us. They're the ones who help keep the bad days in the shadows. They make us laugh, and they love us through anything life throws our way. With Haddie by my side, I'll fight through anything put in my path as long as I have her love and she'll always have mine.

Keep reading for deleted scenes.

If you want to know more about Shawn Lucas and Ryder Stone, be sure to check out *Incognito* and *Only Ever You* by Siobhan Davis.

Thank you for reading *Broken Beats*. If you'd like to read Noah and Sawyer's story and learn more about Bastards and Dangerous, you can start with *Just an Illusion—Side A*.

If you haven't read Jordan's story and would prefer to read another interconnected stand alone, you can find Jordan and Allie in *Interlude*.

Next up in the Illusion world is Eli's story. This story is still untitled but will be releasing this fall. To keep up with release information, updates, pre-orders, and more, please consider joining my mailing list.

http://www.dkellyauthor.com/mailing-list/

To keep up with all things Illusion Series please join our Facebook group -
https://www.facebook.com/groups/1916016678629629/

If you'd like to join my reader group we'd love to have you! Please visit Dee's Dirty Divas on Facebook -
https://www.facebook.com/groups/239952459522719/

To purchase Just an Illusion – Side A or other books by D. Kelly please visit –

http://www.dkellyauthor.com/all-books

acknowledgements

Most of all, I want to thank you for reading Darren and Haddie's story. I know so many of you have been waiting on pins and needles for it, and I hope it was worth the wait.

Siobhan Davis – Thank you so much for believing in these characters and for loaning me Ryder and Shawn. You're a wonderful friend with an amazing heart. I'm so blessed to know you.

Lyra Parish – I love you to pieces. Thank you for being my sounding board, my sprinting partner, my technical guru, and most of all, my friend.

Emilie Couture – Thank you for all you do, especially for keeping me organized and mostly on target. I know I'm a hard one to keep focused, but I try.

Ashley Griffieth – Life is hectic, but you're still my girl! Thank you for all you do. I love you.

Dee's Awesome Arc'etts – Thank you so much for being part of my team. Your support and dedication means the world to me. I love you all.

Dee's Dirty Divas – You guys are the best. Thank you so much for being in the group and for your unending support. I know I've been quiet lately, but that's about to change. Pretty sure you'll wish I'd be quiet. I love you, ladies.

Just an Illusion groups – Ladies, I'm hard-pressed to find words to describe how much you all mean to me. I cherish your love, support, and opinions. You're always so excited to talk with me about this crazy group of friends—no one understands me like you do. There is going to be some fun stuff coming up for our group, and I can't wait to share it with you.

My husband and kids – I don't know how you put up with me most days, but I'm so happy you do. I love you more than you'll ever know.

To all the bloggers, beta readers, and anyone else I haven't listed previously, thank you. I would love to list everyone, but I'd never stop typing. You're all so important to me. If you're reading this, I love you and I'm incredibly thankful for you.

ABOUT THE AUTHOR

D. Kelly

D. Kelly, author of The Acceptance Series, The Illusion Series, and standalone companion novels *Chasing Cassidy* and *Sharing Rylee*, was born and raised in Southern California. She's a wife, mom, dog lover, taxi, problem fixer, and extreme multi-tasker. She married her high school sweetheart and is her kids' biggest fan.

Kelly has been writing since she was young and took joy in spinning stories to her childhood friends. Margaritas and sarcasm make her smile, she loves the beach but hates the sand, and she believes Starbucks makes any day better.

A contemporary romance writer, D. Kelly's stories revolve around friendship and the bond it creates, strengthening the love of the people who share it. For all things D. Kelly, you can visit her website: http://www.dkellyauthor.com

Dating Roulette

Bexley

Seven Dates.
Seven chances to win my heart.
It's not hard –
Don't put ketchup on your eggs.
Don't wear tasseled loafers.
For the love of all that's Holy, don't ogle the waitress.
See? Simple…
Yet no one can get it right.

Tristan

Dating Roulette.
It's Bexley's game.
Correction - it's her life.
A constant rotation of dates.
You might get one; you might get seven.
No one has ever gotten to eight.
There's only one rule –
Don't commit a dating sin.
I've watched for years and bided my time.
Now, it's my turn to play.

Coming July 9th 2019 – pre order open -
http://www.dkellyauthor.com/dating-roulette

Deleted Scene

Darren

Six months ago, I asked Haddie to marry me and she said yes.

Picking a wedding venue was difficult for us. We both love the beach, but after exchanging vows with Belle, that was out. I never want to alter those memories; they're some of my all-time favorites.

Haddie's back yard is out because it's where she and Richie talked about getting married; it's their sacred space.

One day, I had a talk with my grandmother that changed everything.

I push Grandmother's wheelchair into her sitting room and position her to face the window. She wants to watch my grandfather teach Cadence how to tend to the rose garden.

"You and Haddie can have your wedding here. It's been a long time since the grounds were used for a celebration."

"I'm not sure that would be a good idea," I reply as I take a seat on the sofa on the other side of the room.

She looks at me sternly. "And why is that?" she inquires, her voice firm and authoritative.

"Would you have extended that offer to Belle and me?"

Her eyes meet mine, and it's like looking in a mirror—I inherited her baby-blues.

"No, but not for the reason you think."

I snort. "So it had nothing to do with you being racist and hating Belle?"

"I'm not racist and I didn't hate Belle." She sighs softly. "I admired her."

I pause, needing a moment to collect my thoughts. "You were always rude to her and pointing out how different we were."

"*Darren, I grew up in a different era. I'm ninety-two years old and was raised a specific way. When your father married your mother, I was devastated. I lived a good part of my life in a racially tense and divided world. Growing up on a farm in the South, I saw the worst side of humanity at times.*"

She blinks and focuses on Cadence and my grandfather.

"*You have always been my favorite grandchild, and if you repeat that, I'll deny it. You wear your heart on your sleeve, and I've always thought the unconditional love your parents showered you with is why. It's not a secret your mother and I don't get along. For years, you've all assumed it's because I'm a racist old bitty when, in fact, we just don't mesh. I'm allowed to not like people, and I am sorry your mom is one of them.*"

I chuckle, and she smiles at me.

"*I knew you'd understand that. When you and Belle marched in here and announced she was pregnant, I wasn't pleased. You weren't married, and yes, her ethnicity was a consideration for me.*"

"*Which is why you didn't like her.*"

"*No,*" she says firmly. "*It's why I worried for the safety of your family, especially that beautiful little girl out there. I may be old, but I still watch the news. I know there are people out there who are not supportive of families like—*" She takes a deep breath and exhales. "*Like ours.*"

"*Why were you so mean to Belle?*"

"*Darren, it may have come across as mean, and if she were here, I would apologize to her for that. I pushed Belle because I wanted to know she had the passion and drive she would need to stand up for her family if the occasion ever arose. I did the same thing to your mother. She failed though. Your mom has a strong backbone, but her retorts were insults filled with indignation.*"

"*And with Belle?*"

"*Belle was fire and fury backed up with thought and fact. She was quick-witted, sarcastic, and knew how to respectfully put me in my place. Cadence has that same fire. Perhaps that's why I'm so attached to her. I admired Belle, Darren, and I'm sorry she never knew it."*

"So you were testing her?"

"Yes. I'm sure it wasn't my right, but it's who I am."

"Do you like Haddie, Grandmother?"

"I do. She's thoughtful and kind, and her love for the two of you is plain as day."

"Why do I hear a 'but' after that?" I smirk.

She tilts her head and smiles. "She's not even on the same spectrum as Belle. Don't get me wrong, she's lovely, but are you sure she's the one for you?"

"Belle was the woman I needed when I was in my twenties. She was outgoing, spontaneous, and ready for any kind of adventure. I'll love her until my dying breath. Haddie is who I need now. She's the only one who was able to bring me back to life after losing Belle. She's the best of humanity wrapped up in a single soul, and I'm going to love her past forever."

Grandmother claps, startling me. "Would you look at that ... Cady's managed to get herself some roses," she says, gesturing toward the window.

I smile. "It looks like Grandfather is cultivating another green thumb in the family."

"Indeed, he is." Grandmother turns back to me. "Are you going to accept my offer for your blessed union, Darren?"

"I'll talk to Haddie about it."

"Lovely, and remember, dear, all the things I've done have been out of my love for you. Surely, you understand."

I cross the room and kiss her cheek. "I love you too."

Noah's Video

Deleted Scene

Haddie and I had an incredible honeymoon in Paris. While we were there, I decided it was time to watch Noah's video. I think not having him at my wedding really fucked me up. I wanted to do this alone, so I waited until Cadence and Haddie left for school.

I take a deep breath and start the video. Right away, I notice how young he looks, and I have to hit pause. I've aged almost ten years since he filmed this. Though I don't feel old, seeing him shifts my reality a bit. I'm aging while my brother never gets to see his kid grow up. It's not fair, but I owe it to Noah to listen to what he needed to tell me.

I start the video again and get comfortable.

Noah smiles. "Hey, Darren, long time no see! Out of all the videos I've made, I think this is the only one I worry will never be seen."

I laugh. He knew me so well.

"I'm going to guess if you're watching this video it's because you miss me and you're at some sort of crossroads. I can't help you miss me any less since I'm one of a kind and all, but maybe I can help with your problem."

Tears fill my eyes, and I have to work hard to swallow over the lump in my throat, but fuck me if I don't have a constant grin on my face. I've missed him.

"I'd say there are three things you may be conflicted about— music, love, and parenthood. I can't picture you and Belle not being able to work through anything. That woman loves you with an undeniable passion. And since I won't let myself picture Cadence as anything other than the sweetest little girl possible, I don't think I can be much help with parenting. If it is one of those two, just breathe and remind yourself of this: however much you love them, they love you the same."

Man, Noah, if you only knew ...

"That leaves music, and it's probably the most logical issue for you to have. I imagine if I'm gone, you guys are in a rut. None of you probably want to play, and you're seeking other outlets. God, please tell me Sawyer went solo. If that happened, shout it to the heavens. The three of you are far too talented to stop playing for good."

Noah pauses and takes a drink of water.

"Want my two cents? Start a spinoff band. Take all your emotions and make some kickass music with the three of you. Do it indie style, play some clubs, have a few special shows a year, and have fun. Lord knows you don't need the money. Hell, bust out a hologram of me and have a kickass reunion tour. If that makes you happy, go for it."

I pause the video and laugh—the kind of laughter that comes deep from your soul. Sawyer is never going to believe this. It could be sort of fun if we could get past our emotions. I turn the video back on.

"Be fucking happy, Darren. You're the only one of us who lets shit roll off his back easily. You're the first one to go for something you want and not let anything get in your way. Make the music, love your wife and kid, and enjoy your life."

Noah pauses and shakes his head.

"Okay, back to Belle. I can probably give you a little more advice. If you're watching this because you're no longer together, I'm sorry. It's hard to imagine, but I know life happens. If that's the case and you want my advice, here's what I would do if it happened to me. If you guys can't work things out and you need perspective, remember the feeling that drew you to Belle and wait for it to come again. You know as well as I do that love will find us when we least expect it.

"Now, I love the hell out of you, but I want to get back to my wife. Hug her for me, yeah? Give Nate big snuggles and a kiss and tell Sawyer I'm proud of him. It doesn't matter what he's up to—I'll never not be proud. Tell everyone I love them. Just always remember to be true to yourself because that's when you're the happiest, Darren, and you always have been. Love you, brother."

D. Kelly